DESTINY

Jennifer J. Lacelle

To those who want to write their own stories.

Preface

Vasilis looked to the sky as clouds parted for the moon to shine against Earth's black mass. Stars twinkled in the distance but were never close enough to imagine touching. They persistently teased him.

He stood still amongst the creatures as his eyes turned to her. She was a star in her own right, her smile and eyes dazzling. But this time, she was broken, and her golden eyes veiled. He couldn't fix nor change her moirai—the predetermined fate she was never meant to see.

Vasilis knew of her nightmare. His core felt it, and he shared the vision. The fate she saw was one of many possibilities but also incomplete. Knowing he couldn't change her decision, his soul wept for her as the spell's symbol sat atop her chest.

Never had she looked so shattered as she did now. Her soul splintered into ways he could not repair. No amends would change the world, and no catastrophe could change his heart.

She stood on a precipice, eyes turning to the breaking dawn as the earth crumbled around her. Vasilis had always known she was her worst enemy, and her powers would be her downfall. Magic was not for those who feared the unknown.

He called to her, and she faced him solemnly… she only wanted more time. Her longing in life was to give him everything, but her moirai had told her she couldn't have such a life. That was never their fate.

Begging to be heard, she howled, like waves against stone, and her heart whispers hopes of compassion against destiny.

Vasilis spoke her name, his heart pouring forth the compassion she desperately craved.

The sky sparked, stars shifting and flaring, and his eyes turned from her. He fell to his knees in disbelief.

She sang a final note, humming alongside the wind before she released the spell into the universe. The bluff split apart and flattened the earth. The water rose high and surrounded them. He sprang to her, but to his dismay, she stepped into the ocean tide, now waist deep, as her tears mixed into the saltwater.

"Wait," he heard a whisper, "you'll see."

Vasilis knew better. He had seen the destruction of her actions; every piece of civilization would suffer from her fear.

His eyes, watching her vanish, cast another spell. He removed his sovereignty over nature and planted it into the rune affixed to the bottom of the bay as the remaining water crashed down around him.

The symbol, floating above the rune, seemed to mock him. He took it with him and waited quietly, unknowing which of the million timelines was inevitable now.

Chapter One

Professor Marlin Byrne handed out use of force worksheets to his first-year students before striding back to the front of the class and sitting at his desk. His eyes scanned the room but Stella was fixed on him. His easygoingness and knowledge had quickly made the man Stella's favourite teacher.

"What happens when we look at the situation through the victim's eyes? That's what you'll be taking a look at in chapter ten of your textbook. Fill this out and return it to me next session. You're welcome to continue working here, or you can head out. Don't forget there's also a test next week," he said.

His fifty students jumped out of their seats and raced through the doorway into the hall. They were rambunctious and loud, happy to be out of class. Stella held back for a minute and slowly filled her backpack with materials. As she made her way to the door, the professor called her. Stella turned to find Professor Marlin holding a stack of files. Curious, she moved closer to the man and the grin under his large, white moustache.

"Yes, sir?"

"These are applications for the summer semester," he said. "Each one has a recommendation letter from me and is specific to the organization. They're your top five from the list you provided at the beginning of the term."

"What?" Stella said with surprise. "Thank you."

"You might not have the highest overall GPA, but you're the best student in the program, practically speaking."

"Yeah." Stella's eyes fell. "I don't do the greatest on tests."

"People who do better on tests usually don't do as well in the field and vice versa." He leaned back in his chair. "It's rare to find both in equal measures."

She gladly took the file folders. Their hands grazed, and she could hear his thoughts briefly.

Though her mental toughness could be improved...but I can't do that for her in class. She needs life experiences to build that.

"Thanks," she said quietly.

"Can I make a recommendation?"

"About what, sir?"

"While you have excellent academic skills, I think you could use a little extra of a push."

"An extra push, sir?"

"Yeah," he said. "I think it would be helpful."

"What do you have in mind?" Stella asked, her skin growing cold.

"If you're going to be a police officer, then you need more skills than disappearing inside textbooks. Why not try going to an old-school gym? The one over on Paris Street, Hardgrove's Boxing," he said. "Get a trainer. You might be uncomfortable, but I think it'd be good for you."

"Because I don't seem as tough as everyone else?"

He laughed brightly. "You have excellent intuition, but your facial expressions give away your feelings. Usually when you want to cry."

Stella chewed her lip. Her abilities had always freaked people out as a child when she spoke up. It led her to wonder what she was and would bury her nose in mythology books.

Though they did not yield any results, she never discovered tales of people who could read minds through touch or feel emotions through eye contact. She felt utterly alone.

"Now, now." Marlin stood up. "Tell the owner I sent you. He's an old friend. You'll probably see some of your peers there, too."

"I suppose you've sent a lot of people there," Stella chuckled nervously.

"I've sent a fair share." He shrugged. "You're three quarters through your first year. I suggest making the best use of everything you can while you're here."

"I know," Stella muttered as her hands clamped down on the folders.

"Check it out." He smiled and began heading out. "They're open today."

Stella watched him leave and wished she had his poise. She could feel her own confidence grow whenever she used her gift, but there were downsides as well.

Tucking the folders into her bag, Stella left the lecture hall. She walked home and pulled out her computer to look up the gym. The website was superficial at best and only provided an address, number and hours. Reluctantly, she decided to check it out while there was still sunlight.

After planning her route, Stella scrambled outside to catch the next bus. Once on the bus, she pulled out her phone and browsed through some news articles. What caught her eye were rumours of a strange creature attacking known criminals in Brazil. Some journalists and locals thought they were golems created by magic. She chuckled and shut the phone — utter nonsense.

Climbing off the bus, Stella walked down the alley to the entrance of the gym. It was dingy, but the sign was hard to miss. She stepped inside and gawked at the range of burly, tattooed men. They were all ages but shared one clear goal: fighting. Many had scars across their bodies and had seen better days. Crowds waited to get into boxing rings or simply enjoy the match. She could practically smell the testosterone.

"What do you want?" a gruff voice cut into her thoughts.

"Uh." Stella turned to the guy. "Professor Byrne sent me here."

He cocked a brow and tossed a form at her, pen rolling across the paper. She picked it up and looked through it. The form, she thought, let them get away with murder. Hesitantly, she looked around and locked eyes with the attendant. He felt tired, unsure, bored, lustful.

Trying to delve deeper, she realized he had too much brain fog to think clearly. Probably from head trauma.

"You wanna talk to Dean, the guy with the massive eagle tattoo across his back." The man nodded to a ring. "He's the owner."

Stella timidly headed the owner. She stopped a few feet short and watched as the man — Dean — screamed at two boxers wailing on each other. He glanced over and then back to the men before turning and sizing her up.

"Well, aren't you a little cutie pie," he grunted.

"Professor Byrne sent me here," she countered indignantly.

"Ah," he laughed and eased up. "Well, let's go to my office."

Stella followed him through the gym. Her hands were clammy and stuck to the application form and pen.

She was anxious but trusted Professor Marlin knew this man well enough to ensure her safety.

The office was small but roomy, containing only two chairs, a desk and a filing cabinet. Dean sat down and opened a drawer in the desk.

"Okay, kiddo," Dean said. He put a new set of forms on the desk before folding his hands together. "We do things differently here, like the old days. That means no crying, whimpering or talking back. This form protects both of us in case you get hurt and allows me to provide you with the membership and training for a fraction of the cost."

"What else do you get from it?"

"What do you mean?"

She locked eyes with him and dug deep. He was a mountain of a man, expressionless.

Yet, his emotions told a different story. She reminded him of someone, a memory that made him sad, lonely and reminiscent.

"Why do you help his students with discounts and training? What's underneath the surface?"

"You really are a cop at heart," Dean responded flatly. "He's an old friend of mine. We've known each other since we were kids."

"That's a long time."

"Sure is," he said. "You seem smart… but he usually only sends the crybabies to me. You can start today once you fill this out. I'll find someone to give you a hand around the gym for the first little bit. Maybe a trainer."

He got up and left the office but Stella didn't turn. She knew a decision needed to be made, but this decision was dangerous. Shaking her head, Stella laughed at herself. If she were going to work in law enforcement, her life would be in danger more often than training at a gym.

She filled out the form and stepped back into the training area. Dean nodded to her, so she approached and handed him the paperwork.

"Excellent." He looked through the pages. "The changeroom is over there."

Stella changed as quickly as possible. The dank scent of sweat and perfume in the dark changeroom was putrid and worse than the rings. She locked her bag and put the key on a chain around her neck. Walking back to the training area, she found a group of men standing around the closest ring.

"My name is Richard." A tall, lean man approached. "Unfortunately for you, there are practically no women who train here. On the bright side, you'll get stronger faster working with bigger opponents."

"Thanks," she said. There had been brief hesitation but she urged herself to sound confident.

"Dean said you're in school." Richard pushed his hair away from his eyes. "Have you done any kind of combat training yet?"

"Some," Stella said.

"Good. Let's see what you've got then, kiddo."

She noted two of them called her kiddo so far… She enjoyed it because it reminded her of her dad but hated it because she didn't want to be thought of as a kid.

"Right." She inhaled deeply.

Richard pulled the ropes apart so she could climb into the ring. Her arms shook as she watched one of the men follow suit. The man who entered the ring after Stella quickly armed her with foot, hand and headgear then stepped back to put his own on. She observed him carefully. He was calm, collected. This was not his first time, and she was clearly an easier opponent.

"I'm Frank, by the way," he said.

"Stella."

Collecting her thoughts and bringing herself into the present, she put her hands up. She had no idea what the rules were and was about to ask when Frank lunged forward.

Jumping left, she avoided the jab. Standing outside his body, she grabbed his wrist and thrust her free hand into his floating ribs. He coughed, and she released him.

"She's kind of like a little kitten," a voice taunted.

Stella wanted to tell the person where he could shove it but when she realized her opponent was smiling, she let it go. Frank moved forward, zigzagging, before throwing two punches in succession. She couldn't jump out of the way and blocked the first before ducking under the second and straightening her legs, swinging with an uppercut. He dodged and smacked her hand away.

"Wonderful!" Richard called over the noise. "Crank the speed up a notch, Frank."

Stella watched a grin appear on her opponent's face, locked eyes with him briefly, and began hopping. He was excited, happy. She looked back to his chest, recalling the few words from her first class in college. The professor had told the class to use their peripheral vision when fighting an opponent. She also recalled being told to use their energy to her benefit.

He swapped his stance and began forward and backward steps, the smallest of hops on the balls of his feet. His hands protected his face well, but his elbows and arms protected his torso. Stella needed to wait for an opening, but he was fast. His hands moved at a speed where she could barely see them aiming toward her.

Drawing a calming breath, she waited. Frank seized the moment she blinked and sprang into action. His fists flew swiftly and then his foot. She blocked quickly, barely avoiding a slam to the head. The force rumbled through her arm as his shin landed across her folded arm and bicep.

She could feel herself clenching her teeth as pain roared through her body. Knowing she was open, she shoved the foot away and slid to a southpaw stance, her right leg forward. As she settled into her position, Frank moved, suddenly outside of her body and spinning for a kick.

Stella turned fast and raised her knee up to meet the kick. His leg crashed into hers, and she pushed it down and swung at his face. He moved his leg, and the sudden release caused her to stumble.

He paused, eyebrows lifting in concern. "You good?"

The fight had only just begun. She looked at him. "Yes."

Pain coursed evenly through her arm and shin. Her heart pounded blood angrily through her, and she could feel her body pulsating. She shook it off and went back to her stance.

His speed remained even throughout the match as he threw attacks at her. She found herself heaving for air by the end of the five-minute match. The bell chimed, and she took in as much air as her lungs would allow.

Richard stepped onto the ring, grinning at her, as Frank began removing his equipment. Richard took the foot and headgear off Stella.

"Well, you need better cardio," he said. "But you're decent enough. One-minute jump rope, thirty second rest, one-minute speed bag, thirty second rest, one-minute kettlebell. Repeat that ten times. Don't forget water. Keep the gloves for now."

"Okay," Stella said, though she was quite breathless.

"Water first, actually." He pointed and turned to the others. "As for the rest of you…"

Stella was happy to stumble off the platform, ignoring the rest of what he said. She looked at the members as she slurped water. No one cared about her. She was lost in a cluster of giant, testosterone-driven men, and they couldn't be happier than to allow her to vanish into the wall. Normally feeling hidden was an unpleasant feeling she wanted to avoid, but, in this case, she was happy for the lack of interest.

She moved to the small circuit training area that had been fixed up and put the water bottle down. The circuit Richard had instructed her to follow was daunting at best and deadly at worst.

She could hear the clatter and grunts of the men around her, and she slowly pumped herself up with some light jumps on the balls of her feet.

I can do this…

Chapter Two

Stella was quiet as she handed in her final exam to Professor Byrne. He was grinning at her from underneath his large, bushy moustache. Her classmates had already left the exam hall and it was silent in the room, save for the ticking analog clock.

"You never did tell me about Hardgrove's," Professor Byrne said.

"He accepted me," Stella said.

"I didn't think he would deny you."

"Has he ever sent a student back to you?"

"Only once and it was because Dean said he was a bully," he said.

"Well, can't say I blame him."

"Nor I," he said. "So, tell me how you're doing."

"I've gotten faster," she said.

"I'm sure you have. You've changed substantially over the past month."

"You think so?" She asked, hope welling in her chest. Apparently, his approval meant more to her than she'd initially thought.

"I do, but don't let my opinion stop your progress," he said with a slight grin. "I'm just an old man."

"Thank you," Stella said, her eyes twinkling with admiration for him.

She left the hall with a slight hop in her step. She was proud of the noticeable change and knew she would continue. Hardgrove's Boxing had become an essential component in her life in just a few short weeks.

Rather than heading home, she went directly to the gym. She sat on the bus and watched the city pass by while other passengers stared down at their phones. Stella had refrained from looking at her screen as the news she continued to see was harrowing and desolate in nature. It had yet to serve her a meaningful purpose.

The city was less busy with the flocks of college students moving home for their summer holidays. Stella, on the other hand, decided to remain in the city and continue her training. She wasn't prepared to give up everything she had gained for a few months of rest.

It was silent in the gym as she stepped inside. She hadn't realized how many members at the gym were also students of the college. There were barely fifteen people working the rings when she stepped out of the changeroom. That was less than half the average amount.

She ran her newest circuit for cardio before stopping to look at the television in the corner. It was playing the news, as usual, with closed captioning. It briefly showed an amateur clip wherein the tops of trees could be seen rustling, bending, and a black creature leaping between them. Stella noticed her face was scrunching together as the video cut back to the reporter.

Turning away from the screen, she moved to the changeroom and showered speedily. Without Richard, Frank or many other options to spar with, she was content with just the cardio. Hastily, she left the gym and walked into the cool night air.

Her body was rejuvenated as she walked steadily toward her bus stop. The street was substantially quieter, but a young man caught her attention.

She glanced at him briefly, her heart thumping, before continuing down the street. She stopped for the bus and leaned on her knees. He felt familiar, but she couldn't recall where she had previously seen him.

He was handsome, and the aura surrounding him sent delightful shivers through her body. She imagined his hand touching her skin and the inevitable warmth that came with it.

Stella shook her head and freed herself from the imagination encapsulating her. Truthfully, she didn't know what it would be like. Having avoided both touch and relationships her whole life, there was no way for her to know what would be felt upon a lover's graze. Sighing, she looked up from the ground.

Almost nineteen and single for life.

The bus rolled up and she slowly stepped on. Stella locked eyes with the driver as she greeted him. He was tired but at least happy. His emotions were easy to read, though—unlike most people, he didn't try to hide them.

The sun was beginning to lower, casting large shadows around buildings, as she stepped off the bus and toward her apartment. She inhaled deeply before stepping into the building. A glance of the newspaper stand caught her eye, and she paused mid-step.

"Terrible, isn't it?" Mrs. Whittle said, wobbling to the elevator.

"What is?"

"Those sightings," she said. "It's the end of days."

"End of days?"

"God said the end of days would come." Mrs. Whittle wagged her finger dramatically. "The tribulation is finally raining down on us."

"I beg your pardon?"

"Those monsters, the black ones, that are roaming the woods must be God's wrath," Mrs. Whittle said.

"Is that what your Bible says?"

"Well, technically, we're supposed to go up in flames. But I'm sure that's on its way."

"I think I'd rather drown," Stella said.

Mrs. Whittle took a newspaper from the box and rolled it under her arm tightly. She shook her head and waited in front of the elevator doors.

"So much hatred in the world," Mrs. Whittle said.

Stella merely smiled sadly and held the elevator open for the woman as she stepped inside. She was leaning heavily on her cane as she waited inside.

"I'm taking the stairs, Mrs. Whittle," Stella said politely. "Have a nice night."

Stella watched the door shut as her shoulders slumped heavily, her lungs heaving a darkened sigh. A preposterous notion to believe in the wrath of God through a black creature jumping between trees. Though, the woman was correct about one thing. There certainly is too much hatred.

Chapter Three

The sweltering summer heat had given her a sense of renewal each night as the air turned chilly. Though, the news of the monsters rampaging various territories was still running rampant. Online bloggers were filling the world with rumours—unhelpful ones at that.

Her only reprieve from the madness had been the private coaching available to her. It had also dramatically increased her skills.

As she stepped into Hardgrove's Boxing, she could smell the sweat oozing off the men. The building was still dingy, but it now provided her with a sense of home. The autumn crowds were beginning to rise as students returned to school. She smiled to herself as she headed through the people and into the changerooms.

Upon emerging, she found Richard waiting silently next to a ring. He was reading a book though she couldn't quite make out the title. Rather than ask, she walked up to him and pointed to the man in the ring.

"Where's Frank?"

"Otherwise, preoccupied," he said, looking up from the pages. "Climb into the ring."

He was surprisingly cold, and she stumbled briefly for words before accepting the command. "Okay."

Stella kept her eyes locked on her newest sparring partner as she climbed up into the ring; Richard was close behind. He was bigger than Dean but judging from the practice swings, he was faster than Frank. Richard was wrapping her hands up in the gloves and checking her helmet as she kept an eye on the big fellow.

"You'll be fine," Richard said with a shrug. "I already told him if he breaks a tooth or anything, he has to cover the medical expense."

"Gee," Stella said sarcastically, rolling her eyes, "thanks."

"I'm astounded you've done as well as you have." Richard was smirking at her. "You have a natural inclination for this. You've only spent five months here, a chunk of that being your summer vacation no less, and it's like you've been training with me for a year."

"Well, training five days a week helps." Stella grinned happily.

"Kids… it's like you don't have a job."

"I had my placement," she muttered.

"Oh, right." Richard hopped out of the ring. "How's that going?"

"Five in the morning to two in the afternoon," Stella said. "It's mostly paperwork, but I've gone on a couple rides and done some workouts with them."

"Sounds exciting." He turned to her partner. "Time to focus, kiddo. Eric is ruthless."

"Stop calling me that." Stella followed his gaze to the giant.

In times like this, she wondered if giants were true history instead of mythology. After all, the legends had to stem from somewhere. Stella looked him up and down, then focused square on his chest. She knew from watching his other matches that if she took even one hit, she'd be done, so he needed to submit quickly.

Richard rang the bell, and she pounced forward, feinting an attack on Eric's left. Diverting last minute, Stella swung her leg up as his guard came down to protect his gut. Eric's head swung back as she clipped him in the jaw.

Stella let her heel spin and turned her hips, locking her leg around his thigh. Pressing her left leg into his and pushing her weight into him, she tried to sweep the leg.

He grabbed her legs, picked her up, swung and tossed her into the ropes. She braced as she bounced forward and to the floor. She knelt and looked up at him, grinning at her. Sheepishly, she exchanged a smile and got back up.

He charged and swung a barrage of punches at her. She pulled her guard up just in time, and her arms took the beating as she watched for an opening. She could feel her body wanting to pull away from the pain. Stella forced herself to stay put and watch. He clipped her along the face, and she brought her arm back up as the burning sensation cooled. Stella realized through shaky waves of hot and cold running across her skin that blood was trickling down her face at an alarming rate, and she exhaled heavily.

Eric paused for a split second, and she stole the opportunity. Swiftly, she leapt back and yanked his left hand down while shoving his right hand upward, opening his stomach, and delivered a front kick to his chest as hard as she could. He stumbled backward but not before she grabbed his wrist.

Gripping tightly, she rotated under his arm, pulling his hand with her. Her mind went elsewhere as their skin touched. She winced as his thoughts pulled into her mind.

Please don't have a concussion… Dean will kill me.

Gasping sharply, she forced herself to refocus as her grip almost disappeared. She spun to face the same direction as him and pulled his arm behind his back, pushing up as high as she could get it. He tapped quickly, and she breathed as she released his arm.

"I'm not sure that's technically allowed," Dean said with a snort. "Wasn't it supposed to be boxing?"

Richard climbed back into the ring as he sighed, "I'm kind of letting her react. If she's going to be a cop, she needs to trust her instincts. That was probably her best bet at winning."

"You're not bad," Dean called as he moved on.

Richard grabbed Stella's face and ran his finger across the scratch. Her face was pouring blood mercilessly, and he would need to seal it.

"She's done sparring for the day," he declared. The assortment of people who were watching the fight moved along. "What was that pause?"

"Hm?" Her eyes met his.

"You looked a world away," he commented as he held the rope for her.

She climbed down, stumbled in the steps, and he followed close behind with his arms extended in case she fell. Directing her to a bench, he grabbed a first aid kit and began rifling through it.

"I know," she finally admitted. "I get lost in…"

She couldn't exactly tell him that she could read minds or understand emotions through touch and eye contact. Not only would he not believe her, but he might say to her there was too much head trauma to keep training.

"Lost in…?" he waited.

"You know, you guys aren't as old school as Professor Byrne led me to believe," she said.

Richard sighed. "We're old school with the old schoolers."

He moved her head and angled it so he could get to the scratch more efficiently. His hands worked diligently to wipe the blood away and disinfect. Focused, he examined how deep it was.

"Alright." His decision was stated calmly. "I'm gonna glue it shut."

"Excuse me?" Stella barked as her head jerked backwards.

"Relax. You'll like it… old school."

She locked her eyes elsewhere after cocking an amused eyebrow at him. She watched the gym's world move. There were at least thirty guys doing circuit training, drills or sparring. She wondered what they did for work. Most of them were businessmen who needed to blow off steam, but others were too bulky for that.

"Tell me something weird about yourself," Richard asked as he began putting the glue in.

"I can read minds," she blurted in her distraction and then winced as he cinched the cut. "Ouch!"

"Oh, don't be such a big baby," he said. "So, you can read minds."

He looked at her skeptically, and she sighed, kicking herself for saying that. He was busy putting first aid equipment away, but she watched him. He didn't seem bothered by the notion, though she guessed it was probably because he didn't believe her.

"I know." She shrugged and stood.

"Know what?" He said and smirked as he washed his hands. "What I'm thinking?"

"Shut up," she said. Deciding at the moment to take a chance, she reached out to him. "Give me your hand."

"Eh?" He dried his hands.

"Just do it."

"Fine." He relented as he extended his arm.

She took his hand and waited. He was grinning at her, and she frowned. Odd. Nothing. This only ever happened a few times in her life. Stella determined he had no internal monologue. Those types of people could be dangerous, she always thought. Instead, she reached up and touched his forehead.

Inside her own mind's eye, she struggled. She could grasp the idea of what he was thinking but less so the wording. It was predominantly flashing images.

"You're thinking about chilli-cheese dogs." She opened her eyes and looked at him sourly.

"I am actually. But it's not like that's surprising."

"Then think about something else," she snapped.

"Why me?" He looked around. "Frank, come here."

Stella felt her face warm as Frank approached. This would be interesting, to say the least. She instantly regretted her decision, but she kept her breath steady as Richard smirked at her.

"Grab her hand," he said.

"Okay."

Frank was a little hesitant but put his hand out. She released Richard and turned to grab hold of Frank, with her fingers wrapped around his wrist and she looked up at him. Frank was waiting for something to happen.

"Think a very specific thought," Richard commanded with a snort.

"Like what?" Frank exchanged a nervous glance with Richard.

"Anything at all." Richard crossed his arms.

Stella kept her eye on him as he began rolling thoughts around his mind. He went from food to women to training to his vehicle.

What is Stella doing? Oh wow, she has stunning eyes. I know she's single, but I'm not about to bring that up to her. I really want chicken nuggets. I wonder when my next match is going to be. Dean hasn't said anything to me about fights for a little while now. Oh, I have to call mom when I get home today.

Stella released his hand. His tumultuous thoughts had sent a slight headache into her own. "He thought about my eyes, then me being single. He wants chicken nuggets. Dean hasn't said anything to him about fighting for a while, so he's wondering when his next match is going to be. Oh, and he has to call his mom when he gets home today."

She looked at Richard, who was checking in with a stunned Frank. He gasped and stepped backward.

"What kind of psychology is that?" he choked.

"Then she was right?" Richard was amused. "Cute trick."

Stella stood between the two of them. Her eyes firmly ahead of her as she watched their faces from her periphery. Richard still wasn't convinced, but judging by Frank's expressions he could have been having heart failure.

Her attention turned to the television as the sound went up. The room quieted as the news reporter began speaking. They were cutting into the regular broadcast.

"New reports of a single entity from Georgian Bay, Ontario has emerged," the reporter said. "The Canadian Military, local and provincial police are watching the situation closely. They are encouraging people who live along the bay, from Meaford to Collingwood, to stay indoors as the creature is moving across terrain rapidly. It's being described as all black and six to ten feet long. According to reports, the creature is destroying everything it comes into contact with."

The screen went from the reporter to images of slaughtered wildlife. Stella inhaled sharply as scattered deer limbs, grizzly and black bears and smaller animals went across the screen.

"These are different reports than what we heard from Brazil earlier this year." The reporter's face was stark white when it reappeared on screen. "Brazil reported only criminals were attacked during the rampage. Scientists are baffled as to what it is, and there are no confirmed reports that this is the same creature that was seen in Brazil."

The volume went back down, and Dean looked around the room. Stella had never heard the place so deathly silent. She would have been able to hear a mouse in the walls. She locked eyes with Dean and read his emotions. He was terrified.

"Alright," he said. "Let's get back to it. I'm sure the police have this handled. No point worrying about things out of our control."

Everybody moved back to their sections, but their work wasn't quite the same. There wasn't a single person in the gym who hadn't been rattled by the news and images. Stella was shaking. It was different from having it in their own country.

Her chest grew heavy as she thought about it. Something in the reports seemed off. Her eyes turned to Richard, who was looking contemplative as he stared at the screen. Stella could have sworn his pupils had shifted to a cat-like iris. She stepped back in surprise, and he glanced down at her; his eyes returned to normal.

She shook it off and took a large swig of water. The hit to her head must have been hard for her to be seeing things. Taking a few deep breaths, she began walking the gym to prevent leg cramps. She could feel Richard's eyes on her as she moved.

Stella wondered what he was thinking, but she couldn't let him get to her. But soon, he fell in line with her pace and walked the space.

"Do you feel okay?" Richard asked.

"Yes."

"Are you sure?"

"I am," Stella said, eyes lifting to his. "Are you?"

"You don't need to worry about me," Richard said.

He smiled gently, almost encouragingly, as they drifted around the room. His aura was softly humming around him, permeating her own. It was oddly calming and familiar.

"Yet you get to worry about me?"

"I'm the adult in this scenario."

"Yes, I do come across as a child sometimes."

"I was hesitant about trusting you, about allowing you into the ring, when we first met," Richard said. "But you've grown on me."

"Thanks."

"I believe you have great things ahead of you," Richard said. "But you're done for today. That scratch knocked your head a little too hard. Go home."

"Are you sure?"

"I am very sure," he said.

"Okay," Stella said.

She agreed with him. The graze was a little more than a head bop. Her day was hazy from then on until she collapsed into bed, safe at home. Her eyes shut, and she could feel everything stop as she began to drift away.

"I told you not to daydream." A calm voice broke the silence.

"What harm can come from a catnap?"

Her eyes turned about, realizing she was in a garden. It was spring, and the flowers were open and bright. They ranged in colours and shades. The smell was fresh and sweet. Bees were floating about collecting pollen, and a few smaller animals nibbled away on the plants. She saw him, but not clearly.

Her mind could recall who he was, but a great love burned within her chest. She had seen his imperfections and quirks, but they seemed to bring him new life and joy. She could not see his face but knew he was handsome.

"You may see things you do not desire," he warned her.

"What things?" she teased with a lopsided grin.

"The future," he sighed, and the wind swept through the trees. "Or at least… potential futures."

"I think I like our future." She licked her lips. "Even I can guess."

"You think so?" He took a step closer.

"I really do." Stella bit her lower lip.

Stella was about to reach for him when a sudden, jolting alarm rang overhead. She winced and shut her eyes tightly. When they opened, she found herself rolled over in her bed, squeezing the living daylights out of a pillow.

Stella sighed and spun, slamming her hand on the alarm. Sun was creeping through the curtains, and she double-checked the time. Her body ached for more sleep, but her schedule wouldn't allow it. Dragging herself out of bed; she looked in the mirror.

Stella pulled away as she saw her eyes burning brightly like the sun. She gasped and fled to the bathroom. When she checked her reflection there, everything was normal. Her chest and shoulders collapsed heavily in relief.

Using the coldest water possible from the faucet, Stella washed her face. The dream and those eyes of hers had felt real, if not ethereal and elusive, even though she knew they weren't. Stella sighed to herself, desiring an explanation, and knowing she would never obtain one. She had never experienced such realistic dreams.

The piercings along her left ear caught in the fabric, and she stopped to pull the thread carefully. Stella smiled at them, knowing precisely what they meant. She felt calm as she looked at the reflection of them, her fingertips touching the metal gently.

At least her piercings were real.

Chapter Four

The ripple down her arms finally felt familiar as she fired at the target. Pulling the ear protection down, she watched the paper criminal slide forward as she processed the five shots to the head and five to the center of the chest. She smiled to herself and exited into the shop. The owner was watching the news particularly loud as she approached the counter.

Stella handed the gun, ear guards and target to him. He smirked at her as she snapped a photograph. He took the target and tucked everything away before facing her again. Her hand grazed his briefly and she unintentionally heard his thoughts.

She's changed. Not two months ago, she apologized for missing the target entirely. Now she's a sharpshooter.

"How's boxing going?" he asked as he rang up the transaction.

"It's good," she said. "I think I'm okay at it. It's been eight months and I haven't died."

Stella's eyes drifted toward the television as a special news report cut into a talk show. She scowled as the report began.

"There are more mysterious creatures popping out of the woodwork in the Amazonian Jungle along the Columbian border," the reporter announced. "No one knows where they're coming from, but this is the third sighting around the world in the past year. The first was in Brazil back in March. The second occurred in Georgian Bay near the end of August."

Stella drew a deep, heavy breath as the news hit hard. It wasn't nearly as close as the last sighting but third time was always the charm.

"Bodies of animals and humans have been found in pieces. Thus far, there have been at least forty human deaths in Canada due to the creature seen roaming Georgian Bay. Collectively, there have been nearly one-hundred deaths between Canada, Brazil and now the Amazonian Jungle.

"Each sighting has consisted of only one creature, which people have consistently described as black and oily with long limbs, claws and talons.

According to reports, its body is over six feet long and has left footprints as what can easily be described as gargantuan in size yet human. Military officials worldwide are hesitant to allow soldiers closer to the creature without determining its species and origin as scientists are still unclear as to what it is. What we do know is any official military attacks that have occurred have yielded no results in stopping these creatures."

So, it could still be the one that was seen in Brazil, Stella determined. The sound of the television lowered to a mere whisper and she looked at the shop owner. The remote was shaky in his hand.

"If you ask me it's all a hoax," he said.

Judging by the tenseness in his voice, he wasn't entirely truthful. Stella smiled and paid, wondering how much was true in the news report. There hadn't been any clear photos of these so-called creatures. She figured they were just people using an excuse to kill what—or who—they wanted without consequence. Some people had begun calling them furere, though she didn't have a clue what that meant.

"More than likely," Stella said quickly to avoid bickering. "But they've been popping up all over the world. This one, and then the one that showed up in Brazil and even one sighting by Georgian Bay. But they've said nothing further about those separate incidents…"

She momentarily locked eyes with the shop owner who was angry, fuming. He wanted to get involved. Shivering, she looked at her wallet.

He snorted as he handed back her change. "Well, whatever…"

"Have a good one." Stella forced a smile as she left. She considered conducting research of her own but figured there would be far more coverage of the incidents if it ever became a real problem. If they were genuinely monsters, hellbent on destruction, then there were measures the government could take to annihilate them.

Stella's eyes were locked on the pavement as she headed away from the indoor range. She wrapped her jacket around her body tightly. It was a strange business to have in the middle of a city but he made it work. The owner always commented that it used to be quiet, hardly a soul, when the range opened twenty years ago.

Stella tried to quiet her mind as she walked. Her pace quickened as the wind went through her jacket. She wanted to get out of the cold sooner than later and swung through the crowd. Narrowly missing someone who wasn't looking, she tripped and fell into another person.

"Oh, sorry!" she apologized, turning on her heel.

"That is perfectly fine," he said.

His eyes met hers and they stirred her soul. She stood open mouthed and suddenly very awake. But more than that, he was oddly familiar, and she felt reminiscent of different days.

"Have we met?" she blurted.

His face remained expressionless, but his eyes glimmered with knowledge, and they stunned her as they sparkled in the sunlight. She could have sworn they'd met many years ago, but she couldn't place it. They would have been very young. Perhaps three or four, she surmised, from how vague the memory felt.

"Have a wonderful day," he spoke calmly and went on his way. "Be sure to keep on your toes."

She watched him stride quickly in the crowd effortlessly, seeming to float through and between people. Soon he was gone, almost as if he never existed. Stella tried to recall where she had seen him but couldn't pull the memory forward.

Shaking her head and turning away, she made her way steadily to the college with streams of other people and students. The city was bustling as usual, and most of the people probably hadn't even heard the news yet.

She hopped into her classroom, phone ready to show off her latest photo, and walked up to Professor Marlin's desk.

"Hey," he greeted with a wave.

"Hi, sir. Check it out."

Stella put the phone down and opened the gallery. He chuckled at the snapshot and then looked up at her. His moustache tickled his lips as his smile spread ear to ear.

"Very good," he said approvingly. "You'll ace the entrance into the academy. Dean tells me he'd consider putting you in a real octagon with a couple more years of experience."

"Oh, I don't know about that," Stella took her phone back, "but it's been a good time."

"Has it now?"

"Yes." She put the phone away. "Look at these guns!"

She lifted her arm up and squeezed her bicep while laughing. Sound from the hall caught her attention so she moved to a natural stance before moving to her seat.

She watched the slowpokes meander into the room as he began the lecture. She kept her eyes on the board as her hand-copied the notes. Stella wrote quickly to keep up with him, but it wasn't too long before the college's phone rang. He paused and reached for the device.

Stella observed, locking eyes when he turned back around to face the class. His face, although grim, gave nothing away. His eyes, however, told her everything. There was fear and worry digging deeper in his chest.

"Class is dismissed," he said. "Head to the library or cafeteria to study the rest of the lecture. I'll let you know through email if we'll have class this afternoon. There's some business to take care of among the faculty. I apologize."

He hurried to grab his bag, hands trembling, and left the room before any of the students had a chance to get up.

Stunned, Stella went to the cafeteria and tucked her nose into a book. Whatever happened must have been significant. The ding from her phone resonated in her backpack, so she pulled it out and opened it, an email from Professor Marlin explaining that class was cancelled for the day and students were to prep for their test next week.

Sighing, she saw a couple of her classmates walking by. They were laughing about something, and she waved them over, but they continued to pass her. Stella sighed and considered heading home.

Even in a second year of the program, Stella couldn't get people to spend time with her. There had been a few moments of laughter between her and the classmates, but they predominantly avoided her, saying she was too eerie. Stella grumbled to herself and stuffed everything into her backpack. She could always go to the gym.

After jamming her textbook into her bag and rising to leave, the rows of televisions erupted, and news reports began playing. Her eyes stared at the reporters whose eyes were bulged and lips curved downward. The sound of the reporters was muffled as students and teachers began racing to safety. People slammed her shoulders as Stella was shoved and pushed in their panic. Teachers and students alike locked themselves in rooms. Security ran down the corridor as their radios rumbled vague words.

Stella briefly turned her eyes back to the screens, and her breath stopped. Frozen, her heart shrunk as it pounded mercilessly at the revelation: they were real… and in their city.

Chapter Five

Stella's eyes were dark as she watched hordes trample over the walkways of the college. Shaking with fear, she lowered herself from the barred window in the bathroom to the floor. Her phone's battery was nearly dead and there were no outlets in sight.

Her screen flickered to life as she crawled into the bathroom stall where her backpack still sat. Stella closed the door behind her and leaned against it as quietly as possible. The concrete walls and steel door had been lifesaving the past two days, but her stomach was rumbling angrily. She'd devoured the last of her granola bars the day before.

The screen of her phone continued to flash, and she finally checked the screen. It was another news flash. Opening the video, Stella plugged her earbuds in and placed one in her ear.

"The creatures, now commonly being referred to as furere, have continued to plague cities across Canada," the reporter said. "We aren't able to offer a total body count, but it's estimated nearly fifty-thousand people have died over the past two days as police and military attempt to gain control over the situation. People are urged to stay in their homes and await further instructions."

Stella's eyes shifted to the blinking red light in the corner of her phone. Only nine percent battery left. Dumping the contents of her bag over the floor, she scoured for anything useful. She was only bringing her metal water bottle, phone charger and sweater.

The textbooks and binders remained scattered on the floor as she put the backpack over her shoulders and crept to the door. She removed the massive wads of spitballs from the crack between the floor tiles and the door before turning the lock.

Slowly, cautiously, she inched the door open and peeked into the hallway. The college's lower level had always been dark, but now it was near pitch black with little to no fluorescent lights shining. But it was at least silent.

Her feet moved slowly, her body following into the hallway. Her heart was hammering inside her with each step she took. She peered into an adjacent hallway to find it far darker and more ominous than the present one. Looking dead ahead, she decided to try for the lighter of the two options.

She sprinted across the open threshold and toward a small set of steps before a glass doorway. Stella could feel her pack bouncing with each leap of the stairs before coming to a dead halt at the door.

Peering through the glass she looked at the large space beyond. There was blood, blackened, pooled on the floor. Her eyes tilted upward to see bodies hanging by hair, hands and feet. Stella gasped, hands rushing to cover her mouth as the sound escaped.

Tears were running from the edges of her eyes as she looked at the bodies. The creatures weren't just killing everything in sight… they were torturing people.

Her body shrunk to the floor as her breaths heaved unevenly. She put her face in her hands and tried to control her breathing as a panic attack began taking over her body. Stella's body shook and trembled as she curled in on herself tightly.

"Agh!" she cried before wiping her tear-stained face. "Move!"

Her hand shakily reached up for the handle and used it to pull herself upright. Her thumb pushed down on the lever, and she listened, cringing, to the door creaking open. She looked around the space waiting for one of them to come after her, but the only sound she could hear was the wind whistling through the building.

Feet crushing glass as she stepped, she moved forward. Each sound sent waves of fear up her body. Stella's breaths were low, shallow as she finally made it to the stairs. Her hands gripped the banister tightly as she urged herself to the main floor.

By the time she had ascended the spiral stairwell, she was tired and fell into a seated position at its opening. Her body was weakening with each movement, every breath she took. Her eyes drifted shut as she caught her breath.

A sound startled her awake, and she lurched forward, head spinning toward the sound. She scrambled to her feet and went toward the cafeteria, opposite the sound.

Racing through the empty hallways, she barely looked at her surroundings. But when Stella reached the food court, she slid to a halt.

Her entire body froze, mind halting all function. Her body stiffened as her blood ran cold inside her veins.

Every single seat was filled with a human body. They were tied in place by their own entrails, and their heads were all turned to face the main entrance of the cafeteria. Their dead eyes stared Stella down. Limbs were scattered among the bodies. Detached and then reattached to a different person.

Stella heaved bile over the tiles as her knees shook beneath her. The smell of decay was powerful, but it was the sheer sight of the mangled bodies that overtook her senses. The desire to eat subsided, and she looked at the stomach acid lying at her feet.

With a deep breath, she forced herself to rise. She wiped her face yet again and pushed herself by the bodies and into the restaurants. Stella moved slowly as she stared at the human remains surrounding her.

Once inside the kitchen, she opened cupboards in search of any goods she could bring. Stella slung her pack off and filled it with as much food as she could manage. As she was closing the bag, she heard a sound behind her, and she spun quickly.

"Stella!" Professor Marlin gasped. "How in the hell did you survive?"

"Me? What about you?"

"I spent years learning how to hide."

"I uh… I jammed toilet paper covered in soap and water in a door and hid in the basement's bathroom," Stella said, though her face flushed in embarrassment.

"Genius."

Stella looked at him; he was covered in blood and bile. His eyes were gaunt and shoulders slumped. He didn't look as though he'd slept in two days. Granted, Stella hadn't slept either.

"You can't stay," he said.

"Obviously. You can't either."

Stella looked at the remaining articles of food and realized her hunger had returned. Stella grabbed a can of peaches from the cupboard and rummaged silently for an opener. She opened the can and plunged her fingers into the liquid. She squeezed the peach slice between her fingers and transferred it to her mouth.

The juice ran down her throat as she chewed hastily. The sweetness of the peach was almost overwhelming for her senses, but Stella swallowed all the same, holding the container out to her professor.

He reached over her head and took a can of food himself as he took the opener instead. Stella slid down the sides of the counter as she continued to shove peach slices into her mouth. Her eyes watched the old man grab a spoon and begin feeding himself the chopped pineapple.

"A spoon?"

"I'm not a savage," he said with a shrug.

The comment made her smile absently as she turned her eyes away and gulped the juices left in the can. She set it aside quietly and looked at the eerie setting they found themselves in. Knowing hundreds of bodies were sitting just outside didn't help with the unease in her gut.

"What do we do now?" Stella asked in a whisper.

"Where's your confidence?"

"Shot to hell," she said.

"Now's not the time to be meek."

"Tens of thousands of people are dead," Stella said, throat burning with the words. "What do you expect from me?"

"I expect you to do whatever you must in order to live," he hissed.

"What would that entail?" Her voice had raised, but she shifted to a whisper at the thought of the furere returning to them. Stella was wracked in fear, but she wanted to live.

"It will not be the same world once you exit this building."

"It hasn't been the same world for two days," Stella said. "Did you see the food court?"

"Of course, I did," Marlin said. "You want to live? You find a weapon, something you're good at, and a hunting knife. You get a hiking pack and fill it with winter apparel and boots. You find a place you can stay warm in the winter. Stella, hunting and hiding will be key to survival."

"I'm neither of those things," she cried. "I'm not a hunter. I don't kill!"

"Learn how to," he told her. "Think of them as criminals."

Images flashed in her eyes and she held her face tightly, wincing. Stella shook her head violently as faces flashed in her mind as if distant memories. She didn't know who they were but she could see them clearly. They haunted her soul as they screamed at her.

"Stella?"

"Yeah," she said, her head clearing.

"They're not just creatures," he said. "The news has been calling them furere, monsters. But they aren't just animals. They're intelligent."

"They'd have to be to pull of something so malicious," Stella said.

Her eyes were turned toward the food court. Stella shuddered knowing she would have to cross through the deranged garden of bodies once more.

"There isn't much time," Marlin said.

"Why can't I stay here? It'll be warm in winter."

"Perhaps," he said. "But do you really want to live under a horde of bodies."

"Better than running from them in winter."

Reaching across the distance, Professor Marlin touched her hands. Stella gasped at the touch as his thought protruded into her mind.

She can't afford to relax now. I won't last much longer but she might have a chance. If only she retained what she learned with Dean.

"You cannot stay here," he said. "You need to find a safer place. Away from the city, away from people. That's how you stay alive."

"I don't know if I'll stay alive anyway," she said.

"You will."

His eyes were piercing as he said this. She wished for his strength, but she couldn't imagine having such fortitude.

"You have grown so much this year — don't lose that."

A sound from outside froze the pair in their spots, and Stella held her breath. A small whimper crossed her lips as she reached for the cupboard door and quietly opened it. It was too small for either of them to fit, and Stella scrunched her eyes closed, praying whatever made the noise would pass by. She kept her eyes shut as she strained to hear between her breaths.

Stella's eyes opened wide as she waited. Professor Marlin grabbed her wrist and yanked her toward the walk-in freezer. Silently, he pulled the door open and led them inside. He locked the door behind them and waited, ear pressed to the door, for the noise to dissipate.

There was clashing and clanging outside. Each crash sent shivers up her spine, her hand gripping Professor Marlin's hand tightly. She could feel him wriggling his fingers, so she eased her hold as they waited. Stella thought they would be there until their deaths before the door would open again as time ticked slowly.

When the only sounds to be heard were their breaths, Professor Marlin opened the door an inch and peered outside. He sighed in relief, opened it a touch wider before slinking his way out through the crack.

He reached back in, and Stella gratefully took his hand as he led her into the kitchen. The cupboards were fallen off the walls, and items moved aside. They wandered back to the dining area, and Stella fell to her knees in shock at the disturbing image before her eyes. The heads of every single corpse were missing.

"What in the world?" Professor Marlin said, his body trembling as he pulled her forward.

Stella's teeth clenched as her eyes looked at the headless ghosts trapped at the tables. It was disturbing the first time she passed through but now it was haunting. They headed away from the food court and her knees shook weakly.

Tapping on a pane of glass caught her attention and Stella twisted rapidly to see only snow and ice blasting against the window. It was finally winter, she sighed internally.

Chapter Six

"Official reports say there has been no advancement in killing the furere," the radio chimed softly. Stella had found the device while rummaging for supplies. It was small and battery-operated but picked up signals well.

"Military officials have been unable to find attacks or weaponry sufficient to kill the creatures. It's been five weeks since the largest recorded attack that initially stole fifteen thousand lives. After two days, the number increased to fifty thousand. Since then, the onslaught has continued as the current estimated death toll in Canada is nearing fifteen million while the number of furere continues to increase. Military officials are gathering civilians in camps across the country to provide shelter, food and protection. For anyone still listening, you may find yours at the nearest military base to your current location."

The pair exchanged glances upon the news but remained still. The basement of the college was secure and free of the snowstorms.

The few trips out of the building Stella had made over the past few weeks only served to reinforce the fear instilled in her by the furere. Their strength was unmatched as she looked at upside-down cars and toppled buildings. Even pieces of bodies lay scattered in the open.

Marlin had attempted to remain unphased as he took her out for hunting expeditions. But Stella took advantage of his knowledge and expertise over the weeks after the major attack. She figured he meant for her to survive without him soon, but she couldn't give it much thought.

There hadn't been a catch in the past week, but there were still some canned goods left from storage and were heated under small flames in the room they'd called their home.

The small fire sitting between the two of them burned brightly in the darkened space. The basement, concrete and stone, absorbed much of the light from the flame. But the heat was enough to keep most of the shivering at bay.

"You'll be fine on your own," Professor Marlin said.

"What? Where are you going?" Stella asked.

"Surely you know I won't live much longer."

"What does that mean?"

"I'm old, Stella," he said. "This world is not meant for someone my age."

"You're not that old," Stella said.

"Honey," he began sweetly, "I'm eighty-two."

"No, you're not!"

"I am."

Stella was shocked, enraged and frightened. She didn't want to be alone, and his statement had come out of the blue. Pressing her hands into her knees, she kept quiet. There were no words for her to utter that would change his mind.

"May I pass on some knowledge to you?"

"Of course," she said, still dismayed by the previous statement.

"Everything you think you're incapable of is a lie," he said. "You have everything you need to survive, to thrive; you just need to look inside yourself."

"Oh. My. God." Stella's eyes rolled to the back of her skull as she laughed bitterly. Now wasn't the time for cheesy sentimentality.

"You might not think so at the moment, but you're still here, aren't you? You'll be okay, no matter what happens."

She looked at him and smiled, wanting him to think she agreed. The expression on his face told her he could see through the deceptive grin and she lowered her eyes with a sigh.

A tumultuous bang and tumbling clattered above them and both ducked before pushing back from the flames and to their feet. Her heart hammered nervously as the sound grew louder.

"Furere," Stella grumbled.

"Put your boots on," he commanded as he moved toward the sound.

Scrambling to dress in her winter gear, she watched him move cautiously between stacks of desks and tables. Stella stomped the fire out and stood waiting to grab her backpack, her eyes turning as she reached for the coat.

A gurgling scream erupted, and she snapped her face back up. A furere was standing in the doorway, lurking and heaving over Professor Marlin. She watched him yank his pistol up to its face and pull the trigger, all the while screaming for her to run.

Stella was frozen as she stared at the man. The furere stomped forward, arms outstretched and thrashing toward him. The black arms made rough contact, throwing Professor Marlin aside.

"Run!" he screamed, his body rising again.

The furere turned back to him and screeched, the sound filling Stella's body with tremors and sharp pain like ice prickling open her skin. It grabbed Professor Marlin in its massive jaw and lifted him from the ground. The professor turned, his eyes pleading with her, before the furere's jaw snapped shut, severing his torso from his hips.

Stella grabbed what she could and fled from the room. Surging around and under the tables and desks until she reached the second door to the room. She slammed through the door as another echo of a gunshot reached her ears.

She couldn't bring herself to turn and see but that had to be the last of his life force as she fled from the college. Her feet carried her swiftly through the college corridors, the maze of the basement, as the sound of the furere raging through the blockade echoed down the hallway. She ran, turning and guessing which hallway to take until she burst into the winter storm. Stella slammed the door behind her and grit her teeth.

Tears streaking her face, the wind left marks across her skin, she withheld a cry. Stella threw on her coat and pack, eyes shifting backward once more before she began plowing through the mounds of snow.

She raced through the space that was once a parking lot. The sky above was dark, but there was enough light to make out the buildings and rubble. Stella moved fast until she couldn't catch her breath in the cold. She felt her body slowing as she dragged her feet. Turning her eyes, there was no trace of the furere that attacked them.

Stella huffed heavily as she choked down sobs. She pushed Professor Marlin from her mind as the onslaught of dead bodies before her in the streets overwhelmed her. They were torn apart, limb from limb, and deformed. They hadn't been left as a warning but merely too unimportant to be dealt with.

With winter now settled in, the bodies were frozen and their corpses timeless until the spring. Then they would begin rotting and leave their stench in the air. Not only would the furere foul the earth, but so would the decimation they leave behind.

Snow billowed heavily in Stella's face as she slowly trekked through hip-high snow. Her mind wandered as aimlessly as her body.

It had been weeks since the attack on the college, and nothing had improved. There were no traces or signs of the military from what Stella could tell. Of course, she would need to head south to Hamilton to find one of their secure outposts for civilians. But told herself she wouldn't head to a populated area. It was too risky.

Her body slowed as the weight of guilt became trapped in her chest. It burdened her legs into slow, struggling movements. Professor Marlin had been taken by them, and Stella had done nothing to save him. She fled for her life. Trying to tell herself she did as instructed seemed like a lie so she wouldn't feel so terrible. Abandoning him was disgraceful.

As the wind picked up, Stella's mind shifted to finding shelter of any kind in her immediate surroundings. The boots she'd acquired were at least warm enough to endure the temperature and storm. The coat was thick and kept her warm, but her movement was restricted.

Eventually, she stumbled on a shed and walked around it to see a house. The door was wide open and looked as if it had been raided. Stella glanced inside the shed and then the house trying to decide where she would stay.

She decided on the house and stomped through the snow and up onto the deck. Shaking the cold flurries from her garments, she pulled her knife out and stepped into the house. Stella could hear the whistling of the wind as she stepped further in.

In the living room, she found three bodies hanging from the ceiling. They hadn't decayed due to the cold, and she could see their faces clearly as she saw the stripped paint on the walls.

Rather than dwell on it, she moved to the stairs and crept upward. They creaked with her steps, but they weren't nearly as loud as the whistling wind. The master bedroom was still tidy despite the rest of the house. The children's rooms were destroyed, blood sprayed across walls, as the furere had obnoxiously, ruthlessly torn through the house.

Crawling to the floor, she checked under every bed before opening the closets and peering inside. Each room on the top floor she confirmed was empty. She moved back downstairs and checked the basement.

Feces and urine filled her nostrils as she opened the door. Naturally, water lines had stopped working, and they opted for the basement instead of the shed as a waste depository. She pulled her scarf over her face to protect her sense of smell as she went through the basement.

Every nook and cranny were checked, and she still found nothing but air. As she headed for the steps, a creak from above drew her attention. She shuffled backward and looked for a room she could hide in readily as the creaking and steps drew closer.

Shaking her head, Stella stepped into the makeshift lavatory and shut the door with the tiniest of clicks. She kept the scarf rolled high as she pushed further into the room and quietly slipped into the closet. Eyes stinging in the wretched air, she tried to hide in the darkness.

Stairs creaked into the basement, and she held her breath. The door burst open, and Stella jumped in surprise, heart pounding. She watched a long, grizzly snout sniff into the room past the dangling, crooked door.

Holding her breath, she watched it sniff the room. It's claws, long and jagged, ripped into the carpet. The scent of the fecal matter seemed to throw off its sense of smell. Stella remained motionless until the furere eventually turned away. The clack of its claws heading back up the stairs was relieving.

She listened to screeching as it tore through the upper portion of the house. She stood as still as possible in the corner of the closet, waiting for the destruction to end. Stella was saddened to note she no longer smelled the difference in air quality.

After spending hours standing in the closet, she turned slowly, stepped from the room and walked to the door hesitantly. Her eyes searched the main room before she stepped into it.

Stella was terrified, dreading the ascent, as she looked up the steps. The carpet was torn open from the claw marks, and she swallowed dryly. Suppressing a cough, her shoulders and back curled tightly as her torso heaved up and down.

She crawled, hands and knees, up the steps and turned her body near the top to peer into the hallway. A pile of snow had filled the doorway and a vast portion of the hallway. She glanced to the kitchen and continued to crawl down the corridor.

Her backpack was heavy as it shifted forward onto the back of her head. She entered the kitchen and slipped it off. Stella crouched as she looked through the window into the backyard. She saw nothing in the yard and no sign of life in the trees beyond, so she stood upright and began opening cupboards.

There was a bag of uncooked noodles and a can of bean chilli, she took them both and shoved them into her bag. She took yet another can opener and went up the stairs to the master bedroom.

She locked the door and crawled onto the bed, covering herself with the comforter, yet, unlike the name, and the heat building around her body, Stella felt no comfort as she couldn't find it in her body to relax. Stella opened the can and dipped a metal spoon in. Despite the chilli being partially frozen, it still had flavour, which returned saliva to her mouth.

She hadn't expected to eat the entire can, but she placed the empty tin on the floor and curled up in the bed, her hands spinning the spoon in circles, mind on Professor Marlin.

It had been forever since she'd felt such comfort and pulled the blanket up to her face. Stella brushed it up against her skin and enjoyed both the warmth and softness it provided.

Stella cried into the blanket with large, hiccupping sobs. She realized, sitting in an abandoned house, how utterly alone she was. Her teeth chopped down on the blanket to stifle the sound emerging from the depths of her throat. She watched the blanket change colours as the tears and spit fell onto the surface and burrowed into the fabric.

The room fell dark as the light faded from the sky. She turned her orange eyes to the windows and quickly wiped her face down. Now wasn't the time to cry. It was time to rest, she decided.

By the time she awoke she could see the sun creeping up through the windows. She stretched and then paused as she realized how long she had slept. Anyone could have come in and killed her. Particularly a furere.

The thought of being relaxed was harrowing and Stella couldn't afford to let things slide. She spun around the room and realized she hadn't even set up warning bells for trespassers. She slapped her face hard and stared up at the ceiling.

What am I doing?

Standing, she walked the room and drew the curtains so nothing would see her movement. She paused in front of a family photo. They were smiling, happy. Her heart burned as memories of her family emerged to the forefront of her mind.

Stella hadn't seen them in nearly half a year when the country was overrun by the furere. There had been text exchanges before it was cut off, presumably their deaths or the inevitable power outage.

Banging her forehead off the mantle in frustration, she let out a low growl. It took her aback and she stood tall. A stab in her chest caught her breath and she toppled to her knees.

The thud echoed in the house, but it was dull in her ears as the stabbing pain coursed repeatedly through her heart. The sheer pain of slicing was so sharp, so enigmatic, she forced herself to look down and ensure there were no object protruding from her chest.

She could hardly breathe as her hand rested overtop. Stella's hand could feel the beat it was so thundering. Unable to resist, a small cry escaped her lips as the pain echoed down her body.

Pulling upward on the foot of the bed she pulled herself to it and stood breathlessly. She sat on the mattress and looked for anything that might help.

Is it a panic attack?

Her body moved relentlessly to the door where she stumbled out of the room. Her hand scraped along the wall as she moved to the bathroom. Despite knowing water wouldn't come out the spout she hovered over the sink, prepared to vomit.

She caught her eyes and stepped back in startlement. The colour of her eyes burned as flames of a fire, bright as the sun itself.

This again? Am I still dreaming?

Her hand gripped her chest tightly as another surge of pain stabbed through her body. Her esophagus closed tight as she stared at herself.

North.

She spun, looking for the owner of the voice but there was no one else present in the house. No ghosts or spirits to be seen as she peered into the hallway.

Go.

The insistence pulsed in her heart bitterly. She felt the scorch of a burning blade with each word the unknown presence uttered. Stella imagined herself turning insane as she finally heaved into the sink.

Tears blurred her vision when her head came back up. Though she could still tell her eyes had returned to normal. Stella's airway slowly opened, and she leaned into the doorframe, her back to the corridor.

She tilted her head to look at herself. Stella looked deranged in the dim light. Her hair was a tangled mess and her eyes were sunken. Cheeks once chubby, were now gaunt. She blinked once. She looked weak and she detested it.

One glance at the row of piercings along her left ear would have normally made her smile but today the sight of them made her weep and long for better days.

No more. She decided defiantly.

Stella opened her mouth and exhaled deeply. Her hands wrapped around drawer handles as she looked speedily for a brush. As a family home there had to be spares lying around.

Upon finding unopened toothbrushes and toothpaste as well as a hairbrush, Stella smiled brightly. She took them in hand and went back to the bedroom. Locking the door behind her she began preparing her new self.

She scanned the room and realized a number of plants were sitting around the space. Stella had wondered what the scent in the air had been and now she knew and couldn't believe she hadn't noticed them earlier. They should be dead, but they were thriving in adversity. She smiled softly, *at least something is alive.*

Chapter Seven

A large group of people, probably close to three hundred, passed through the abandoned town and by the house. The herd was flocking south, toward a known military base, through the remainder of the snow. Stella barely moved the curtains as she watched them trek through the street. Her eyes were wary of onlookers and curious passerby.

She hoped none tried to enter the house. They would surely know she was present after a quick search. If they moved to the master bedroom and checked the closet or under the bed, she would indeed be found.

She had spent nearly a month residing in the abandoned house, and despite making the exterior, and general areas of the interior, appear unlived there were bound to be traces.

The people were slow and varied in age. Most wore layers of thin fabric rather than proper winter clothing, and Stella shivered at the thought. They appeared to be zombies themselves as they moved. There was no true life in their movements. Even so, the furere would track them easily and remove them from the world in one fell swoop.

But their tracks would also lead the furere to her. A pang in her chest burned, and she sealed the crack between the curtain and the window frame as she gasped for a breath.

She felt her chest jump up and down as she struggled for breath. It had come every so often, and it was coming in more rapid succession as time went on. Stella thought she had developed a heart problem, but the more she thought about it, the more she realized the pain in her chest burned when she considered fleeing far from their first sighting in Canada.

But it eased when she considered going north… toward the furere. It was ridiculous as she imagined going into the nest of the enemy only to be ripped into pieces and left to desiccate and rot on the surface of the earth.

Once the string of people had passed, their tracks clearly leading the way, Stella could breathe more easily. Though, she feared for her safety as much as theirs. The furere would surely find her as simply as them if they merely stepped off their trail a fraction of an inch.

Her hair was pulled back and twisted together tightly as she prepared to leave. Her stay had been long enough, and she needed to get away from the tracks as soon as she could. Packing her freshly airdried clothing into her bag she stopped to listen to the screaming outside.

The wailing echoed into the house and she brushed the curtain aside a touch to look. Screeching took over and the sound burned through her skull as she shot her hands over her ears to protect herself. However, the loud shrieking burrowed into her body as her lungs burned as though sitting in a house set ablaze.

Her body moved slowly as her vision spun. She packed as much as she could into her bag and stumbled into the hall. Stella's feet whipped together, and she tumbled down the stairs with a loud thud, her body pressing into the floor.

"Ugh," Stella said, before she managed to roll to her stomach and push onto her hands and feet. "Get up…"

Stella pushed herself as the screeching and wailing sounds closed in. She wondered, briefly, if they were dragging the people back to the houses. Crawling, her bag looped around her arms, down the stairs to the basement she managed to make her way back to the closet of the lavatory where she managed to fit herself. She sat, tired and sore, away from the howling outside.

Her hands were pressed into her ears so hard her ear drums could have popped. The cover didn't offer much reprieve as the sounds above rattled the house.

The destruction outside violently shook the structure of the building and Stella thought the whole house would collapse on top of her. She felt the walls shudder and she closed in on herself as debris above began scattering over her.

This is it.

Stella couldn't tell how long she sat in the putrid fumes of the fecal matter, but she was intensely dizzy by the time she decided to move. Her body moved on its own as she mindlessly left the room.

Her eyes stung, lungs coughing and sputtering, as she looked up the hallway and then the stairs. It was pitch black at the top, but she decided to chance it anyway. Her pack dragged behind her as she crawled pitifully to the top. The wind struck her face, billowing her hair back, as she made it to the main area.

The cold stung her skin as she sat and turned about. The entire top portion of the house was toppled. Stella was astonished as she moved to her belly. The floor in the kitchen was broken through and the hallway didn't appear to be in good shape.

Her arms stretched far over her head as she dragged herself flatly across the crackling floor. It was beginning to cover in flurries as the night sky above was hidden behind clouds. Reminding herself it was almost spring, she pushed onward.

Her body finally tumbled onto the porch and down to the ground. She sloshed in the mud and looked at her surroundings.

The houses were all demolished and bodies hung from the remaining beams and doors. They draped over broken houses like dolls left by a child.

Stella gaped at the damage, her eyes running down the street, left in their wake. She hadn't known the screech of the furere could freeze her in her tracks, but they had done more than that. The trail of blood in the moonlight glistened darkly against her eyes. She realized then that the creatures had done far more than scare. She had heard them in her soul.

Her bag was heavier than she'd recalled as she attached it to her back and looked up at the stars. Despite the clouds above she thought it possible to at least see the stars, but her hopes faded when she realized she wouldn't see them.

Her breath came in heavy sobs as she sat in the muddy ground surrounded by death.

Chapter Eight

Stella held the rifle up to her shoulder and aimed for a small rabbit. Green vegetation was scarce, and she could tell the animal was struggling to survive. The winter had been bitter as well. She told herself it was a mercy killing as she pulled the trigger.

The shot rang out, echoing over the hill and through the valley. Birds scattered into the air and other critters scuttled as far from the echo as they could, their feet and hearts slamming in their bodies. Stella also paused, fearing the noise would bring forth the furere.

Slowly, she walked to the rabbit. She sighed in relief as she picked it up by its hindlegs, slit the throat to drain the blood, and waited for something to hunt her.

"Didja catch something?" a voice called.

Turning on a dime, dropping the rabbit, she aimed her gun toward the sound. Her heart pitter-pattered in fear as she waited for the person to reveal himself.

"Come on out," she called back sternly.

A man, no older than her, emerged. He wore an old leather jacket adorned with a gold infinity symbol over the heart. He held up his hands innocently and smiled. Stella felt her lips curl downward.

"Hello," he tried to sound nice.

"If you want it, you can't have it," she said.

"Not at all. It's just… I was heading north when another furere came through." His voice lowered, eyes looking away from her as if to hide the shame. Placing his hands in the pockets of his jacket, he shrugged.

"Well, I'm sure you know what happens with furere."

"How long ago?" Stella's grip became sweaty. She hadn't seen any bodies.

"Two days?" he guessed.

"How did you survive?" Stella didn't try to hide her suspicion.

Furere didn't leave survivors, but there was no trace of the creatures. There were, however, very large animal prints in the grasses. She scanned the area more clearly and saw a dark, burned portion of the field.

"I… uh… there's a large hole under that tree." He nodded to his hiding spot. "I pulled in as much dirt as possible and held my breath."

Stella lowered the gun. She didn't believe his story but would let it pass for now. Taking a deep breath, she nodded and slung the rifle over her shoulder.

"Where are the bodies?"

"They took them," he said, shuddering. "I have no idea why, but all the bodies were snatched."

Her nostrils flared. She could only guess what would happen to all those corpses, human and animal, when they arrived at their destination. It wasn't as if the Valkyrie of Norse mythology had come to save their souls. This was a furere.

"Where up north did you say you were headed?" Stella changed the subject.

"I'm not positive, but I feel compelled to go." He ruffled around his pockets. "I have a map."

Stella was cautious as his hands shuffled in the unseen. She put the rifle back to the ready position while he searched. He whipped the map out and offered it to her freely. She walked to him carefully and let her fingers graze his skin as she took it from him.

Please take me with you.

She glanced at him curiously; his thoughts weren't distasteful but fearful.

She opened the worn paper, careful not to tear it. She could see the dented, folded edges and pencil marks discerning it was a map of the Bruce Trail. At least, part of a map.

"You've been using old trails?" She was surprised.

"Yeah." He pointed and tapped the star drawn on the map. "That's where we wanted to get, and this is where we are." His finger ran down along the paper until it stopped near a river. "We're just past Halton. The trail crosses to Sixth Line Nassagaweya. We can follow that and some sideroads until we hit Georgetown. I'm sure I can find more maps that can finish taking us up to Georgian Bay."

"It's an idea." She folded the map and handed it back to him.

"You don't like it," he noted with a frown.

"I'm not entirely comfortable with being in places where there are more people. More people mean more furere. That means more death and the odds of survival decrease significantly."

"Okay," he said. "I understand that."

"However," Stella began walking, making the decision to bring him along, "that being said — it would at least keep us on course."

He brightened up and jumped into a pace with her. She scanned him sidelong. He was slender, not much taller than her, and his jeans were clearly expensive. Overall, she guessed he had gone to a decent school, and his parents were made of money. Jock. Frat boy. Smart but not enough to boast about it. His hair had obviously grown out, but she could tell he used to maintain it. A small line along the side of his neck could have been a tattoo. She wondered what it was but decided not to ask.

She thought of her appearance… long, dark blond hair snugly braided all the way down to her thigh. She thought of cutting it almost daily but had rather masculine features otherwise.

Her shoulders were far squarer than those of her female peers, though her frame held substantial muscle despite the lack of sustenance and training, so she didn't complain. Her training at the gym had given her a serious edge. She noted her square jaw once had chubby cheeks. They had hollowed out and made the cheekbones more prominent now.

But it was always the eyes that made people take a second glance. They could be mistaken for brown or hazel at first look, but a second look made it clear they were golden — not a plain, tainted brown or sullied gold.

They glowed, even in her darkest mood, and shimmered like crystal in sunlight. Stella tried not to think about them so much after they turned ablaze.

Ruminating, Stella kept her thoughts quiet. She hadn't thought much about it lately as there was no one to impress anymore. Well, she supposed that couldn't be too true since she still couldn't bring herself to cut her hair.

Despite the end of the world, she kept her row of piercings down the left ear, still unable to bring herself to remove them for sentimental reasons. One for each year of high school and one for each college semester. A reminder of better times—both grim and happy. Richard had given her the last one as a gift for her excellence at the gym.

"You look lost in your own world," the man said.

"What?" She pulled herself back to reality.

"I'm Ari."

"Ari?" She bit her tongue briefly. "What's that short for?"

"It isn't short for anything."

"Well, Ari, nice to meet you. I'm Stella."

"Oh, like from that movie." He snapped his fingers.

"Stella." She repeated and looked at him with a grin. "From the Latin name meaning star. Or so my parents told me."

His voice lowered as he spoke, "were you close with your family?"

"Not particularly." She adjusted the rifle, and his brown eyes shifted quickly from her to it and back, as she continued. "I moved out at sixteen, emancipated, then finished high school, got a bunch of scholarships and rocked college. But I did visit them, kept in touch."

"What did you study?"

"I was taking Community Justice and Outreach," she said. "Policing."

"Oh, that's why you're handy with a gun," he said. "I was taking Social Work in university. Almost done… just needed to finish my thesis."

"You were so close. What were you going to do with it?" She kept her eye on the horizon as they walked, beginning to go uphill.

"I was going to work with children with disabilities," he said. "You know, autism or physical disabilities, anxiety, depression. I was specializing in mental health as well. Double major."

She smiled. He was smart, determined, but perhaps more intelligent than she'd initially given him credit for.

"Do you know what I miss the most?" he asked after a brief period of silence.

"Pizza."

"Well, yes," he snorted. "I was thinking more along the lines of smoking."

"Tobacco or weed?"

"Both I suppose." Ari pursed his lips. "Mostly the weed though."

"How's your cardio?"

"Decent," he said.

Stella thought she heard more than a little hesitation. "Hm... very convincing."

"Well, it's not like I was habitual. I did track all through school, and vaulting, some wrestling."

"So, it should be okay," she said.

"Considering we've been in this isolated disaster of the earth with no means of transportation apart from our own legs, yes, I'd say my cardio is good."

"Well," she breathed heavily as the rugged terrain increased, "someone's offended."

"No. Just frustrated. Your questions seem more interrogative than interested."

She paused and looked at him. He was certainly handsome. But this was not a time for romance. There were things that needed to be done for survival, not pleasure.

"We're not exactly on a date here," Stella snapped. "I need to know if you can take care of yourself. I barely manage my own survival. I haven't even had to fight a furere — I've been lucky."

They paused as the sun began to fade away. She was looking at him intensely, and he stepped back, eyes shifting from hers and away quickly, wanting to both avoid and maintain eye contact. When she caught a glimpse of his emotion, he felt his sadness.

"Sorry," he said. "I was just hoping you didn't hate me."

"Uh," Stella stuttered. The retort she had prepared was not in expectation of that. Shaking her head, she clomped through the trail. "Let's just find somewhere to cook this thing and sleep."

"I like food."

"Me too."

She glanced backward at him. He had a strange aura about him, but she liked it. He was different, though clearly kind and smart enough to keep himself safe. Nodding to herself as she began searching for a decent hideaway to rest, she thought perhaps he could be trusted in time.

Chapter Nine

Stella turned in her sleep restlessly. A voice was once again speaking to her, but she wasn't able to wake now. The dreams had become pervasive and insistent since the collapse and they left her unrested each day.

You know what will happen if you go there.

The grasp on her arms tightened as her pulse quickened.

If you do not stop, you will die.

"I know," she finally sputtered.

Then why do you go?

"Because… it's important."

Now you bring another soul to perish?

Stella felt the hands loosen and she pushed away. Turning on her heel, she ran and kept the wind in her ears to block the voice. Noise burst through the silence as she screamed and stopped her body before a cliff. Her arm caught a tree as her feet slipped over the edge and she hoisted herself away from the earth. Stella felt tears sting her eyes from fear.

She grasped the tree tightly and turned around to see a figure standing not far away. He was ghostlike and haunting. She gasped and wrapped her arms around the tree for stability.

He spoke calmly. "You should not be in this world."

"What world?"

"You cannot simply enter this place." He approached.

She looked at his broad, tall figure before settling on his eyes. They were the brightest glistening blue she had ever seen. A quiet calmness resided behind them but the further she delved into his emotions she found there was worry sitting amidst his soul. His shoulders were the apex of his form as he loomed over her protectively, arms outstretched to cover her from the open air below.

Stella feared using her gift until she remembered it was no more than a dream. She lifted her eyes to his again and looked into his eyes quietly, firmly and with purpose. She laughed at herself as she began admiring him.

"What are you?" She asked.

"I am merely a guardian," he whispered.

"A guardian of what?"

"You should not be here," he said, emphasizing each word.

"You say it as if I want to be here."

Stella's lips curled into a small snarl; her eyes locked on his.

"Then go home," he commanded and reached up.

She meant to swipe at him, but he poked his finger into her forehead. Stella awoke from her dream, bolting upright, breathing heavily. Disoriented momentarily, she placed her palms firmly on the earth to ground herself in reality. When she looked up, Ari was gawking at her. He looked like he was going to vomit, release his bowels or cry as he hugged himself.

"Ari? Oh, thank God…"

She rubbed her face hard to push the sleep from her eyes. Shaking her head, she sighed and felt her heart return to normal. When she looked up again, Ari was still staring at her.

"What?" She asked.

"I don't know what kind of dream you were having or what was going on but…"

"But what?" she urged.

"Look." He pointed and tossed her a compact mirror from his pocket.

She opened the small mirror and held it up to her face. A mark just above her eyebrow was bleeding. She creased her brows and touched it. Stinging across her forehead prompted her to stop and she gently leaned back. But the tree felt hollow and she spun quickly. Directly behind her were a row of trees with perfect cylindrical holes through them.

"What the heck?" she muttered in disbelief. "What did you see?"

Her head snapped back to Ari who she was fairly certain had just shat himself. He shook his head as his eyes grew wider.

"You were crying and then out of nowhere this enormous light pops up in front of your face. The next thing I know you're bleeding and there's this awful sound as the light swoops literally into and out of the trees!"

"What was the sound?" She turned to the trees again.

"It sounded like wailing people."

Eyes large, she looked at him. In that gaze she read all the fear, amazement and wonder in his body. She jumped to her feet and lunged toward him. He clambered to his feet and backed into a tree as Stella grabbed his face. She didn't think as she let their skin touch.

Holy... what is this woman? Is she part of the furere? Am I going to die? What have I gotten myself into? This is not what I signed up for. Why am I even going north? There's nothing there. There's nothing anywhere. God... she has beautiful eyes. No. Stop. There's no way she's human. None... of this can be happening. I'm in a coma. That's what it is. This has all been a dream. I'm in a coma and this isn't real. But on the other hand, the pain is real.

She released him and stepped back. Squatting down, Stella debated her next steps. Ari watched nervously as she rocked her legs restlessly and looked at him again. An aura about him lingered, hovering as if protecting him.

"Why are you going to Georgian Bay?"

"I have no idea," he told her shakily. "Why are you going?"

"I don't know," she admitted. "It's like someone's calling me there and I have no choice."

"Me too," he said. "Except... I don't have light spewing from my head destroying trees."

"I don't know what that was." Stella shook herself and rose.

"What are you?"

"As far as I know I'm a person," she muttered.

"Wow, thank you." He snapped his fingers. "Clears everything up."

"If I had an answer, I'd give you one," Stella retorted blandly. "Besides, it's not like you're perfectly normal either."

"What does that mean?" His hands rested on his hips.

"You have this… haze around you." She gestured to his frame, but Ari remained silent. "Do you believe in auras?"

"As in the personification of one's energy around the body," he asked as he rubbed his eyes. "Everyone has a different colour."

"Yeah, more or less…"

"I don't know," he said. "I guess anything's possible at this stage."

"Okay, let's say for a minute we believe anything and everything right now. Yours is different."

"Fantastic! You're also a nutjob," Ari said.

"No, well maybe."

The two paused and stared at one another. Stella's bright orange eyes were watching him closely as he chewed his lips. She sought words but nothing came to mind.

"So how do you explain the light? Third eye?" he snapped sarcastically.

"Chakras?" She was exasperated. "It was a dream… a man poked me in the head."

"Where you're bleeding?"

"Yes."

"Oh my God, your manifesting level: pristine."

"I don't need your sarcasm, thank you," Stella said. "We're both probably going to die whether or not we go north, south, east or west."

"I know," he answered. "It's not like I ever expected to survive this long."

They exchanged glances and Stella felt more trusting of him as the truth unfolded between the two of them. She leaned back into the tree and smiled for his benefit. Her hair rippled down her neck and back as the braid began unwinding. The loose strands tickled her exposed skin as she turned her face upward.

The sky was still fairly dark but she could see the beginnings of dawn. The yellow mingled with purple and pink was started to ripple over the horizon in a delicate haze. She missed the peace that often came with early mornings.

Chapter Ten

Galen swung his sword toward the furere as it lunged. His massive stature never deterred them from attacking.

The sword sliced the creature's head clean off as the other furere leapt down from their perches in the tree. He met them with a jump as his saber made its way through the chest of one and his fist thrust through the other's skull. The beasts screeched, but the wailing never affected him.

A quick jab of his spare knife through the eye and to the back of the skull finished the fourth and he sheathed his blades. Sighing, he dragged their bodies away from the forest line and lit them on fire. The corpses burned, though the flames didn't change their figures much. Their black, charred and oozing bodies were similar in life.

He encouraged the fire to burn intensely until they were no more than ash. A sharp ray of light caught his attention. His face flatlined as he sighed internally. Was it finally time? Would he meet her now?

He had wondered for many years which one it would be to restore the world to its natural order. Not that the earth had known a history where man did not assert its will over others.

He took a heavy breath and carried on. A deer darted past him, away from the light, and he smiled. At least something was still alive. He struggled for food himself but couldn't bring himself to kill the lone creature. Especially a doe. She had the potential to bring more to their species.

Galen moved through the forest at a slow pace, his head playing tag with the branches. The evening was dangerous, but more so was allowing furere to find his home. He would never know quiet if that happened.

His crossbow sat across his back and shoulders, reminding him that he had intended to find a small animal for breakfast. But they had fled the area in fear when the furere arrived.

"You've wandered far," a voice said from the shadows.

"You've wandered farther." Galen faced the voice. "It's been years, Charon."

"It has," Charon said.

He stepped forward so they could speak face to face. The two men exchanged concerned expressions as they waited for the other to mutter anything conversational. Finally, Galen broke the silence in an attempt to make light of the situation.

"No painting this time?"

Charon turned his face to the sky before tilting his head back down with distress ridden over his eyes. He paused before speaking, choosing his words cautiously.

"She has no true magic yet," Charon said. "It's hidden this time."

"Surely that's not true," Galen said.

"She has some. But she doesn't know what it is. She doesn't know the extent to which she's capable."

Galen watched him writhe in concern and pain. He knew Charon felt more deeply than the average person yet rarely did his emotions rise to the surface for all to see.

"Charon," Galen said, finally breaking the silence. "What do you need?"

"Can you help her?"

"Why can't you?"

"You asked what I needed," Charon said, his face calm but voice tight.

Galen was bitter about the request, but Charon wouldn't ask without cause nor would he expect more than what could be handled. However, it certainly put them both at greater risk. Galen could see the weariness in Charon's eyes and made up his mind.

"I'll do what I can," Galen said.

"I thank you."

Charon evaporated into the wind like a ghost and Galen's eyes watched closely until there was nothing left to be seen.

"You're welcome," Galen sighed, shoulders sagging. Quests had not been on his list of things to do before welcoming death, but magical elements were beginning to rouse, and he too had his part to play. He could feel the earth beginning to pulsate magic as it once did.

Chapter Eleven

Stella let her feet fall into the chilly water as she and Ari took a break. The air was hot, and the two companions had walked since dawn. Her eyes moved to the sky before scanning the area. Ari was happy to splash about the water childishly while Stella let her back roll onto the earth with no predator in sight.

She looked over to a small flower and reached out to touch it, running her finger up the stem and to the bulb. She paused as the light went up the stock. Turning her body, she watched carefully as she did it again. Another sparkle of light went through the plant, and the bulb began to open.

A small humanoid creature came and sat on the flower, tiny legs swinging as she watched Stella.

"Hello," the tiny person greeted her.

Stella felt her mouth turn dry as she stared at the small creature openly. Its wings were fluttering effortlessly, but she still sat on the flower. Stella could feel her heart flicker uneasily, unsure if she had fallen asleep or was hallucinating.

"Wha… what are you?"

"Wow, well, I'm a pixie," she said.

"Right."

Stella pinched herself — it stung. She looked past the little pixie to Ari, who was gleefully going on a tirade in the water, and chuckled a little to herself. It was like watching a toddler. It was comforting knowing he was off in his own world and could happily ignore what she was doing.

"Are you still going by the same name, false queen?" the pixie asked dryly.

The statement drew Stella's attention back to the small person. The pixie was watching her with a snarl on her lips.

"Excuse me?" Stella asked.

"Are you still calling yourself Stella?" The pixie sounded a little more irked.

"My parents named me that."

"I'm sure they got the idea somewhere."

"What's your problem?" Stella withdrew, annoyed with the little creature. She decided, given her past experiences, it was real and opened her mind to the possibility.

"Well, isn't that a conundrum," the pixie popped her words. "Considering you're the one who caused all this, you really should know what my problem is."

"What does that mean? What are you talking about?"

Stella leaned her face in so close her nose could have poked the creature. She tried to make eye contact with the pixie, but the little creature was having none of it. The magical being crossed her arms and turned her nose upward.

Stella sighed and sat up. "You're really real?"

"Indeed." The pixie fluttered across the water and sat on the rock opposite Stella. "You really don't remember anything this time?"

"This time? What am I supposed to remember?"

Stella dropped her hands into her lap as she waited for a reply. Of course, she didn't know if she would get one. She also did know if any she did get would be sufficient or explanatory.

"Many things," the pixie said. "This is your sixth life, after all."

"Reincarnation? If that's what happens after people die, I assure you there's no memory."

"Not people, you."

"Me specifically?"

"Geeze," the pixie said with a scowl. "Yes. You should have six life-based memories."

"I have nineteen years of life experience?" Stella offered hesitantly.

The pixie's shoulders slumped, and she flew down to the water. She swept in and out then sprung up into Stella's face.

"I guess it'll come back when it's supposed to." The little creature pouted then flew off quickly.

Stella lost track of her within seconds, but the words left her reeling. She shook her head. Things that cannot be explained by science were magical to people. She supposed her abilities fell into that same category, but what utter nonsense. Six former lives.

"What's with that face?"

Ari had meandered over; his boxers clung to his skin, revealing every curve of his body, and she turned away quickly with wide eyes.

"Oh, come on." He plunked down.

"Nope." Stella shook her head. "Do you believe in magic?"

"Well, given what we saw the other night it's possible but there could be other explanations."

"Such as?"

"I haven't gotten that far," he admitted. "Why?"

"Just curious." She shrugged.

"Okay," he said without looking at her. "Did you already wash your clothes?"

"I washed them before I relaxed." She pointed to the tree above them. "I'm happy to carry a spare t-shirt and undergarments, unlike some people…"

"It's not as if I've had time to go shopping," Ari snorted, wringing out his wet clothing. "But while we're at it… I could go for a haircut."

"Yeah, you could use one, couldn't you?" she teased gently.

"What are you trying to say?"

"Oh, nothing."

He finished flattening the fabric and turned to her. She was troubled but the peace and quiet bothered them both. It suddenly felt unnatural.

"Do you think it's weird we haven't seen any furere?"

"I was thinking that." She nodded. "If they want people then they'll have to go where people congregate."

"How do we know it's people they want?"

"They've killed off the planet." Stella scowled. "What else could they possibly want?"

"Think they're aliens?"

"Without spaceships?"

"I see your point," Ari conceded. "Demons?"

"Plausible," Stella said. "Legends and myths come from somewhere."

"That would also make magic a reality."

They locked eyes quietly before he shrugged the suggestion away. He was being honest and open, but she could feel the worry building in his body. Confusion. Distress. She let go and sighed internally.

"Do you wonder what we're doing?"

"Going north?" he asked.

"Yeah."

"I dunno. Just feels right."

"Me too," she whispered.

Though Stella was unsure if she should tell him there was a voice in her head telling her to go there, even though she had no idea who it was talking to her. Stella also didn't know if she could trust him to believe her if she told him, that when she thought about going the other direction, she felt sharp stabbing pain in her heart. Rather, she opted for silence.

"Are we believing in magic?"

"I think so," Stella said.

She chanced a quick, nervous glance up at him. Given the pixie she had just talked to her was perhaps more open to the idea. Stella thought of her own abilities, biting her tongue, and drew to a conclusion she needed to accept magic as real.

They sat quietly together as water washed over their legs, sending goosebumps up their skin. A small amount of stress was released as it worked through their skin and toes. Stella knew she would be wrinkly, but she wanted to feel clean at least a little longer before sweat, dirt and grime layered on her body like a medieval fortress.

Chapter Twelve

Charon wandered through the deserted prison as he shoved rubble aside with wind. The jail could no longer hold back their rage. His magic had waned with each century Stella's spell renewed her bodily form. It stole magic from the fae, humans and nature itself.

Usually, a barrier between the two worlds allowed fae their natural forms and magical incantations. Humans had never accepted them as they were and often hunted them down, either from hatred or a desire for power. Sharing the world was difficult with the growth of human civilizations, but the barriers had provided protection.

However, the release of the prison's walls shattered all defences over time. Human and fae were caught up in the rampage, and he held himself responsible. Had his magic been more potent, he supposed it could have kept them at bay for another century. It was too large of a magical force to contain. They were pure madness, their minds long gone in their lividity.

He could attempt restoring the prison, but it would do no good. Capturing the furere was impossible, and only a handful of humanoids could kill them. If Stella's latest rebirth gained her power back, she would be able to end them once and for all by undoing her spell.

If she restored the world to its proper place, the sovereignty and rights of Vasilis would also be returned. Had the rights been hidden as they should have been, instead of bestowed on her rebirths, many things could have been prevented.

Charon reached the stairwell that descended to the mass pit the furere had resided in for two centuries. Their cells had once been separate but as numerous prisoners, criminals in the queen's eyes, were passed through the prison walls, it hadn't been possible to keep them apart.

He sent the rubble down the stairwell until the massive pit was filled with the walls' stone and dirt above. The earth was flat and deathly, he noted as he raised his eyes from his work.

He swept across the earth and allowed himself to mourn silently. His heart yearned for peace before death became a plague. Before, death was something to be feared. Before Stella had interpreted her end.

He did not desire her to return to innocence. Instead, he wished she had allowed herself understanding which would have led to knowledge and wisdom. Had she done that, she would never have cast such a ridiculous spell, nor would the rebirth containing rage have tortured fae to this state.

Charon could hear the sky mocking him. Despite knowing it could not be changed, his own desires to reverse the world's timeline were pitiful. Destiny could only write itself through every individual's choice. Nothing was ever predestined that he could see, and every person in the world influenced the timeline through their decisions.

Unwittingly, he chuckled to himself. None ever thought the smallest of their choices would change anything. He had watched many fae and humans rise and fall through actions and deeds. Many of those persons had influenced the world, none of the least being himself or Stella.

Chapter Thirteen

"Well, that's what I would call a castle." Ari peered through the woodland; eyes wide with surprise. "It's very… fairy tale, if you ask me."

"Is there a road near here on your map?" Stella looked at their surroundings.

She could only see the forest and the castle-like mansion. It looked almost ancient, abandoned since at least the Second World War by the look of the wood and stone that held it together, but the style seemed more like antiquity Greek or Roman.

"There really shouldn't be," he said, opening the map. "We're too far south to be at that ranch on here but we haven't crossed enough ground to make it anywhere near the Sixth Line."

"Does this place show up on the map? What if we haven't been following the directions properly?"

He scanned the image shaking his head. Stella let out a frustrated sigh and then shrugged. She moved out of the way of the trees and onto the edge of the property, hands at her sides casually.

"What are you doing?" Ari hissed. "Are you dumb?"

"Dumb would imply the inability to speak." She gave him a teasing look.

"You know what I mean," he said.

Stella glanced his direction to find him scowling heavily. She grinned, to herself, before turning back the lonesome structure.

"It looks like it was abandoned a really long time ago, Ari."

"So does the rest of the world." He folded the map and crept toward her.

"Thank you for reminding me that our lives were interrupted in the worst way possible in the prime of our lives." She walked toward the massive structure. "Let's just check it out."

"I'd like to live a little longer." He protested.

"Fine. You stay here, and I'll look." She took the rifle off her shoulder.

He stood by the edge of the trees debating the idea. She took a quick peek at him; he must have been thinking of all the possible ways he could die inside. Floorboards breaking beneath his feet, threatening to swallow him whole. The opportunity for bandits to find them, tie them down, chop them into pieces slowly and eat them alive: cannibals, the worst of the worst. But it was also plausible they could find some canned goods… or nothing.

"Ugh," he rolled his eyes, "fine."

He caught up and walked next to her as they paced themselves quickly but cautiously across the vast property. Stella kept an eye out for traps but only saw what used to be maintained gardens… and graves.

She faltered in her steps and took a moment. Curiously, she altered course and approached the graves to read a cenotaph.

"Oh God." Ari mumbled when he glanced over. "Why graves?"

Stella took a sharp breath as she read the name. *Stella Martin.*

She shook her head and licked her lips, palms sweaty. What was her name doing on a cenotaph? She consciously exhaled and steadied herself.

"Eighteen-hundred, May twenty-third to nineteen-hundred, May twenty-third," she said. "Nineteen-hundred, May twenty-third to two-thousand, May twenty-third."

"Why are you reading those?" He finally approached and leaned over her shoulder. "Hm… that's interesting. Precisely one-hundred years old. To the day."

"Yeah." Stella nodded.

"Oh, and she has your name." He hummed while mulling the thought over. "Wait…"

"Yeah."

"Same last name or different?"

"Same." She bit her thumb nervously.

"Excuse me?" Ari straightened up, hair standing on end.

"I was born May twenty-third, two-thousand-three." Stella was biting her lips now. "They're in order. One dies and the next is born the same day of the same year."

Stella sucked in a tight gasp of air as she read the cenotaphs on each headstone. It was eerie how they corresponded to each other and distressing that they all shared her name. Lost for words, she remained squatted before them as the gears turned in her mind. Was the pixie really telling the truth?

She had lived six lives according to the magical being and if Stella assumed the pixie spoke the truth then that meant she, herself, would be the next in line. Except there was a three-year gap.

"Okay," Ari said. "Creepy."

"A little." She was grinning at him, trying to ease both their fears. "Scared?"

"No… Are we still checking out the rest of this place?"

"Why?" She prodded him with her elbow. "Want to see if you have any graves?"

"I'd prefer not knowing, to be perfectly frank." He turned and headed toward the house. "Can we just go through this mansion so we can leave?"

"Just a second."

"Stella!" Ari called.

She spun on her heels, rising from her squat, and looked at Ari. His arms were crossed and waiting for her impatiently. Stella smiled at him in an attempt to convince him that it was worth the wait as she told herself it was nothing.

"Can we go inside now?" Ari asked.

"Look who's growing a pair," she joked but the tension in her chest was rising.

"Shut up." He strode toward the entrance, legs and back stiff.

"Okay, grumpy." She followed him, eyes still scanning for traps and now ghosts as her mind wandered. She swept her gaze around the property once more before focusing on him. Her teeth grit together harshly before screaming loudly, "stop! Ari, don't!"

Her screams went unheard as the door swept open and swallowed him. She stared, open mouthed, at the space he once occupied. She surged toward the entrance and barreled through it, door swinging and banging against the wall. He had simply vanished.

"Ari?" her voice crackled from the outburst as she looked around. "Ari!"

Her heart pounded ruthlessly as panic set in. Her limbs stiffened as she replayed the incident in her mind. She sought clues she might have missed upon first glance. It was difficult to focus as the thought of ghosts crept into her mind.

Stella's breath shook as her body fell into a dirty, old wall. Her memory churned from the graves to the house and then back to the graves. She grabbed her head tightly, fingers tangling in her hair, as the vision of Ari disappearing replayed like a broken tape. The form of a man inside the house came to light as she slowed her breath and focused once more.

The man was ghostly, tall, broad… was it the man from her dreams? He had appeared to her more than once, she thought.

She pinched herself in the arm. It hurt. Stella decided it couldn't be a dream this time. Her body shook as she commanded herself to move. Working up the courage to take the first step and then each one after that grew easier as she moved deeper into the house.

Eventually she managed to get to the center of the foyer. Looking down, a dusted, old pattern in the floor stood out to her. She paused briefly, her heart fluttered nervously, as she recognized it was the same symbol as the one embroidered into Ari's jacket. She looked up at the chandelier then to the hallway at the top of the stairs. Frantically, she began running and stormed through the house's rooms and hallways hoping to find her friend.

She slammed through each door and opened every closet and cupboard. Her heart was beating faster than it ever had before, even during sparring matches. When she couldn't run anymore, she stopped and keeled over, her stomach threatening to heave. Her hands slapped her knees as she attempted to catch her breath. Dizzy, she sat down with her back to the wall. She must have been running for nearly an hour and still hadn't found all the rooms in the castle.

"Oh my God!" she cried. "What do I do?"

Her head tilted, eyes shut, as she rested against the wall. She thought of the pixie as she remembered Ari's disappearance. It had to be some sort of magic. But what magic makes someone invisible?

Stella opened her eyes and looked at the hallway she'd slumped in. Who even owned this house? There was no artwork or furnishings. It was plain as a model house.

Taking a moment to decide which way to go, Stella slowly pushed herself to her feet and began her march. The rest assisted in calming the bile threatening to rise so she headed down the hall toward the furthest, deepest space of the house. She thrust open every door only to find empty, hollow rooms. The only living things were bats, spiders and rodents.

As she grasped the handle of the last door, Stella paused. It didn't budge no matter how much she tried to force it open. It was dark in the furthest reaches of the house, but she could tell it was locked and no key sat in the keyhole. It was the only sealed room. She caught her breath then cracked her shoulder into it heavily. Knowing her square, muscular frame would be okay, she continued smashing her body into the wood. Stella felt the sting each time, but the cracking of the frame gave her hope.

The latch finally gave way, and she pushed it open, stumbling into the room, and the hinges creaked until the door hit the wall. She entered the room and the floorboards creaked with her weight. But her mind was focused on the portraits staring back at her.

Stella stepped closer as her chest heaved with pain. She felt connected, yet detached, from the portraits of herself. She knew these women, but they were entirely unknown to her. She inched closer, hand outstretched delicately, as her body turned heavier and sluggish.

Each one was dated, reminding her the graves outside.

Five tombstones.

Ten portraits.

Two for each.

Twenty years old and the day they died; one hundred years old.

All exactly one hundred years apart. And yet they looked exactly the same. They were not aged in any imagery. The only difference was clothing, hair and jewelry. Each to match the time period they lived and died in.

Shakily, she touched the golden frame of the last one. Death: year two-thousand, May twenty-third. She moved the dust off the frame as her lips quivered. Beneath her fingertips she felt grooves. Wiping heavily, the grime pushed away and she found an inscription etched into the frame.

Moirai and then *Cowardice.* She felt her stomach fall as her eyes moved to the face.

"You should not be here."

She spun fast, hair whipping around her as she shifted for her rifle. She was so close to the wall the butt of the gun struck and scraped against it, slowing her turn.

"Why do you continue to return?"

She stared up at the man. It was the same from her dream. She knew it was him which also meant this very moment wasn't occurring in reality. She had to be asleep. But she couldn't recall when she had allowed herself to ease into such a state.

"Why do you keep showing up in dreams?" She pushed back but her arms were solidly in place.

He held her firmly with ease. Her neck was craned ever so slightly. Despite his ghostly, immaterial appearance, she could feel his hands as though they truly existed. She studied his face closely. Her head pressed into the artwork as she realized how familiar he was, as though she had bumped into him in the street or seen him at the grocery store.

"Who are you?" she asked angrily. "What are you?"

"A guardian."

"Guardian of what?" she snapped.

Stella could feel her heart angrily pumping blood throughout her body. She watched him glance down at her as her veins pulsated in his grasp. Stella's body grew hot from the effort her heart was making. Her cheeks began flushing a bright, rosy pink as she stared at his face.

"I suppose nothing anymore," he said.

"Where is Ari?" She twisted her hands downward, toward his wrists and stretched her fingers so they would graze his skin. Fear was gripping her chest tightly and shallowing her breathing as she continued to reach for the man's skin.

"That boy?"

"Yes, obviously him."

"He should not have touched the door."

"Well, how would he have known that?" Frustration took over, replacing her fear. "What did you do with him?"

"I have done nothing to him."

Stella paused as she contemplated the man. He was sincere, but she still could not discern his thoughts. Her fingers brushed across his skin before taking a firm hold but there were no thoughts she could pull from his mind.

The more she stared at him, the more she found him dangerously handsome. He could calm a storm or raise one with a single expression. She was both in admiration and fear of his power.

Frustrated, Stella pushed her mind from him. Instead, her thoughts rolled through her experiences in life — being an outcast because of her abilities — the pixie's statements and now the portraits of her.

"Why do I look like these women? Who are they to me?"

He withdrew, his grip lighter but still firmly in place. The man glanced past her to the portraits. Stella watched him, his bright and crystal-clear blue eyes possessed knowledge. His gaze turned downward to her and once their eyes connected and she saw a storm of emotions. He was sad, confused, hurt, angry…

She could feel his emotions fill in her limbs and stomach. Shame, though she didn't know what for, rippled through her bones. She wanted to vomit from the agony. Her legs nearly gave way as she turned from him and took a slow, cautious breath.

"Who are you?" she repeated her first question.

"You seek a name?" he asked, his fingers wrapping around her flesh nervously.

"Yes." She matched his gaze, his emotions hidden away once more.

"Charon." He released her and stepped backward.

"Charon," she murmured and scrutinized him. "What is this place?"

"It was a home."

"Can you tell me who she is? Or who she was?"

"I could tell you many things," he said with sadness. "You must go home. I will return the boy to you. But I must ask, how far do you intend to take him?"

"He's choosing to go with me."

"As you also choose to go and you decided to bring him."

His eyes shifted and the glint of a smile, sad and longing, passed his lips. He stepped further away until he was no more than a glimmering crystal then nothing. She drew a breath of relief and fell against the wall.

"Stella!" She heard Ari hollering. "Stella! Where are you?"

"Ari!" She stumbled before she raced toward the sound of his voice.

Her feet and legs propelled her down the hall swiftly. She finally crashed into the railing and looked down into the foyer. He was running through the castle searching for her. She could see the fear in his body.

"Ari," Stella yelped and began taking the stairs two at a time. "Are you okay? You disappeared!"

"Stella." He began trotting up the steps.

Their bodies clashed against one another and he grasped hold of her tightly. She hadn't expected him to hug her, but she allowed it and gently put her arms around him. The symbol in his jacket pulsated against her chest but she ignored it for now as she focused on him instead.

"Are you okay?" He asked her, pulling tangled hair from her face. "You were gone for a good three hours. You were following me and then poof: nothing. You were gone."

"No," she said with a shake of her head. "You touched the door and it was like you never existed."

"Nah." He stepped back. "I turned around and watched you vanish. It was like a movie."

She shook her head and grabbed his hand. "Come with me."

"I've already seen the whole house. I went through every single room."

"Even this one? The door had been locked until I broke through." She dragged him up to the room. "It was locked. I had to break the frame."

He was silent as she yanked on his arm. She needed him to see what she had seen even if, in his mind, he had checked all the doors and rooms.

"Yes, even this one. I'll admit, it has a creepy vibe, but the door wasn't locked. The frame is intact, Stella. What about this room has you so wound up?"

"There were paintings of women, with the same names as the tombstones." Stella walked up to the wall and pressed her palm against it. She was haunted as she stared at the blank wall before her. "My name. But they looked the exact same age. From twenty to one hundred, they still looked twenty years old. But they looked exactly like me."

Stella thought of the pixie's words once more. Had she told Stella the truth? Was reincarnation possible? She thought that, given the images and dates, she could have potentially lived several lifetimes. But the idea that she had caused the end of the world… she was not the kind of person to do such a thing. Nor would she know how to even if she wanted to.

"You're tired." He approached her calmly. "Maybe you dreamt it? Or hallucinated it?"

"If I hallucinated the pictures, the locked door, the man that was here, then maybe it was something I ate. But I don't think so." She turned and leaned up against the wall. He was right, she was exhausted. "Let's stay here for the night."

"I think that's a bad idea."

"Ugh." She pushed off the wall but stumbled as it shook.

Stella turned, eyes wide, and pulled the rifle off her shoulder. There was a hidden doorway now visible to them. She half expected eyes to be peering at her from the darkness in the shifted wall as the butt of the rifle poked through the entrance.

"Oh great." Ari slapped his thighs as his words poured out sarcastically. "There's a secret passage. Perfect. We're never leaving, are we?"

She glanced at him briefly and saw his aura shifting uneasily. He was chewing his lip and his hands were rolling into fists.

"Stay here," Stella said. "Make sure the door doesn't close."

"You stay here." He pulled her backward. "I'll go."

"What?"

"Honestly, watching you vanish was enough to give me nightmares for a week. But I should really be the one to do this." Ari began to push the door wider.

"Hell no." Stella wanted to smack him.

"Hell yes," he said with a frown.

"Why?" She crossed her arms.

"Well, I'm a… you know…"

Stella's eyes grew wide with both shock and annoyance. "A man?"

His shoulders fell sheepishly and he didn't look her in the eye. Stella inhaled sharply as she thought about a proper response. Instead of being angry, she chose to stay calm.

"That's a horrible reason."

"No, it's not. It's chivalrous."

He crossed his arms as they faced off. Hands on her hips, Stella debated with herself. The disappearing man, Charon, had warned her that their lives were in danger. She didn't want to be responsible for him. But Ari would never believe her if she told him what she saw, who she spoke to, or what was said, so there was no way to convince him to stay put.

"What's the plan?" he finally asked.

"We both go. Flashlight."

"It's amazing you still have batteries." He pulled the flashlight out of the small bag affixed to his side.

"It's compact, uses sunlight to recharge when the lithium batteries die and the batteries themselves are small enough that they're not a hassle," Stella said as she pushed through the door first.

The secret hallway was covered in dense spiderwebs. Stella cringed but swept them away as they moved quickly. The door hadn't sealed… yet. She glanced back. Some light still crept into the tunnel from the room's large window. She felt a little more at ease, knowing there was an escape and kept going.

The tunnel wasn't small, but she couldn't picture it within the structure of the mansion. However, she knew that it would be relatively easy to stay out of sight in such a massive place, and people were fond of hidden places.

Even as a kid, she loved to find nooks and crannies to hide in. She could escape from the crazy family for a while. No screaming or yelling. Just quiet.

She heard movement and paused. There was only one tunnel, no offshoots, so where was it coming from? She looked up and shone the light.

Nothing.

Nothing by their feet, no rats or mice. She turned around and shone the light toward the entrance, which was long gone and a mere dot in her vision. How far had they gone?

She felt relieved to see the door still open. But then she saw it, movement in the dot. She turned off the light. Ari began to object, but she covered his mouth.

The space was too small to put up a good fight and too dark to see where it planned to strike. Her heart was hammering hard.

They stopped briefly and Stella kept her eye toward the entrance as she pushed Ari, trading places with him. She kept pressing her hands on his back until he started moving again.

"Keep it off," she said as quietly as possible as she gave him the flashlight.

Her rifle sat in her hand comfortably as she edged deeper into the tunnel. There was still a flickering shape in the light, and she could tell it was moving nearer them as it closed the space in the light.

"Faster," Ari whispered.

They shuffled quickly down the tunnel. She kept her eye behind them, her head turned. A gruff, angry growl echoed against the walls and shook the building.

"What the heck?" Ari shuttered and stumbled.

"Don't stop," Stella hissed. "Go. Go!"

They began sprinting down the tunnel, not bothering to turn again. She couldn't risk tripping over her feet. But she could feel the ominous figure moving more quickly now. It wanted them but wanted to play for a little bit. The growling was deeper, closer.

It was a furere.

She felt herself shaking as she urged Ari from a sprint to a full-blown run. Thankfully, the furere's size kept it from moving too quickly down the passage.

She huffed the stifled air heavily, ignoring the webs that caught and stuck to her, as they made their way into what she imagined was the lair of the furere. Being hunted sent shivers up her spine. Having seen the destruction and death the furere leave in their wake she knew they attacked with cruel, malicious intent.

The growl turned from anger to a raging screech and they covered their ears, screaming at the sudden pain flaring through their ear drums into their brains. The screech bellowed in their bodies, sinking deep into their bones, like bass sprung too loud in a small room.

"Run," Stella screamed, trying to overcome the sound drawing from behind. "Move, Ari!"

They stumbled through the tunnel at a slower pace than Stella would have liked but were moving nonetheless. Still, she could feel it getting closer, could hear its claws scraping on the walls and floor.

Furere enjoyed terrorizing their victims. It could have caught them already if not for its sadistic love of fear and pain. She knew this and yet she continued to run even if she didn't know where to.

"Fresh air," Ari gasped and took hold of Stella, flinging them forward.

They crashed into wooden planks and what remained of the day's light. Stella and Ari grabbed the wood planks, fingers slipping through the slits, and began yanking them from the wall with their body weight.

They could hear it moving closer, howling and screeching, as it inched towards them. She could smell it now: tar, burned flesh and mold. Bile rose up from her stomach as she continued to yank on the boards.

Finally, the planks budged and fell backward. Scrambling, they crawled through the tiny opening. Her back caught the wood, and she pushed into the dirt to scramble through. As she fell out, she sprung into the forest.

Stella barely caught the fresh air as her foot entangled itself in an extended root, and she fell forward onto her hands and knees. Unable to catch her footing, she scrambled and tripped again. She felt strong arms tug her up and push her into the forest. Ari was moving quickly.

The sky was darkening as the sun's warm glow began to dim. She could feel Ari running nearby as her feet quickly caught onto the idea of moving wildly through a forest. She dashed over roots and under branches. Her lungs were burning, but she refused to acknowledge it. She couldn't. If she did, then she would stop. If she stopped, she would die.

Her face burned, and she knew it was purple, but she needed to press onward. It didn't matter. At least if she passed out, she wouldn't feel the furere digging into her body and rip it apart like a jigsaw puzzle.

Her eyes quickly scanned for Ari who was still moving but something in his movement was off. His body moved too smoothly through the rough terrain for it to be natural. Ari didn't just run; he leapt and soared. Moving elegantly and swiftly through trees and bramble he carried onward while Stella stumbled in her distraction.

"Keep moving," Ari shouted at her.

She shook her head and sped up again. What she saw almost looked like an animal, not a person.

Every inch of her body was aching and stinging as she flew. The branches grabbed hold of her skin and peeled layers from her body. She didn't know for how long they'd run but she knew it would never be far enough from a furere. So far, she had been lucky enough to simply hide. Now there was no choice in the matter but to flee like a mouse from a cat.

Then she felt it. A sharp hand grabbed her arm.

Stella was tossed in the air as if she weighed nothing at all. She tumbled into the brush on the descent and felt the tree limbs cut into her flesh. Eyes open, she gasped for breath as she attempted to aim the rifle at the furere. The pain in her arm stung as if a nest of hornets was swarming her skin as she pulled the rifle up.

"Stella!"

She could hear her name being called frantically. It was still in the distance as it echoed ever so slightly in the air.

"Go," she called back. "Go!"

Stella was scrambling to her feet as she watched the furere edge closer. It was on all fours, looking at her curiously, ravenously. She heard it lick its lips, almost purr, and she cringed.

She darted out of the shrubbery with her rifle ready. The beast screeched, and she dropped to her knees as it took her balance from her. Her ears felt like they were bleeding, and her brain reverberated in and out of her skull. Her chest emptied of air with each inhalation.

"You're fun," the furere said as it slammed its clawed hand into her chest.

It spoke? Her mind turned chaotic. *It's not an animal? It can speak.*

A hardened stab to Stella's chest stole her breath before flinging her into a tree. Her back and spine tingled with the shock. If this was how she died, she wanted to know what the furere felt, if it felt anything.

It came in close, face to face, and opened its gaping mouth of razors, teeth that protruded like stalagmites from the soft tissue. Even its tongue appeared sharp, writhing like a snake's, but it too had teeth protruding from flesh. But that's not what she wanted. She moved her hands, hoping to distract it momentarily.

It cocked its head downward like a bird and then its eyes landed on hers. She locked its gaze and stared with as much effort as she could muster. Her mouth turned dry as she focused her attention.

Its eyes were black, nothing but a vortex of empty awareness. As it inched closer, she could smell its ragged breath on her skin and clothing.

It reeked of blood, soot, decaying flesh… Bile moved up her esophagus. But she held onto the stare angrily. She would not die without knowing.

As if it knew what she was doing, it screeched angrily. In that screech, she could see all of its emotion. There was rage and confusion in the creature. But the most discernible and disturbing was familiarity. It was as though she knew the beast.

Confused, her face distorted, and she released her gaze.

"You can speak," she shouted, and the furere shut its mouth.

It licked its lips again, the teeth on its tongue cutting open its own flesh. She pictured a cat waiting for its prey to do something. It was more fun to hunt prey that wanted to live.

She had distracted it once and thought perhaps it would work again. She moved her hand in its line of sight and, when it focused on it, jammed a stick into the other eye. The furere recoiled and screamed in pain.

She could have sworn it spoke to her. Why not speak now? She took another deep breath, holding the bile down, as it lunged for her. She meant to close her eyes and allow her death but instead grabbed the tree branch above her and swung her body up.

It moved quickly, curling its body to the tree. She squinted, knowing it would reach up and grab her. But nothing came.

A howl pierced the air and Stella opened her eyes. A magnificent beast stood before her; its jaw was clamped down on the furere's throat.

She let her feet down and dropped to the ground as the beast kept its eyes on her. With one motion its jaw, easily the size of Stella's body, closed and severed the head of the furere, thick black blood oozing out of the furere's now lifeless carcass like cold molasses.

The beast dropped the remainder of the limp corpse and spat the blood out disgustedly. Stella began hyperventilating as she took in the situation. She let herself sit as pain began coursing through her limbs.

She could feel her blood burning as it ran through her body and into her chest. The sensation inside her lungs changed as her inhalations turned ice cold. The chill moved up her neck then down to her stomach. She thought perhaps this is what death felt like.

"Stella," Ari said.

Her eyes, and jaw, were clamped shut to keep the pain and bile at bay the best she could. But soon it was too much. She felt the vomit explode out of her mouth through a scream of agony. Stella's bladder loosened as her stomach pulsated.

The fire ran through her blood to all portions of her body. She could taste the acid in her mouth and then the metallic taste of iron—blood. She gasped for air, but every breath was ragged and empty.

"Breathe," Ari said. It was the last sound to resonate in her ears before the world around her turned black in the madness.

Chapter Fourteen

The sweet smell of roses floated into Stella's conscious mind. She opened her eyes slowly, her body comfortably rested. It was bright, the sun warm against her skin. She wondered if this was heaven.

"Oh good. You're awake," Ari said.

She began sitting up but changed her mind as pain vibrated down her shoulder and arm. Her chest felt heavy as lead.

She looked around as best she could, head on a swivel, as her eyes strained to see. They were surrounded by a tall brick and concrete wall, but she couldn't see where it began or ended.

"I climbed it," he said. "It's just a giant circle. No doors. For the record, you're heavier than you look."

"That's kind of rude."

He left her and sat down an arm's distance away. She kept her eye on him suspiciously. He was plucking petals off different flowers. Stella could see the roses in the distance. Eyes back to Ari, she noticed he was placing the petals on a large flat stone.

"What are you doing?" Stella asked quietly.

"Nothing much." He shrugged.

She nodded, unconvinced. "Where's the dog?"

"Excuse me?" He looked up at her.

"You heard me." Stella crossed her arms then decided against it as pain jumped up and down her arm and collarbone. "The giant, massive dog that killed the furere. It was at least the height of the forest. You couldn't have missed that thing. Where is it? Why didn't it eat me… why didn't it eat you?"

"I don't think you have to worry."

"Why not? Have you seen it before?" Stella looked around again and noticed Ari looking at her peculiarly. "Don't look at me like that. What happened?"

"What do you remember?" He shifted his gaze back to the petals.

"The best question is: what was real?"

"I guess all of it." Ari shrugged and began smooshing the petals between the flat rock and another. "Except me disappearing... because it was you."

She turned over to watch Ari work, trying to ignore the pain in her body, as she let the comment go. She didn't want to bicker with him.

"Why aren't you freaking out?" Ari asked.

"I'm not actually sure this is real," Stella said. "I mean... people don't usually experience pain in their dreams and I'm hurting but this is too peaceful to be real."

"Okay." Ari glanced at her. "If this isn't real, what would you like to do?"

"What do you mean?"

"I mean... if this is a fantasy all up in your head, how do you want it to turn out?" He stopped what he was doing, grinned and winked.

Stella sighed. "I'm in too much pain for that, thanks though."

"Women have found yet another excuse..."

"Shut up," she chuckled. "It's impossible that we survived. Something killed a furere. Which is not possible. I've never heard of a furere being killed... or even injured. Do you think that thing was a government experiment?"

"The wolf or the furere?"

Stella needed to pause before offering an answering. Either case was possible, she determined. "Both I guess."

"Well, at this point I have to ask, what government?" Ari put the petals into their small plastic travel cup and stirred with his finger. "Everyone is dead. Well, I guess not everyone, technically. Now, drink this."

She finally sat up and hunched her shoulders over her legs to keep upright. "I appreciate the thought, honestly, but I'm not drinking that. Tea wasn't really my thing when the world was normal."

"It'll help."

He squatted in front of her and put the cup to her lips. She recoiled as her nose scrunched at the strange aroma. She was skeptical.

"Why does it smell like piss? Oh my God, are you trying to get me to drink urine? Seriously?"

"Is that what you think of me?" He frowned. "Hurtful."

"You're trying to make me drink pee made pretty with a few flower petals." She fought back. "How am I being—"

"That's it." He turned her head for her and dumped the tea into her mouth while he could.

She coughed as it went down her throat unexpectedly. It didn't taste nearly as bad as it smelled, but she still glared at him as her body shook with the coughing. He rubbed her back as she finished coughing on the liquid.

"Now that was mean," she said hoarsely.

"No, it was logical. It's you that smells like piss, by the way. Not my drink."

"What?"

She pulled her clothes up to her nose. He was right. She stank of body odour and excrement. The rot and decay of the furere was also fused into the fabric.

"Sorry."

"At least you didn't soil yourself."

"Why?" She grinned. "Did you?"

His face contorted. "None of your business."

"You did!" She laughed until pain stopped her. "Oh, ouch... that hurts."

"Serves you right," he said.

Stella half-smiled at him. At least she had someone to banter with at the end of the world. Taking full advantage of the situation, she breathed gently.

"What are you thinking about?" Ari asked.

"Where were you when it first happened?" she asked.

"The first attack or the first time I saw the news of it nearby?"

"Nearby."

"I was home with my parents. I was trying to finish writing my thesis and I couldn't focus. So, I went home for inspiration. The wing of the university they decimated was where I would have been working.

"The campus news crew was doing a report on it while I was in my car driving back to school the next day. They weren't sure where the furere had gone. All they knew was that there were at least five hundred people dead and two hundred more injured. I considered turning around but, when I pulled off the highway, the police weren't letting people back on. They told us to find a place to hunker down."

She thought of her own day. Georgian Bay had been nothing compared to the attack that followed it. Stella watched people trample each other to death, shouldering her out of the way, just to get themselves to safety. Their selfishness hadn't been surprising.

But the food court had been traumatizing all on its own. The stench of rotting corpses and blood had offered some protection from the furere. Especially in the first few days.

Her mind pulled her back to the kitchen. Stella had wanted to hide in the cupboard but Professor Marlin had insisted on the walk-in freezer instead. The clack of claws on tiles sent chills down her body before he completely sealed the door.

She hated leaving the bodies in such a disgraceful, disrespectful manner but Professor Byrne had insisted on leaving the bodies as they were in case furere returned. He had explained the need to lessen their footprint in the college.

"Where did you pull off?"

"Ingersoll." He finally looked at her. His eyes were large and ridden with sadness as emotion rolled over his face.

"You were so close to London…"

"I know… I almost never listen to the radio. My parents don't watch the news. I had no idea what was going on. Anyway, I found a small, cheap, dingy motel by the highway and kept my eyes peeled on the news. I didn't turn it off, not even when I started falling asleep. It was utter chaos the next few days. People were packing up and trying to escape, but the police wouldn't let them go anywhere. Not that there was anywhere to go anyway. I watched tanks roll through. I was there when the furere turned the bypass bridge into rubble and threw tanks around like they were toys."

"You survived that?" Stella's heart was turning heavy.

"Yeah." Ari rubbed his hands together. "A small group of us managed to get away on some dirt bikes and quads we stole. Is it weird that I still feel guilty about the theft?"

He began laughing melancholically. Stella wished she hadn't asked him to dredge up his trauma. She knew they were both in a permanent state of fight or flight and it was stressful enough on the body and mind.

"I'm sorry," she whispered. "Why do you feel guilty?"

"The people we stole them from… what if that's what would have saved them?"

"Do you know for sure they're even dead?"

"No, but…"

Ari was fiddling with his fingers nervously, clearly upset. For someone who had wanted to work in a place that was meant to assist people, he had done the complete opposite. Stella could feel the guilt and shame he was plagued by.

"I get it," Stella said. "I've done a lot of horrible stuff to survive."

"Anyone who is still alive at this point has," he said.

"Maybe not you; if you feel that guilty about stealing a dirt bike."

"Thanks," he said. "Do you mind if I ask… about yours?"

"I, uh…" Stella hesitated. Her mind turned to her professor and tears welled in her eyes. "I was at the college. Something had happened and my teacher cancelled the rest of our classes. I didn't think it was the furere. When I saw one through the window, I knew it was real. It was ripping apart the building and throwing chunks of concrete at cars and people. Everyone began screaming and running all at once. I watched one tear someone in half with a single motion.

"The students, and teachers, tried to lock themselves in the classrooms and offices. They shoved people out of the way and stomped over bodies. In the long run, I suppose they did those people a favour.

"I raced to the basement and locked myself in one of the bathrooms. Because the school was older, at least this part, the door was metal and still had a lock on the inside. I didn't see anybody down there, so I locked it and jammed spitballs in the creases. Rule number one: diminish your scent. Then I went and sat in a stall, feet up, and waited. I spent two days locked in there before I had the nerve to leave.

"When I did head up, the building was chaos. Everything was destroyed and bodies were everywhere. Blood was dried and so thick it looked like paint. They were taunting survivors."

"I'm so sorry."

"Thanks."

"Who was the last person you saw?"

"You," she laughed.

"Apart from the obvious, smartass."

Stella squirmed uncomfortably. She had spent the last few months alone despite the agonizing pit in her gut for company. Groups were dangerous, as her mind recalled the mass of people wading through slushy snow, so she'd rather be alone and allow that gnarly pit to fester.

"It was outside the city. I stole a car and drove to the woods. There was this little old grandpa. I don't even know how he'd managed to survive. Well, I kind of do; he was self-reliant and lived in the middle of nowhere."

"So, they didn't even think to look for a human out there," Ari murmured. "Smart."

"I think he just wanted peace and quiet in his old age," Stella said. "Peace and quiet sounds good at this age… Anyway, he was a hermit and I watched him for a few days. He just took care of his garden and carried a couple guns with him. But he mostly used a crossbow to hunt. If I had to guess, he'd been doing this for many years until it was routine. I decided against getting close. He didn't seem aware of what was happening in the world. I kind of wanted him to keep living that way. It didn't seem fair to take that away from him. He looked to be about ninety, if I had to guess."

"Do you think he's still going?"

"I imagine it." Stella kept her smile. "But probably not. If they're coming out to places like this now… any scattered civilization left is doomed."

There was a brief pause and Stella watched Ari chew over his words. "What did you really see in that house? In your dream?"

"Are you religious?"

"Not in the least."

"Churches all over the place were claiming the furere were demons."

"I don't know about demons," he said with a shrug.

Silence filled the space and Stella's body ached. There were undoubtedly torn muscles from fleeing and being flung by furere. She ran her fingers over her chest. The grooves from its pointed palm were still there. She could feel the open skin and knew it would bleed given the chance.

"I cleaned them the best I could," Ari said. "And the one on your arm."

"Thank you."

The pair were still in silence as Stella stared ahead. She could hear Ari's breath as she steadied her own. Stella's heart was murmuring softly in her chest but she was still weary. To her, the beat was weak.

"I miss people sometimes," he said softly, breaking the silence.

"I miss cars... and chicken balls," Stella said, the corner of her lip curled upward in a slight smirk.

Ari laughed, "I could go for some chicken balls."

"Oh, and bathrooms." Stella leaned back to a lying position, her body weakening. "I miss a lot of things..."

Stella's eyes closed as she drifted from the waking world to the dreaming one. She could feel her body give way to sleep, the aches and pains drifting away. Despite hearing Ari's voice, she couldn't discern the words.

Chapter Fifteen

Aurella bound down the forest toward the ocean. Very few animals were left on the west coast, but the lack of boat traffic encouraged aquatic creatures to emerge. However, if any furere were nearby, they would dive into the water and scoop up the animals.

She slowed as the ocean came into view. Quietly emerging from the trees, she tread across the sand, allowing it to meld between her toes. She could feel the vibrations of the earth humming up into her body. She took the energy willingly to refresh her powers.

A reverberation shook her, and she turned on her heels to the east, eyes wide. Her breath was sharp as she felt the magic whir about the trees. It was far-off in the distance, clear across the country, yet it could be felt. The owner of the magic was indeed powerful.

Magical creatures emerged from hiding and watched with her. Their cluttered presence was sure to attract the furere, but they were entranced and worried. The pixies fluttered over to her and molded together until they formed a humanoid.

"Is that coming from the mansion?" the pixie asked.

"I think so. You felt that shockwave, right?"

"Unfortunately. What do you think she'll do this time?"

"There's no way of knowing." Aurella looked over at the clustered human form.

"There's no way of knowing, or you simply won't tell us?"

"If I told people everything I know, there would be no secrets left in the world."

"Should there be secrets?"

"You see many things, pixie." Aurella began trekking east, toward the mansion. "You have recorded history better than anyone. You should not stop now."

"We have no more history!" the pixie argued vehemently. "There is nothing left"

"We're left," Aurella said without so much as a glance. "That counts."

"You suggest we continue then."

"I advise you to continue living, observing and recording. There will never be history if it is not watched and written."

"Then you go to the mansion."

"Yes," Aurella said. "I have tasks I must complete."

"That's to be expected as you were her lackey."

Aurella stared backward at them with a warning glance. Her face was scrunched and tight, eyes glimmering with anger. The fae side of her temper was beginning to show and the pixies took to the sky, scattering into the wind and above the tree line.

She watched them fly high and inland. She knew what they would see below. A world of crumbled ashes. Remnants of homes humans had designed, and remains of nests magical creatures concocted. There weren't even graves for the departed. What bodies not snatched by furere lay scattered in the open.

Aurella found herself hurrying across the country to reach the mansion. It had once been her home and had taken her many years to forget it. But when called, like a dog, she went running. Such was her life. Free but enslaved by her own impractical hope.

She had been given responsibilities beyond her desire.

Aurella supposed she should be flattered by having the trust of those above her station, but she felt indignant instead. What she had been asked to do was incomprehensible. However, she did it nonetheless.

Chapter Sixteen

When Stella's eyes opened, it was dark, and her limbs were numb. She quivered, goosebumps covering her skin, and wrapped her sleeves around her as best she could.

Turning her head sideways, she saw Ari sitting cross-legged, hands cupped over his stomach in a small ball. She blinked because she wasn't sure what she saw. She grunted and pushed up onto her elbows, joints creaking, and her jaw dropped. She ignored the pain fluttering up into her shoulder as she watched.

There was lightning inside his hands. It was perfectly contained and danced about his palms and fingers. But it didn't harm him, it didn't even seem to bother him, like nothing more than fireflies caught in a glass jar.

"What in the actual…"

His eyes opened and the lightning vanished. He rubbed his hands on his pants and smiled. "What's wrong?"

"There… you… lightning… hands…" Stella couldn't find the words.

"I meditate," he said. "It helps with anxiety."

"The lightning?"

"Lightning? It's just energy." He shrugged as though it was nothing. "Ki, or qi, even chi, depending who you ask."

She shivered. "Sure. And you think I'm nuts."

"You are," he said. "The light shooting out of your head proved it. Then there's the portraits that only you saw, plus your vanishing act."

"There was lighting in your hand."

She sat completely up, her body cracking every which way. The burning in her blood had eased some but the muscles were tired and didn't want to move.

"No." He corrected. "Just energy."

"I know what I saw." She wagged her finger, eyes glued to his belly.

"Okay," he said.

She chanced a glance up at him, curious who he really was underneath that cool exterior. What was he really like past the facade? Not to mention that strange aura of his.

Ari was watching her quietly, his eyes fixated on her wounds. He looked sickened but compassionate. His quiet demeanour made Stella hesitate asking him questions at the moment. She realized too that she was scared to get answers she wasn't prepared to hear.

"Would you like some heat?" Ari moved closer. "Come here."

Stella realized her body was shaking in the cold and nodded, choosing to trust him even if she couldn't ask questions. Ari grabbed her good arm and pulled her closer as he scootched toward her. She fell into his chest heavily and let her body absorb his warmth.

The shivers across her body began to settle as the sound of his heartbeat soothed her. It hummed evenly in his chest. It proved there was still life in the world — life she was jeopardizing by being nearby. The symbol on his jacket continued to pulsate as it had previously.

It pained her not to know why she clung to her journey north. If they changed direction, would they last a little longer? What distressed her more was the thought of watching him die because of her. She quickly wiped away the tears that stung her eyes.

The night air had grown chilly despite the weather deepening into spring. The flowers developed in the cylindrical space's protection were much further along than their surrounding counterparts. Despite the chill, it was a pleasant evening to enjoy.

Stella figured he had to have seen the tears as he rested his chin against the crown of her head. She could feel his muscles move and wondered if he was smiling as he tightened his arms around her, locking them into a security blanket. She wondered what his thoughts were milling on as her body laid on him limply as though she were a little, lost girl.

Both life and death were sitting in Stella's wake, and she could feel it despite her pitiful and injured state. The grass around her had been brown when she'd first awoken but as she came to life, so had the vegetation.

Stella opened her eyes and brought her fingers up to touch the symbol on his jacket. She felt its smooth but worn outline against her skin. It made her feel sad, broken as Stella traced the infinity symbol over and again. She was looping it rhythmically, obsessed with the pattern, as her mind churned.

"Moirai," She murmured incoherently.

"What?" Ari asked.

"Moirai." Stella's eyes began to shut. "Cowardice…"

"Okay," Ari said.

She continued to trace the golden pattern on his jacket until she fell asleep. The words stuck in her mind and tongue as she escaped the world and fell into one of her own making.

She was naked and walking along the edge of a creek in an open field. It didn't feel like her own body. It felt lively and bright, golden.

The sun was hot, and birds were chirping. Wind whipped by her, pulling her hair away from her body, before stopping to speak with her.

"Hello," he said.

She turned to gaze at him and was stunned even though she couldn't quite make out his appearance. Regardless, Stella knew he was magnificent, ethereal.

"What do they call you?" he asked her.

"Stella." Her tongue and lips moved but she didn't hear herself.

Her body ached for him to reach out to her. Her flesh longed for his fingers to trace her bare skin and run his hands across her.

She was starved for a mere graze against his celestial, exquisite form.

"Stella." He repeated her name, a simper on his face. "Beautiful as the owner… yet you are still very corporeal in your desires."

Coming to her senses she looked at him but could still not discern his face. She felt him recognizable but could not place him.

"Does that offend you?" Her smile was coy as she asked.

"Certainly not. It simply creates curiosity."

"What are you curious about?" She could feel the throbbing in her loins become heavier, more desperate.

"I can feel the heat rush through your body." He inched closer teasingly. She could smell the cool pine of the forest resting against his skin as he spoke. "Your cheeks are flush and grow more sensitive to physical sensation, your eyes give you away. I wonder… is that what you equate love to?"

"I do not love," she laughed. "You misconstrue me. My physical body has its own desires that do not always align with my mind. It is a curse of flesh."

"Then you refuse to love anything?"

"Love is a decision as much as it is a feeling," she said, disdain dripping from her tongue. "It leads to disaster. Have you not watched humankind for centuries? I have seen plagues, wars, famines incited all for the sake of love or God.

"For the sake of a beautiful woman, though no more than an object in man's eye, they would topple each other's countries. That is a pity. But perhaps no more a pity than refusing to give in to desire when it happens to strike." Her chest burned as she spoke. It wasn't anger that filled her body but distress. The lack of understanding eroded her body at an alarming. "Does the male form believe the female has no desire contained within in it? This physical form, magic or not, female or ungendered or male, still craves satisfaction regardless of my mental state. It is a conscious decision which determines other factors, such as acting on it. Yet I have more control than man."

"My apologies for the offense," he said. "Though I must disagree on one note. Love does not lead to disaster. Lust, anger, jealousy and hate lead humankind to act selfishly. Not love, dear one. Never love. If it is unconditional and truthfully given then there can be no malice in it, no lust or anger or hate which leads to selfishness. It is giving."

"You speak as though you have never considered it as it is presented: business," Stella said.

"If it is presented as such, as a trade, then should one consider it love?"

"I would not."

He grinned at Stella before preparing to leave her as she had been: in peace. "Perhaps I will see you again." He whipped away into the wind and trees.

Stella stood, humbled by the experience and curious. He was clearly more than a fae in the wind. He was too steady to be only that.

Her eyes fluttered and she was back in the dark. She was still warm and Ari was humming something, presumably falling asleep. She shook her head and smirked to herself. At least it wasn't a nightmare this time.

"Can't sleep?" she asked.

"Hard to sleep sitting up," Ari said.

"Sorry." Stella began to push away.

"You're cold, and frankly, I'll be too if you move." He kept his arms locked around her, preventing her from shifting further.

A howl tore through the air and their hairs stood on end. Fear prickled her stomach as the sound vibrated over the sky. The brick wall around them wasn't going to keep furere out. Rather, it would keep the pair trapped inside if they were found.

"Do we run?" she asked.

"No." He shook his head. "No need to attract attention. Besides, you're not ready yet."

Stella scowled at him before sighing and letting it go. She shivered and nestled in closer as their heat melted together. The sound of the creatures vanished and her body relaxed.

"Well, if we're going to die, I'm doing it in my sleep," Stella said. Her eyes shifted to his jacket and her curiosity overcame her. "What's with the gold infinity symbol anyway?"

"I dunno. My dad got it from his dad and so on and so forth. Family crest, technically. It's the only thing I got to keep through all this."

"I wish I had something from home."

"It is a reminder of home and that makes me both sad and relieved. The people I was with died only days before you came along," he said. "The whole ordeal has been a nightmare, but I was never by myself at least. I'm not sure I could bear that. From the sounds of it you were mostly alone this whole time."

"I was," she said. "Not at first."

She considered telling him about Marlin but the thought of him haunted her. She was quiet and let her breath fall in line with his.

Her eyes turned upward to the stars twinkling above them. The stars' freedom in space mocked the pair of humans and their pitiful existence. Despite not being omniscient and mere balls of gas there was a lifelike presence in their appearance in the heavens.

Stella's breath came easier as her body began healing. She was thankful for the lessened whistling in her airway. Furthermore, her thanks needed to go out to that giant wolf. She would certainly be dead if not for the massive wolf that had torn through the trees and severed the head of the furere.

There had never been reports, not even whispers, of anyone killing a furere in any news report Stella had managed to hear. It was as if the skin and flesh of the furere were impenetrable armor. Yet, a wolf the size of a house had stormed between the two and decapitated the beast to protect her.

A small shift in weight sent stinging sensations through Stella's veins. Judging by the continuous burning and chill that coursed through her blood after the attack it was likely their claws had venom or poison like a snake's bite. She pushed the thought from her mind and counted sheep until she fell asleep.

Chapter Seventeen

A petite chickadee bopped across the grass toward Stella and Ari. It chirped at them excitedly as the sun began to pour into the small enclosure. Stella's eyes flitted open and she saw the little bird looking at them curiously. They had fallen backwards and were sleeping in an awkward pile-up spoon.

She pushed off Ari's chest carefully, crawled staggeringly over to the bird and leaned, arm extended as far as she could reach. It jumped into her palm and cheeped at her once. She smiled.

"I don't have any food for you, little bird."

It cheeped again and bounced up her arm onto her shoulder and sat there. It looked at the sky to the north and cheeped once more.

"Yes, north is where we go." She shook her head at herself for talking to a bird.

Two small chirps were returned to her, as if to say, "why wait?"

"Are you talking to a bird?" Ari spoke up groggily, his voice both annoyed and amused.

"Yes." She glanced back teasingly. "Apparently I have two little birds in my life now…"

"Hey, that's rude."

Smirking, she looked to the chickadee. "I feel like if I'm going to have a familiar, it should be a cat. A black one."

"Dear God, you're not a witch… are you?" Ari muttered as he got to his feet.

"No," Stella said. "Okay, little fella, time to fly away."

The chickadee opened his wings and fluttered away as Stella rose and moved to the other side of the concrete structure to relieve herself. Plucking at large blades of grass and leaves she could find, she sighed to herself. She spent some time examining the wall. It was smooth, a few crumbles here and there, but overall stood firmly in place. She wondered who built it and why.

There was nothing remarkable about the space and, if people couldn't leave easily, what was the point?

Perhaps she had it wrong. Was it meant to keep something in? To hold something?

Her eyes moved upward. The air was stifled as the wind ceased to run through the trees. She forgot how long it had been since she felt wind on her cheeks. But the sky was a brilliant blue and held hardly a cloud. In the current moment it seemed as though nothing was wrong in the world.

"Okay, so the way I see it we can jump down and keep going," Ari yelled, capturing her attention. He was sitting on the top of the brick enclosure.

Stella wiped quickly and hoisted her pants back up. She went to a different area on the wall and examined it. Ari raised himself to his feet and walked across the top like a gymnast on balance beams. Once he reached her, he sat down again, one leg on either side, and offered his hand.

"Time to head off to the wild," he said.

"Yeah." She realized he had the rifle and bags.

"Good, but first things first, a bath," he said, coiling his nose. "For both of us."

"You see any tubs out there?" she responded dryly.

"No. But I heard water earlier."

She planted her feet on the wall and grabbed the brick as high as she could before dragging herself upward. Ari held one of her hands, but the pain coursing through her veins made the climb difficult. He grabbed hold of Stella's clothing until she was half over the top and hanging limply on either side.

"Thanks."

Her lungs begged for air as she pushed herself up and into a seated position over the wall. The injuries to her arm and chest burned, causing Stella to wince between quick, raspy inhales.

"No problem." He swung his feet over to the outside.

"How did you get up? It's at least ten feet."

"Well, I'm already over half that height," he said smugly.

"Barely." She followed suit and let her legs dangle from the top. "How does someone who's maybe five-foot-nine climb a ten-foot brick wall that's basically flat?"

"There were… etches on the other side," he said. "Besides, I used to rock climb with my dad. A lot. I was kind of a spider on those walls going left and right, or upside down."

"I got it," Stella said, if only just to calm him.

He swapped positions, allowing his hands to catch him as he hung over the edge. Once he was straight, Ari opened his hands dropped to the ground. His legs bent strongly, catching himself in a squat, before standing back up and waiting for Stella.

"The little bird is full of surprises," she muttered sarcastically.

"Okay." He walked over and reached up. "Can you trust me for thirty seconds."

"Fine." She turned over and slowly began hoisting herself down.

The side of her body that felt the sting of the furere were screaming at her to stop, but she clenched her teeth and told herself she was stronger than that. Ari's hands touched Stella's hips, steadying her as she made the small descent.

She let go of the wall and fell into him, forcing a small cry to crackle from deep within his throat as they tumbled into the grass. Ari chuckled lightly as Stella scrambled to get off him.

Chest burning, arm numb, she rolled away with a breath heavy. Ari stopped laughing and crawled to her with his hands extended.

"You okay?"

“Yeah.” She winced.

“I think I should have shown you this earlier,” Ari said.

He pulled out a handkerchief and opened the corners to reveal the black, insidious pieces hidden within. Stella’s face scrunched together tightly as she inspected the items. His arm remained steady as she looked at them.

“Are those claws?”

“I don’t know,” he said, sitting back. “I was pulling these pieces out of you too.”

He reached into his pocket and ruffled out a small, bundled up patch of bloodied fabric. He opened it and revealed the spikes. They were forked and black like sludge. She examined the items slowly. They looked like dark cacti.

“You plucked those out of me?” Acid rose from her stomach in disgust.

“Yeah. I’m sure I got them all. But they’re nasty little buggers.”

“I imagine so.”

She tossed the corners of the fabric back over them. Stella leaned back on her hands and stared at the sky lazily. Sitting up, she rolled her shoulder gently. She knew Ari was watching quietly as she tested her mobility. She wondered what pity he had for her in this state. Rather than ask, she merely turned away and began to rise.

“What are you doing on my property?” a loud voice boomed from the tree line.

Ari and Stella scrambled to their feet, though Stella’s sight blurred, and sought the man. He emerged slowly and kept his bow drawn. Stella’s heart stopped. He was massive. Beyond massive, he was comparable to an old oak tree. Or a troll. Though… not nearly as ugly. Not gross in the least, actually, the more she looked. Her vision cleared and she noted he was quite a handsome man.

“Sorry,” Ari apologized. “We were attacked and needed to recover. We didn’t know this was someone’s property…”

"Didn't know anyone else was still alive for that matter," Stella muttered.

The man paused and licked his lips. His bow remained steady as Stella watched the gears turn in his mind. She kept a close eye on his hands. If the man released the arrow there was no way she could move fast enough to dodge. Her eye twitched to Ari, he was ready to leap but he wouldn't be faster than an arrow in what appeared to be a one-hundred-and-fifty-pound draw. It was designed to catch fast, large animals such as deer and moose.

"That used to be a sanctuary for magical creatures," the man said. "Only magic gets you in."

Stella's mind turned to the pixie as he mentioned magic. She furrowed her brow and looked at her hands, daring to turn away from his bow, as her thoughts turned to the flower that blossomed and glowed upon her touch.

"I can go on a little faith," Ari said, "given all the crap we've seen."

"Humans don't survive the touch of a furere," the man's words were released through a sigh, laden with sorrow. "Their bodies can't handle the toxin."

Stella examined his skin as best she could, wondering if he too was magic. There were marks along his arm, similar to the ones left on her body by the furere. As her eyes scanned him, she realized his hair wasn't quite… hair. It looked more like long, thin strands of fur. He was tall, broad — she imagined him as a bear or perhaps bigfoot.

"So, what are you?" she asked him, chancing a step forward.

His bow shifted, lowering, as he answered, "caelum."

"Ca-cae-what?" Stella stammered.

"Caelum," Ari said. "Is that your name?"

"It's Latin." The man turned his back. "Let's go then, kiddos."

"Kiddos?" Stella whispered. "How old does he think we are?"

"Come on," he called as he began walking into the forest.

"Alright." Ari shrugged; eyebrows raised. "Couldn't get much worse, right?"

"You're so optimistic."

"Kind of have to be in a world like this," he said, chasing after the man.

Stella's throat echoed a small growl before following the two of them. It was too easy. She had a sneaky feeling it was a trap. Walking behind them, she kept her eyes and ears alert. Her body's strength was beginning to wain but she pressed forward regardless.

"What is a caelum?" Ari asked.

"I will explain when we get there," he spoke quietly.

"Well, I'm Ari! That's Stella."

Stella held back a chuckle as he made introductions. Ari was almost too friendly and trusting but in a cute, endearing way.

The man glanced back at her. They made brief eye contact before she quickly turned away, not wanting to see his emotions. But his eyes didn't have a specific colour. They seemed to be made of the galaxy: sparkling and dark.

She thought of the guardian, Charon. His eyes were bright but they too sparkled like crystals in the sunlight. Then she thought of her own eyes… had what she'd seen in the mirror been real?

The man paused before he turned frontward. Ari glanced back at him.

"She's a bit of a grouch," Ari said. "But somehow still likeable."

Stella restrained an eye roll and said nothing to redeem herself. No one would willingly show them their home if they intended to keep them alive. She was suspicious of the strange man, just as much as she was curious.

The man snorted as they came to a clearing. He strode right into it, Ari close behind. Stella paused and looked at the area. A cabin, barely the size of the man himself, sat by a waterfall. Ari was right about the sound of water.

Stella watched the man crouch through the door into his cabin. She checked the surroundings for traps. From her peripheral vision she could see Ari dipping his hands in the pool of water. Upon the man's return,

Stella noticed his arms were bundled with blankets. She reached out as thick fabric was tossed her direction.

"Bathe," he said. "You both smell of death. I'll be back soon so don't take forever."

"What?" Stella was stunned as she watched him leave. "Where are you — where is he going?"

"I don't know," Ari said. "But I'm taking advantage of the water."

She watched the large man tromp through the woods, strangely making no sound, until he was no longer visible. She assumed he was hunting or leaving them in a trap. If the latter, there was no time for fun.

Ari stripped without hesitation and jumped into the pool of water beneath the falls. Stella looked at him momentarily and then looked away as his bare body bounced in the water. She could feel her face turning red.

"Get in," he said. "It's nice."

"You've got to be kidding me… first he aims his bow at us, then leaves us on his property, next to his house." Stella dropped the blanket next to the water. "How are you not suspicious?"

"What's unbelievable is that you're not taking advantage of the water," Ari shouted before dunking himself under the surface and swimming behind the waterfall.

Stella stripped cautiously; suspicious the man may be watching for a moment to strike. She placed the rifle carefully along the water's edge and slipped into the pool. Her undergarments clung to her skin, and the chill of the pool burned into her injuries.

Her teeth chattered as she held onto the side, fingers clinging to dirt and grass tightly as tears stung her eyes. She could feel the water rippling against her skin like insect stings. She couldn't hold on and felt herself slither under the water.

She didn't breathe; her body burned in the water as though her blood were fire itself. Paralyzed, her eyes saw the light at the surface, but she couldn't reach it. Panic set in and air left her lungs. She convulsed helplessly, choking on the liquid flames.

A whirlwind enclosed her, spinning her around, until a strong grip took hold of her shoulders. She tried to open her eyes but couldn't see.

Bursting from the water, Stella's body was flung carelessly onto the grass. Her skin was stinging mercilessly as she coughed out water. Body shaking, she kept her eyes closed, both wanting to and not wanting to see her rescuer.

"Stella!" Ari yelled and sprung from the stream of water. "What the hell?"

"What's… what's in the water?" she sputtered.

"It's old magic," the man said as he draped a blanket over her. "It removed what was left of that poison in your blood."

"What do you mean?"

"Dry yourself and come inside," he said to Ari as he picked up Stella.

***

Ari grabbed his blanket and dried rapidly, tripping over himself to get to the door of the cabin. It was left open, so he stepped inside. He stopped and caught his gasp mid-inhale. The blanket hung around him like a toga as he stared inside the home. The man had already disappeared down a hallway.

The inside of the cabin was massive, two stories tall, and had all the makings of a real house. Ari stepped backward and looked at the outside once more. The building's exterior was no more than ten feet tall by ten feet wide. Waddling around the corner, blanket dragging behind him, Ari peered along the sides to be safe of his assertion. Heading back inside the cabin, he stopped to look at the man who was now waiting impatiently with his arms crossed.

"Care… to explain?" Ari asked.

"Close the door."

"Uhm…" Ari was unsure of locking himself in a strange house. "Are you going to eat us?"

"You think my house is made of candy? Do I look like a witch?" he snorted.

~ 105 ~

"No," Ari said. He slowly shut the door and winced when it reached the frame and clicked.

"I have no interest in eating you," the man said dryly before he moved down the corridor.

Ari moved his feet quickly to follow him, looking at the walls only to see blank white paint, then turned his gaze downward to see plain hardwood flooring. There were lights in the ceiling that sat in straightly aligned, affixed rows, but they were crystals not bulbs.

"What are those?" Ari asked.

"Young people know nothing anymore."

They entered a smaller room where Stella lay under the covers, unconscious, on a bed. Ari swallowed tightly as he watched her chest rise and fall heavily.

"She'll be fine." The man fell into a seat at the foot of the bed. "Why don't you tell me what your power is, little fae-el."

"Excuse me?" Ari held the blanket tighter against his body.

"Caelum are creatures, human or otherwise, that were infused with magic carried by fallen meteors," he said. "You provided your name earlier, I'm Galen."

"Nice to meet you."

Ari said the polite thing but internally he wasn't sure how to proceed. He considered briefly dragging Stella from the cabin overnight. He tried imagining what she would do, or want, but drew a blank.

"Are you going to stand there and tell me you haven't seen magic with your own eyes?" Galen said. "What about that mansion a little way back. Surely you passed by it."

"We... uh..." Ari stopped himself. "Yeah, we did. We've seen a few weird things."

"I'm sure you have. You are also magic," Galen said.

"How do you figure?" Ari looked between the man and Stella as he sought similarities.

"You think there is only one type of magical creature?"

"I've been to magic shows, but this takes the cake. Are the furere magic too then?"

"Of course."

The amusement on Galen's face wasn't appreciated by Ari though he noted the man was chewing his words carefully. He wondered what knowledge the man was withholding and as much as he wanted answers, he didn't think Galen would provide them easily.

"What did you see at the mansion?"

"It was some rundown old house. Well, mansion more like, it has a few castle-like features," Ari said.

"What are you not admitting though?" he pressed.

"Well, what do you know about the house?"

Galen smirked before responding. "I know it belongs to the fae. I know it was the queen's home for many centuries. Around the start of the colonization in North America, I suppose. Though, I suspect the fae knew of this place for centuries prior to the settlers' arrival."

"Do you know how crazy you sound?"

"Do you recognize how crazy the world has become?" Galen said sarcastically. "Do you even recognize yourself when you… shift?"

"Excuse me?" Ari cocked a brow.

"Never mind." Galen was rubbing his eyes.

He hoisted himself up and strode, two steps, clear across the room. Ari could feel the heat emanating off him like a fireplace.

"I assume you want to stay in the same room as her," Galen said. "I'll let you keep watch."

"Thanks." Ari went and sat on the bed, whispering to Stella, "you're gonna love this guy."

Chapter Eighteen

Stella awoke to a heavy weight covering half her body and the sound of snoring. Tilting her head, she saw Ari sprawled across her. She sighed and dropped her head, eyes closed. The little bird had turned into a giant puppy. It was at least nice to be resting in something soft, she told herself.

"Ari." She opened her eyes. "Ari!"

Stella shook her legs and pushed until he fell off the bed with a thud. She rolled over and looked at him. His arms were sprawled over his head as his legs began moving like a fish out of water. He began groaning.

"What was that for?"

"I do not like passing out and waking up in random places," Stella hissed.

"But it's so much fun," he said sarcastically.

She threw her feet over the side of the bed. "Is this a house?"

"Yeah, sort of." Ari stood up. "It's that dude's cabin. Get this… it's giant inside… "

"This room is the size of the cabin. How does he fit? Where is he anyway?"

"Probably in the other rooms. The big guy, his name was Galen, anyway he says magic exists."

"I believe anything at this point," she said.

"I don't know what to believe," Ari said.

Stella picked herself up and proceeded to march out of the room and into the hallway. She paused and looked up. "What's with the lights?"

"I asked that too." Ari followed close behind, scrambling and checking his breath.

"About time you two got up." The man's head popped up from the edge of the hallway. "We should talk."

"What did you do to me?" Stella stopped walking.

"The magic in the water healed you," he said. A sly smile crept across his face as the rest of his body appeared. "What did you see in the mansion?"

Straight to it then, Stella nodded, drawing closer. "What have you seen?"

He cocked his head. "You first."

"You're the one that sees magic." She crossed her arms. "And where is my rifle?"

"It's by the door." He nodded toward it. "You still don't trust me?"

"You knew the water would do something to me," she said, less than impressed.

Tension in the room rose as the two of them faced off. Stella wasn't quite ready to lock eyes with him and delve into his emotions but she was reading his body language perfectly. He was calm, collected, but wouldn't budge on his position in the matter.

"Okay, let's just take a break." Ari bounded between the two of them.

Stella glanced at him as her stomach suppressed a gurgle. Her body was growing agitated. She watched Ari try to stop an onslaught of vicious, entangling words and probable violence all while Galen was smiling at the pair.

"What do you think I saw?" she snapped.

Stella could see the debate playing in his mind as it riddled his face: how to handle the kids? Finally letting out a loud sigh and uncrossing his arms, it was clear he came to a decision.

"I think you saw your former selves," he said. "Or am I wrong?"

He knows. Stella could burst at the seams with anticipation. Her eyes were locked on Galen as she began her parade of questions.

"Is it a horror house? Did you see yourself? What is it?"

"No." The man shook his head. "I saw you. Five of you, actually."

"What exactly did you see?" She moved closer, making strong eye contact.

She delved deep into his mind to see anger, exhaustion, frustration and, surprisingly, hope. But he held himself together too well for any of that to show on his face. She let go of the connection.

"I saw your portraits, your graves, the dates. I've spoken to Charon," he said.

Galen moved to his dining table and sat down. Stella watched his eyes scan her over as he was waited for a response to his last statement. She could feel Ari in the background, his nervous energy was drifting toward her.

Stella slowly inched closer to Galen in curiosity and wonder. She didn't just want answers, she needed them. Her innate yearning to understand was so strong she wouldn't be able to rest until she had the knowledge.

"What did he say? How well do you know him?" Stella asked.

As she came closer, she noticed he was still easily her height even from his chair. Their faces met nearly equally, and Stella made contact again, but this time she reached out and touched him.

So that's your trick…

He was grinning. There was a thick pause in the air as Stella drew back. She didn't sense any danger coming from him, but his facial expression suggested he knew much more than he was letting on.

"You can read," Galen said.

"For the record, I can read too." Ari pointed out loudly. "English, French, some Spanish…"

"That isn't what he meant," Stella said, her eyebrows raising ever so slightly with amusement.

"No, it isn't." Galen pushed to his feet, forcing Stella backward. "I haven't met someone with that magic in nearly two centuries… he was very interesting."

Galen moved across the room. Stella followed him with her eyes as he disappeared into another room and she exchanged confused glances with

Ari. When Galen returned, he was carrying a platter of food. Her stomach growled angrily at the sight as she salivated.

"How old are you?" Stella asked, ignoring the aroma of food as her mouth salivated.

"About two-hundred and eighty?" He brought the food forward and placed it on the table.

"So, what is a caelum?"

Ari sprung into a seat and waited expectantly for Stella to follow suit. The anger in her stomach reminded her of her humanity. She sat between them hoping for an invite to fill her plate as much as an answer to her question.

"Eat, "Galen said. "Caelum are beings infused with magic from meteors and meteorites. Typically, we're twice to three times the size of our ancestors. Anything from people to animals to plants to bugs."

"Is that where the idea of giants came from?" Stella leaned back in the chair.

"I suppose," he said. "It's very rare. Please eat something."

"You called me fae-el before," Ari said. "What does that mean?"

"Fae-el are humans with one fae parent or fae lineage. Fae are purely descended from fae. I haven't quite figured out your lineage, but I have a clue."

"So, you think I'm fae?" He choked.

"Fae-el," Galen said. "The mansion belongs to the fae. Charon is the protector of it, among other things. His job is rather daunting, if you ask me."

"To protect a decrepit old house," Ari said.

Stella glanced over at him then back to Galen. She sighed and reached for some food off the platter. She had to admit it smelled delicious. Her hand shook as she realized it had been a couple days since she'd really eaten anything and took the food

***

Galen left the room muttering under his breath and went to his private library as the pair devoured the meal. He scoured his collection of books and scrolls for the one that Charon had given him at the death of the fourth queen in nineteen hundred. She had been the cruelest of all the rebirths.

Fae were not known for compassion and kindness in human tales. Rather, they were known for their spite and cruelty. But the young man in his dining room was another story all together. He did not know his magic; he could not see himself as he was.

"Fae-el are often diagnosed as psychopaths or sociopaths," Galen called to them. "Their humanity was often what left them unprotected in both worlds. Fae would do nothing for them, and humans could not save them, though many have tried. However, there are very rare cases where the brain develops normally, and instead magical prowess is unwittingly developed. Fae-el are usually not magical. Except in that they could lie or charm extraordinarily well."

His nose twitched and his ears perked as he heard one of the furere nearby. They were close but not close enough for him to worry just yet. He grabbed the book once he found it and went back to the dining room and observed the pair.

Stella was studying the inscription in his hidden mirror while Ari watched her, but Galen noted the food practically demolished. Judging from Ari's perplexed gaze, he couldn't see the mirror, as it should be.

"Do you know what she's looking at?" Galen sat down.

"Your empty wall." Ari tapped his fingers. "Did she go crazy?"

"Hardly," Galen said with a smile. "She can see magic, unlike you."

Stella spun on her heels and watched the two men. Galen smiled at her as he watched the gears in her mind turn. He suspected she couldn't read the language inscribed in the frame of mirror.

Though, given she had seen the portraits in the mansion it was likely she could make out one word. *Moirai.*

Galen watched her eyes turn to the book he had brought back with him. Her thirst for knowledge continued to grow. He could see the fire burning in her eyes as she watched him.

"Let's say I believe you. Sure, it would provide insight into what I've been able to do my entire life. But I've always tried not to use it."

"I can't imagine why," Galen said sarcastically. "Reading people's emotions is tricky. Especially if you also end up feeling it. It can make you extremely empathetic and sympathetic."

"It isn't just that." Stella shook her head. "I can read thoughts… or hear them, might be more accurate."

"Excuse me?" Ari's voice squawked as he sprung up, chair flying behind him.

"Through touch." Stella explained. "It's difficult to not hear other people's thoughts when our skin comes in contact. I have to fight every urge and impulse in my body to keep their thoughts out of my head."

Galen was grinning as he watched relief flood over Ari's face as he looked to Stella. Leaning against the table, Galen opened the book and began reading.

"May twenty-third, nineteen hundred, death of the fourth queen of the fae. One-hundred years after her birth, eighty after ascension.

"The fourth queen of rebirth was murdered by those whom she trusted most: royal advisors, generals and guards. Her rule was denied by all fae, pixie tribes, caelum, sylph and wizards. In her abominable acts she tortured her own people, beyond that of the reasonable permittance for criminals, until they were no longer themselves. Her line was not meant to continue, due to the assassination, for fear of another plague queen. However, she was reborn yet again."

Galen closed the book and looked to Stella calmly. It hadn't been the first time his eyes had read the words yet they still stood out to him profoundly. He hadn't imagined he would witness firsthand the reincarnation of the fourth queen. However, given her prior rebirths it also hadn't surprised him to learn of the one standing before him.

"Charon took responsibility and tried to keep order best he could in his grief. But he took on too much and now… we're here."

"You're saying it's his fault?" Ari snapped. "Because he bit off more than he can chew?"

Galen frowned. "Fault is a strong word. He is the only person who has kept the world even remotely alive over the millennia. I'd like to see you do that."

"You said the fae own that mansion and Charon is the protector of it. But I have the feeling there's more to it than that. So, what does he actually guard?" Stella's face twisted as she spoke.

"He guards magical criminals and protects magical creatures," Galen said, suspecting where she is going with the conversation.

"He was there during this fourth queen's reign?"

"He was."

"And you're saying we're fae-el," Stella said. "Half fae and half human."

"He is. You're reborn, though not complete."

"So that makes us the exception, not the rule, Stella."

"Clearly," Stella said, withholding her laughter.

"Does that make us cool?" Ari leaned back.

"As a cucumber." Stella smirked before turning serious. "Who is pulling us to up north? Why Georgian Bay?"

The question confused Galen, making him pause a moment. His eyes peered between the two of them. "Both of you?"

"Yes," Ari and Stella said in unison.

"Does that symbol on your jacket mean anything to you?"

"Not really." Ari shrugged. "The jacket was passed down from family though. Our crest."

"Do you feel connected to Stella?"

"Sure, she makes me feel safe."

"How about you, Stella?"

"Yeah, I'm comfortable with him. He has a weird aura and controls lightning, but I guess it's pretty cool."

"It's not lightning."

"Right, chi."

Galen wasn't focused on them. He shifted uncomfortably and held onto the book a little tighter. "Let's discuss this once the furere has left."

"What?" Ari stiffened.

"How can you tell?" Stella ran for the window and peered out.

"I can smell them, mostly." Galen disappeared into another room. "They don't exactly smell great. Nor are they quiet. They're presently chasing down a doe."

"Can you kill them?" Ari asked.

"I can," he said with an indifferent shrug. "As can you both."

"And yet here we are." Ari pushed the chair back as he stood. "We almost died the other day and who knows how many other times since this began last year. It's only random coincidences that have saved us all this time. Because we can't kill them."

"That giant dog killed them, most recently." Stella added. "First time I've seen one die. Reports from the military when this began were calling them indestructible."

"Wolf."

"Whatever." Stella shook her head. "Canine."

"Then stay here if you feel you can't help," Galen sighed. "If I'm not back in three hours, take whatever supplies you need and head out."

"Wait." Stella walked to him but he remained unchanged as he opened the main door and left the pair alone in his home.

***

The door closed and the cabin filled with silence. Stella and Ari exchanged nervous glances. Stella was unsure what to make of the man but she knew for certain he had a vast reservoir of knowledge he'd not yet shared.

"Do you believe him?" Ari asked.

"I don't know yet. It's hard to believe. Though, your aura is something else." She looked at him. "But it worked with that lightning."

"It's not lightning." He was exasperated.

"Sorry. We still don't know much but this information explains what I saw in my eyes, what I can do, the pixies, fae, furere. It explains my dreams, the mansion, even Richard's eyes."

"Who's Richard?" Ari asked.

"Oh, he was my trainer at a gym," Stella said. "It only happened once but I swear his eyes changed. They looked like cat eyes."

"That's pretty cool," Ari said.

"I suppose. I never asked him about it."

"Why not?"

"I thought I'd imagined it at first. We were distracted by the news too."

Stella moved back to the table and sat with Ari. But she stared at the mirror. It was taunting her. It tempted her with that word and the reflection that wasn't quite accurate.

She moved to the mirror again as Ari barked at her, but she ignored him. She ran her fingers across the word.

In the mirror she saw Charon looking back at her. He was amused but didn't say anything. Stella opened her mouth to speak but another person came into view. She blinked; it was like watching herself walk away physically while mentally bound to her spot before the reflection. He was smiling faintly at her and it was like the sun lighting the world at the brink of dawn.

"As effervescent as ever," she breathed.

"Flattery?" His hands caressed her arms.

"Not flattery," she said, shaking her head. "Simply the truth."

His eyes were soft, gentle as they gazed at her. She was turned upward to see him and she craved to reach out and feel his heat against her. His hand rested over her heart, fingertips entwined in her hair, his lips murmured echoes of spells.

She could feel the nature around them move. They answered his words with dances and songs of their own. But there was a sadness around her that she could not explain.

Her eyes closed as she rested her ear to his chest and listened. He was more than a man of magic. He was the chime they answered to.

"Stella." She was shaken out of the image.

"What?"

Stella faced Ari, eyes large, as his hands wrapped around her shoulder. He pulled her away and forced her to look at him.

"Where did you go? You were off in your own little world."

"I was. What proof would we need to know, for sure, that magic exists?" Stella's eyes welled with fear. "That all of this is magic. That I am."

"I don't know," he said. "A miracle. But I'd really rather blame science."

"Because science is explainable?"

"More or less," he said. "There are definitely things that cannot be explained. Such as that light through your head and the trees."

"Your aura of lightning."

"You vanished from sight in a haunted mansion."

"First off, that was you. Then the giant wolf."

"Galen and his abnormal size," he said.

"The mansion itself."

"This cabin."

"The mirror." Stella glanced at it. "That you apparently can't see…"

"Nope."

"I can read minds and emotions." Stella crossed the room. "The pixie I saw last week."

"Pixie?"

"Yeah, it came to me. She blamed me for all this."

Ari chewed his fingernail. "Okay, so we're saying magic exists."

"I guess so." Stella spun on her heels.

"I don't like the sounds of that." Ari frowned at her. "If magic exists then what happened to those furere? What made them so… volatile. Who did what? Where did they come from?"

"Apparently me." Stella's eyes fixated on the mirror as she felt that unknown sadness creep into her chest. She was biting her inner cheek as she considered the giant's words.

"Do you believe that?" Ari asked.

"I don't know yet…"

Chapter Nineteen

Stella made her way to the library where she immersed herself in the books and scrolls. They contained ancient and secret languages, mysteries and riddles that she couldn't solve. Some books wouldn't open no matter how hard she tried. As a result, there were more questions than answers.

She could hear Ari rummaging for supplies. Curiously, she set the last book she'd scanned through back on the shelf and peeked out of the room. She moved up the staircase and toward the only room on that floor.

The door opened easily, and she peered inside to see a portrait. She gasped quietly as she walked in. It was a study, but Charon's portrait stood alone against a blank grey wall. She searched for a date on the frame, but she only found *Ventus Vasilis*.

Her heart quickened as she touched the portrait. The room shook and she flinched to protect herself. She spun as the light dimmed and she was no longer in the office. It was a small bedroom with a canopy over the mattress and flower vases in every corner, though the flowers were now dried and dead. She looked at the portrait again. It sat quiet and untouched.

"I do not have time for this," Charon bellowed as he burst into the bedroom.

Stella tumbled over her heels as she turned and fell backward into the portrait, disturbing its peace. She felt herself well up with fear as he paused to look her up and down. Her nostrils flared as she wondered what he might do with her now.

He stopped mid-step and gawked at her before begging, "stop touching things… you really can't help yourself, can you?"

She straightened the portrait frantically. "Sorry."

"Where is Galen?"

"Went to fight furere," Stella said. Her nerves were rising as he glared down at her with anger and frustration. She withered under his gaze as she waited for his response.

"Of course," Charon said heavily, his shoulders sagging.

"He said…" Stella began speaking but her tongue slowly stopped moving as Charon's eyes, sharp and stunning, locked onto hers. She could feel his pain, curiosity and, oddly enough, affection. Stirring uncomfortably, she shook her head and looked at the portrait.

"What is this?"

"It's clearly a painting of me."

The sarcasm would have shocked her had she not been distracted by his sharp-tongued comments. Stella rolled her eyes and looked back at him. She was still beguiled by his appearance but hadn't given much thought to his personality or intellect. She couldn't decipher what kind of man he was: soldier, follower, leader, trickster? Galen said he was a protector but not of what.

"Portraits retain memories," he said.

"Kind of like Dorian Grey?"

"Wilde learned fragments of magic from us," Charon said. "Emotions. Thoughts. They are powerful and they can be stored in objects."

He moved about the room easily, floating rather than walking as he moved. His legs carried him but the movement was inhuman and flitting.

"So, it is magic," Stella said.

"Everything is magic."

"Everything?"

"Yes. Humans, animals, forests… everything is compounded with some form of magic. Though, humans prefer the term science. What has Galen told you?"

"Not enough. But he did mention you."

"And what did he say?" Charon leaned into the wall opposite her, arms crossing and eyebrows rising a twitch.

"You've been trying to hold everything in place. You're supposed to be the gatekeeper to hell, or so I gather."

"Is that what he said?" Charon laughed; it threw her off guard. "That's one way to phrase it."

Stella paused as she considered the stabbing, electrical pain in her chest. Her need to head north had been gathering in her stomach heavily the closer they became. However, her desire for answers was in equal measure. The pain now rising as she considered retracing her steps caused her to falter momentarily.

"Have you ever felt like you absolutely needed to do something? Like your whole life depended on it?" She paused as her heart opened up to him. "There's this madness inside me that's driving me to Georgian Bay."

"I am aware." He smiled at her sadly. "It isn't madness."

"Then what is it?"

"An undoing."

"What happened?" she asked after a brief pause.

"Two worlds collided." He turned away. He was peering out a small window absently. "You saw something that frightened you and you acted irrationally. You were terrified but you never saw the entire dream. Your haste and terror changed you, and you changed the world."

He crossed the room before she could speak and rested his hand on her forehead. She was stunned by the gentleness and lost her ability to speak momentarily. He allowed his fingers to run through her hair before giving her a gentle nudge. Stella fell to the floor as she snapped back to her space, in Galen's house, and out of his.

"That again?" she muttered angrily as she dusted herself off and stood.

Stella descended from the top floor and saw Ari sitting at the table with two bags. His leather jacket was sprawled over the table carelessly.

"Wow." He shot her an accusatory glare. "You sure enjoy leaving me in the dust. It's been about five hours since he left, three of those you were gone."

"That long?" It had felt only minutes.

"Yeah. What was it this time?

"I keep touching things I shouldn't?" she offered jokingly.

"Ugh." Ari sighed. "Should we go?"

"He hasn't returned then."

"No."

"We're going back to the mansion."

Her chest seized but she growled internally and pushed it as far from her mind as possible. It eased some and she exhaled delicately as her eyes locked with Ari's.

"What?" Ari froze. "Are you mad?"

"Yes." Stella moved into the library and opened a small wardrobe. "I want answers."

She pulled out a thin coat and tried it on. It fit perfectly. She zipped the side and clipped the collar together. It made her shoulders look broader, but she didn't mind. It would keep her warm and she could move in it.

"What answers do you think you'll find at an abandoned, haunted, magical villa?" Ari snapped.

"You can stay here." She emerged from the room; her eyes gentle as she looked at him. "But... I don't think I'm done with that place just yet. I need this."

"Of course, you aren't done," he said. "Are we bringing the bags?"

She mulled it over for a minute then decided yes. If they couldn't make it back to the cabin, they would need those extra supplies. She was worried for Galen, who had been gone long past three hours, but she needed to focus.

Chapter Twenty

Galen sat high up in the trees and watched the sky roll over the earth in glistening colours. His life in his younger days had been relatively difficult. Often, Christians accused him of demonic possession due to his stature. They would have no part of him and described him outlandishly.

It stirred quite a debate about the monster, bigfoot, from the early nineteen-hundreds and beyond. Now there were other monsters to tell scary stories about.

Galen chuckled to himself as he recalled the original tales of the large, hairy monster roaming forests and eating people. He couldn't see the resemblance at first but the more he looked at himself, the more he could understand their paralyzing fear.

Eyes black as night yet littered with crystals reflecting light back at them in a starry array; hair comparable to strands of feathers and a frame larger than a bear. It was surely a nightmare to their small children who believed all the tales from the Bible.

Yet, being compared to the Nephilim or Goliath had always left a terrible taste at the back of his throat. In his almost three-hundred years he'd never met any Nephilim. Though, a wizard had named himself Goliath ironically from his tall, human stature.

The Indigenous peoples, however, rarely gave Galen a second thought and gladly traded with him. They had no tales of him, for which he was thankful. His desire to remain unknown had been respected through the centuries and lineage.

His eyes turned downward toward his home. Stella had inadvertently called Charon to her. He could only imagine the scene that took place.

He was curious to see what they would do. Would they head north on their journey or would Stella be driven back to the mansion now? She had new knowledge but surely it wasn't enough for her. He wondered if she felt the past versions of herself edging her toward her own doom.

Granted, she had done it to herself. But he knew too many secrets of their world that he could drown both her and Charon.

He knew Charon's deep knowledge encompassed more than human's written history. Yet he always desired a path far from either world even if it was not always granted to him. Galen did not know if it was due to his former ability to see the timeline of this world. He did, however, know Charon suffered far more than he should have.

Galen squinted his eyes as he watched Ari and Stella head back to the mansion. He nodded slowly and smiled slightly. It may not be the best decision to allow her back into the building, but he knew he couldn't stop her.

Rather, he chose to see what she would do inside her old home. Would she begin to remember, or would it take the power Aurella was granted? The gap between the last version's birth and the current was vast compared to the few hours between the others.

He found himself quietly watching them tromp through the woods. Even from afar he could tell they were squabbling. He imagined them as siblings as he couldn't picture Stella as the lover of someone other than Charon.

A swarm of pixies flew up to him and sat across the branch facing him, gathering into a single humanoid.

"Hello."

"Hello." He repeated.

"Have you been watching her too?"

"She has no idea," Galen laughed as he rubbed his eyes.

"The others were born with the knowledge, weren't they?"

"Indeed."

"How many furere have you killed?"

He paused and eyed the cluster. They really were difficult to see individually when they grouped themselves together. It was no wonder they could fool humans so easily.

"Too many." He was tired. "Yet, not enough. Have you been attempting to kill them?"

"We don't kill them. We can't," the pixie said.

"There aren't many who can kill them," Galen sighed as his back pressed into the tree.

A heavy, saddened pause filled the air between them. The pixies longed for their former safety and lives. Galen wished the same… to an extent. In this world he was freer to roam than the one filled by humans.

"They ruined their own world," the pixie said.

"The furere had no choice but to destroy the fae dimension." Galen could still remember watching the magical doorways shatter. "Once it was gone there was nothing stopping them from entering the human domain."

"Where was Vasilis?" the pixie lamented. "The fae army had only generals. No king. And Charon… he could not keep the prison closed."

Galen could feel the anger and fear emanating from the pixie. He guessed they had been on the outskirts of the battles and watched the magical armies defeated shortly after facing off with the creatures.

"And you fault the girl down there?"

"Shouldn't I?" the pixie snarled, teeth sharp and glinting.

"Perhaps. It would be easy to put blame on her, certainly. What the original did was based on fear. I do not believe she acted out of malice. She merely desired to live longer… though the process by which she decided to act I do not understand. To die and be reborn six times… that is far crueler than one death, is it not?"

The pixie remained silent for a moment. "Why can't she use magic?"

"I would guess the space between death and birth," Galen said with a shrug. "The prison break occurred shortly after the death and the fae spent the next twenty-three years struggling to hold them within their world, to kill them, to imprison them again. All while this version is born almost purely human, three years after her predecessor's death, and then raised entirely oblivious to magic and the fae world."

"Yet, humans are magic themselves, aren't they?"

"Not in the same way as us. They have always been particularly unaware of the magic coursing through them, as it was only meant to keep them alive. It's simply borrowed time before it returns to the fae world. Now… they're combined."

"Is the fear of death really so painful?"

"You hide from the furere for fear of death." Galen began to lower himself from the branch.

"Is it the same?" The pixie eyed him.

"The fear is."

"You intend to follow her?"

"I made a promise. Besides, this may be our best option to save ourselves."

"Then you are okay sacrificing her?"

"She will know and understand her own moirai eventually."

Galen finished climbing his way down the tree to the earth. His feet planted evenly on the moss and he tread through the forest softly. His shoulders swayed and his hair blew behind him with each step.

The wind carried him far and it would not take long to reach the mansion, but Stella would arrive first, of that he ensured.

Chapter Twenty-One

Stella stood outside the garden and drew several breaths before grabbing Ari's hand and pulling him toward the mansion. She tried resisting his thoughts as their skin pressed firmly together. However, she was unable to push them aside as they neared the door.

She's crazy. This isn't what I signed up for. I just want to get up north. It's safe there... right?

She pulled him up the steps and down the hallway to that final room. She took a deep, albeit shaky, inhalation as she crossed the threshold. She stared at the portraits and smiled. They had returned.

"There are pictures," Ari said.

Stella's eyes glanced backward. He was in shock and awe at the sight in front of him. She couldn't blame Ari, seeing as he hadn't seen them before now.

"They really do look like you," he said. "It's incredible. You believe these are the women whom the headstones corroborate with?"

"I do," Stella said.

"Cowardice," he said. "What does that mean?"

"She was a coward?" Stella suggested.

Making a disapproving face at her, Ari moved along the row of portraits uttering the inscriptions, "rage, compassion, childishness, wisdom. Is that what each one represented?"

"I don't know," she said. "I didn't get a chance to look at them all last time we were here."

"Yeah, speaking of that," Ari began, his skin crawling at the memory, "are you sure this is safe?"

"Probably not," Stella said.

"Of course not," he said. "They are quite pretty though."

"Thank you. Not what I was expecting from you."

"I suppose they do look like you, don't they?" Ari crossed his arms and stared across the wall of portraits. The gold frames were glinting in the remnants of light seeping into the room. Stella watched him admire the artwork before moving closer to portraits. Her hands reached out and Ari frowned before asking, "do you even know what you're doing?"

"Nope."

"I hope we didn't come back here for nothing…"

She glanced at him and scowled. "Give me a second."

Please work… she told herself as she moved forward shakily. Slowly, she reached up and touched the portrait. The only word that seemed to have a recurring theme from this mansion to Galen's cabin appeared the most appropriate to attempt saying, "Mor-"

She felt herself lift off the ground as the remainder of the word failed to escape her lips. She could feel hands grip tightly around her shoulders as she fought to see. The room was a storm as it flung dust, glass and abandoned fixtures.

She glanced back; Ari was protecting his face as he was pushed up against the wall by the overpowering wind. Slits of glass sliced open his skin and clothing. He covered his face with his arms and curled up best he could as an unfamiliar voice echoed through the wind.

Stella jumped as she realized there was a tall, broad man behind her with his arms wrapped around her tightly. It was the guardian.

"Do not do this." Charon squeezed as tight as he could as he pleaded with her to stop. She felt his fear ooze into the air as the storm around them raged. "Not now!"

"Then tell me!" Stella screamed over the howling wind.

"Even uttering the smallest of charms in this state is dangerous," Charon said. "This is not how you should regain what you've lost."

"Tell me!" Her voice crackled as pain dripped down her body like rain.

"I cannot," he hollered over the sound of the storm.

"Moirai!" she yelled as loud as she could until her lungs were empty and burned.

The room stopped. Everything hung in the air and the paintings looked at her. Charon was no longer holding her, and she dropped back to the ground. She turned to see Ari gawking at her, fear and awe escaping his body. His aura was zapping around him like a shield, bits of white and blue electricity was rippling in circles around him.

"Don't leave," she whispered and pressed her hand into a frame.

They watched the painting light up around her hand and begin dispersing outward from the contact. The dust and glass mixture in the air pulsated around her. It moved close to her skin, tickling her, then pushing away in rhythm to her heartbeat.

A golden, shimmering light coursed from the painting into her hand and through her veins. The surrounding flesh reddened from the light. Her body was stiff as she was enveloped in magic and capsuled in time.

***

Ari could see her veins pulsate. He was entranced by the beauty that became her. The strength that overwhelmed her. The power that controlled the world around her echoed like her heartbeat. She hung limply before him as the pressure in the room changed.

Looking up in disbelief, Ari watched Galen enter the room nonchalantly. His hands were steady as he sheathed a sword and looked dead ahead.

"What did she do?" he asked.

"How did you know we were here?"

"Lucky guess," Galen said. "I followed you two. Now, what did she do?"

Ari shook his head. "I have no idea."

"She is a foolish child," Charon spat in his frustration.

"And who are you?"

Charon glanced down at him, his expression showing no particular interest, and then looked back at Stella. His shoulders slumped slightly as his eyes fixated on the portrait she touched.

"What should we do?" Galen asked.

"We have to wait," Charon said.

"Wait for what?" Ari scrambled up to his feet.

"For this to be finished. In the meantime, there could be furere who come to us. The magic is intense. Be ready."

Charon and Galen exchanged glances, choosing to remain silent. Galen went to the window while Charon's eyes were glued to Stella. Ari watched the stranger carefully. He appeared calm but his face was wrinkled with worry.

"What is she doing?" Ari finally asked.

"She's reliving memories."

"Because it's magic," Ari said.

"I've never seen anyone access memories," Galen said, moving across the expanse of the window. "Am I correct in assuming you've never left behind memories, Charon?"

"I've not stored them in an object," Charon said. "I have retained every memory in my lifetime."

Being excluded from the conversation led Ari to sit back and watch the room as the light faded. Dust and glass were slowly hovering to the floor though still danced around the room to soundless music.

"They approach," Galen said.

"How many?" Charon's eyes finally peeled away from Stella and toward the window.

"I see three," he said.

"Very well."

Charon turned on his heel and exited the room. Galen followed suit and smiled down at Ari as he ducked through the doorframe.

"You're leaving?" Ari asked.

"We'll return."

"Okay!" Ari slapped his thighs as his words dripped with sarcastic.

He strode to the window and looked through the dirty pane of glass. He could see at least two pairs of eyes staring him down. The third pair Galen had mentioned eluded Ari's sight. But he didn't doubt it was there.

From around the side of the building, on the far right stretch of glass, Charon and Galen appeared. Ari chewed his lip before crossing his arms. He watched nervously as the pair moved toward the forest.

His skin crawled, eyes widening, as a shimmering light surrounded Charon's arms and hands. It extended far past his hands and sharpened to a point as it reached the ground. To Ari, they appeared to be swords. Though, their lack of substance made him curious what it truly was.

Galen's own sword was drawn and Ari half-smiled. The man's weapon was easily the length of Ari's leg. He could only imagine how heavy it must be.

Without notice, the two lunged into the forest, Galen directly in and Charon going above the tree line with a mighty leap.

A screeching howl shook the old building and Ari stumbled backward in surprise. The trees rustled, branches snapping from the trunk, as the foray began.

His heart thumped violently as he watched the shimmering blades flying around Charon's body. The man fought as though it were a dance in the wind and Ari's mouth fell open at the sheer grace and speed at which he was moving.

Galen was far less elegant but he moved just as quickly. His blade swiftly cutting through limb and tree trunk easily. Granted, being nearly half the height of the forest and obscenely muscular would make that aspect easier.

A furere, the third one Ari presumed, lunged toward the house. In a single leap, it reached the window and its claws dug deep into the structure.

Stumbling backward, Ari glanced at Stella to see her body still frozen and attached to the portrait she rested her hand on. "Not good..." He moved further into the room, placing his body between the window and Stella.

The beast snarled at him, black teeth protruding from its jaws, as they stared each other down. His stomach was tight as an electric pang rolled up into his shoulder and down into his hands. He would have vomited had he not been so frightened.

The fear was encompassing, his breath shallow, as the furere's massive clawed hand reached backward. Ari flinched as the hand moved forward but he gawked as Charon appeared behind the creature and thrust the iridescent blade through the furere's face. The tip of the weapon hit the glass and shattered it.

The blade dissipated and the furere fell from sight and Charon floated into the room. Ari's hands shook violently as he fell to his knees in relief.

He watched Galen climb into the room and he controlled his breath. He wanted to thank them but he wondered if they would even appreciate the thanks. Ari heard a shift behind him and he glanced sidelong at Stella.

Her hand finally fell from the portrait as her body tumbled backward. Ari moved to catch her but Charon reached her body first. They stood over her and watched her eyes flicker behind the blinds, trying to catch her breath.

Sweat began pooling in droplets along her forehead and neck before dripping and falling from her skin.

Her body gasped for breath as her eyes bat open, and she looked about the room lazily. Ari reached out and allowed his hand to rest against her cold cheek. Her body was ice to the touch. Her mouth opened and closed but no words came out, rather, she sobbed as tears pooled and streamed down her face.

"Was it worth it?" Charon asked quietly.

Ari grumbled to himself at the harsh implication sitting in the statement. He watched as Charon moved to the side of her, arm still wrapped around her back keeping her upright. She looked at him with no words. She took a gasping breath as tears continued flooding her eyes. Stella's face changed to anguish and her teeth clamped together, her eyes rolling far backward into her skull.

"What's happening?" Ari felt his heart flutter nervously.

"Memories are rising to her conscious mind," Charon said.

"Memories? Whose?"

"Her own," Charon said, his eyes flitted to Ari for a split second. "From that portrait."

"What do you mean?"

"Thoughts, memories, emotions even, can all be stored in objects of someone's choosing," Charon said. "She's born of all magic. It's what caught my initial gaze."

"What does that even mean?" Ari shouted, his hands balled into fists, as he watched Stella roll onto her stomach crying.

Stella turned away from them, hands pressing into the floor as she stood up, and stalked out of the room. She pushed the snot and tears from her face and grabbed her backpack. Her eyes were glued to her feet as she proceeded to exit the room.

"You should relax," Ari said.

"No."

"You don't look so good."

"We need to get north," she finally said.

"This is insane." Ari chased after her, his pack hanging from his hand.

"You were heading north," she spat. "The plan hasn't changed."

"Whoa." He stepped back. "You're right. It hasn't. It's just gotten more complicated."

"It's always been complicated." She marched out of the mansion down the stairs. "How far do you think we can get before the sun falls?"

"Sun falls?" he repeated skeptically, still chasing her. "You mean dusk? We have an hour or so at this point."

"Let's get to it then." She hiked the rifle back up onto her shoulder as she crossed the foyer.

Ari glanced at the two men with a pleading expression as he moved fast to keep pace with Stella's surge of angry energy. He couldn't believe how quickly they'd exited the mansion; it had felt like a mere blink of the eye.

Ari could feel Charon and Galen watching him and Stella heading away from the mansion. Though, he could also sense they were following slowly. He strained to hear their whispered voices as they moved.

"She will be okay," Galen said.

"Are you sure?" Charon tensed. "She was not raised as we were. Why couldn't she have waited? If she needed to follow her hunch, then why couldn't she have chosen the first one?"

"How could she be raised as a fae when that world was in disaster? She is unaware of many things. How could she know which to choose?"

Ari glanced back to see Charon's eyes turned sharply, they burned with rage at those words. Though he knew they were not accusatory, there was always meaning behind words.

"I have no desire to watch her perish," Charon whispered. "But especially not as a destroyed entity. She needs all of who she is returned to her. It should not have been this first."

Galen glanced at him. "I cannot return her magic."

"Nor can I." Charon shook his head. "I don't know where Aurella is."

"Stella won't fracture her mind that easily." Galen attempted to be reassuring but even he didn't seem sure of his words.

Chapter Twenty-Two

Stella's eyes shut heavily. They were perched atop a mountain of rubble. Her hands were bruised and scratched from pulling herself over the piles of buildings, trees, logs and vehicles. She couldn't believe the monument of destruction they stood on. It was at least three stories high and ran for miles on either side. Over the top had been the only way.

"This is what happens when the fae and human worlds collide," Galen forced the words out.

"This is what happens when cities of two dimensions collide," Charon said. "The magic the fae once possessed was too diminished to keep themselves hidden any longer."

Stella's teeth clamped down on her lips as she stared at the two cities piled overtop the other. Some magical elements were still visible as floating debris hung like pendants from the sky. She would have loved to see the fae's world in its prime.

"Why haven't we seen this sooner?" Stella let herself settle into a sitting position.

"The fae do not have many cities," Charon said. "They mostly live in the woods."

Scattered between the rubble were arrays of rotted, decomposing corpses. The residents must have perished in the collateral damage. Stella shook with the knowledge contained in the memories she took back. Before the furere became dark, malicious creatures she knew each of their names.

The group watched a lone wolf trudge through the rubble. She felt a tug of pity for the gangly creature — it surely had once been magnificent to see but now barely clung to life, famished to near skin and bones. Its eyes were dark and showed hardly a sign of life.

"What did the furere do to the fae world?" Ari was hesitant to ask as he glanced at Stella's breaking eyes.

"The fae," Charon sighed, "tried to kill them. We spent twenty-three years trying to keep them within our world. We'd rather have kept them imprisoned but that was no longer possible."

Stella's golden eyes turned to him curiously. She could see the pang of war deep in his eyes. He hid it well from the world, but she could see it more clearly than she had seen anything.

She turned away and her mind went to Richard, her trainer. Those eyes of his had not been human, of that she was certain, but he never told her he was fae. Not even after she told him of her abilities.

"What creature has eyes with pupils slit like a cat? Are there fae who can do that?"

"Certainly." Galen nodded. "Those eyes are the Antelucio's."

"Though they disappeared from the fae world nearly six centuries ago." Charon crossed his arms. "Not one of our Generals, nor myself, could find a trace of them."

"Why did they disappear?" Stella asked.

Charon locked eyes with her decidedly. She had never asked about them in any previous life and she certainly wasn't from that line.

"There is no definitive answer. It was presumed they used their gift to see the future threads of their line and chose to separate from the fae world."

"Gift?" Ari chimed in.

"Those eyes are only seen in one family," Galen said. "It's rumoured they're able to see a person's future if they look at them through those gifted eyes."

Stella frowned. What had Richard seen when he looked at her?

It was silent as the air sat heavily, digging into their skin and lungs, before a screech echoed into the sky. Squinting, Stella could see the black of the furere storming through the trees. The branches shook and snapped as they leapt and crashed.

"Furere," Galen muttered.

"Stella." Charon took hold of her arm. "Go hide. You do not have your magic yet."

Stella wanted to argue but she looked at the furere raging ever closer and her heart crumpled in her chest and agreed quietly. "Okay."

She tumbled down the slope with Ari quick behind her. Heat rose in her body as blood pumped quickly. It was easier to navigate once they hit solid ground. She burst across the field and into the woods, slowing only at the bigger trees to look for a place to hide herself away. Hastily, she dug herself into a hole under a tree.

Ari filled the gaps with dirt and scrambled to his own hiding spot as Stella held her breath. The screeching and howling sent shivers over her body. Fear wracked her mind as the screams became louder and clearer.

She could hear the commotion outside as she turtled her body. The sounds of clashing and yelling, and what she assumed was death, took over the sounds of nature. Her hands clamped over her ears as she shut her eyes.

Her mind toiled over visions of what the fourth queen had done... what *she* had done. The memories began haunting her mercilessly as the shrieking of the furere continued. Faces and howls of pain continued to race across her mind.

She bit down on her tongue to keep from screaming. Her rage against herself was more intense than that against the furere. Fresh air hit her face as a sudden gap in the dirt forced her attention. A large, oily black hand slithered in between the dirt and roots trying to grab her.

Stella's heart jumped as she lunged backward. Scrambling to grab her knife, she pulled it from its scabbard and stabbed the hand. A high-pitched wail reverberated in the small space. She winced and pulled the knife back, nearly cutting her face as she tried desperately to cover her ears. As the furere disappeared, she pushed the dirt out and crawled into the open. The furere came running at her and she scrambled to get onto her feet but stumbled forward. Her rifle was useless from this position. She crawled backwards, hoping to find leverage to get up as she toppled over and sprawled away.

She heard movement behind her and regretted looking as the furere sprung at her. Stella kicked the hands as hard as she could and then the face. She could hear cracking but the pain in her legs told her it might have been her body, rather than the furere's, that was snapping.

Its eyes turned and watched her. It was growling, teeth bared and rage increasing every step of the way.

"Fun," it hissed.

She paused. That was the second time she had heard one speak. She was confused. All the memories in her head sprung to the forefront of her mind and she doubled backward, spine arching as the memories took over. As she began to uncoil, she peered at the creature though her eyes were blurry.

"Hm, delightful," it jeered again.

Time seemed to pause as, for a split second, she didn't see a creature. Rather, she saw a young girl, perhaps ten years old, with stark white hair and eyes, her pupils the only colour.

She was crying and, blood seeping onto her clothing, begging for mercy and forgiveness. It was out of Stella's control as a harsh but garbled voice resonated. The girl looked behind her and then brought her fingers up to her mouth. She was sobbing now and dropped to her knees.

Stella looked past the child and saw two people wrapped in thorns and clamped to the ground with chains. Stella thought they were the girl's parents.

She focused on the little girl, whose shoulders were bobbing as she screamed and cried. The harsh, mutilated voice barked words. The girl put a couple fingers into her mouth, still crying, and Stella screamed.

"No!" Stella's hand flung forward as she cried. "Don't!"

The girl slammed her jaw shut and blood seeped out of her mouth, through tears and wails, as two fingers vanished from her hand. Stella's mouth hung open as tears freely fell from her face. The next thing she knew, the girl was a furere again and was hurling infuriated screams at her.

She could hardly catch her breath as she watched Charon leap in front of her. He swiped his hand across the chest of the furere and wind cut through the body like a hot knife in butter. It collapsed to the ground limply, but Stella could only see the girl.

"What were you thinking?" He twisted to see her.

She didn't look at him as her eyes were glued to the slick, tar-drenched body. It was motionless but her mind shifted from a dead girl to a furere. She tried to tell herself what was real but found it tough to differentiate. Voices argued in the back of her mind.

"She needs magic," Galen said.

"She doesn't have magic. Not at this moment," Charon said.

"Perhaps it's time to teach her." Galen looked at Ari. "And him."

"Me?" Ari dusted the dirt of his body from his own hiding spot.

"Yes. It's amazing either of you are even alive." Galen cleaned his sword.

"Well, I'm good at hiding." Ari sounded particularly proud of himself.

"Clearly." Galen sheathed his blade. "Charon, it's time."

"Ari, yes. Stella, we must wait." Charon lit the dead creature on fire before muttering, "I told her not to touch that portrait."

Stella's mind was slowly coming back to her as the furere disappeared into the flames. She could feel the stiffness of her body and the scent of the woods.

"Can't you teach her to get into their minds until that happens? You would think a gift like hers, before having her magic restored, would come in handy at least." Galen protested.

"I think she just did that." Charon was sitting in front of her steadily. "It did more damage to her mind than the furere's."

"How is she so frail?" Galen nearly shouted. "Isn't she the—"

Charon shot a warning expression toward him before looking back to Stella. She was catatonic and in shock. Her body was frozen, processing what she had seen and listening quietly to their discussion.

"She did things in reverse." Charon leaned back. "If she had obtained her magic first the memories would have slowly crept in and melded into her mind. Taking a portion of the memories in a giant wad, before magical stability, is damaging. It's like trying to shove a cube into a circle. She chose the worst one to recall… rage."

"I don't think she really chose that one in particular. It seems to me she selected it at random." Galen walked away. "I'm going to finish the rest of them. There are two more closing in on our position."

Stella worked on breathing as she racked her brain for the name of the child. Their conversation has passed her by as a blip but she was acutely aware of the argument. She ignored it as she sought the name of the child. It was on the tip of her tongue as the flames chiseling the body began to die, the body disintegrating to ash.

Mind churning, Stella couldn't believe a part of her was so cruel.

Her eyes shifted uneasily to Charon as he placed his hand on her forehead. She felt a tingle in her skin, along with the warmth of his body.

"What are you doing?" Stella asked.

"Infusing my magic into your mind," Charon said. "I'm trying to weave your mind back together so that you don't lose it."

"What did I do?"

"You'll see all your memories soon enough," Charon said.

Stella's eyes grew dark as she watched Charon's face remain still. She could discern no emotion from his expression as he kept his palm pressed to her forehead. The magic coursing from his body into hers was a respite for her mind and body as it soothed her, albeit temporarily.

Chapter Twenty-Three

The road was quiet, eerie. Cars left in ditches and on the sides of the street were destroyed beyond use. No animals could be seen or heard as they made their way quietly north. The few houses and farms they passed were dilapidated and rotted through.

Stella felt as still and broken as the planet. Returning memories haunted her and distinguishing her life from the past was growing difficult.

The group kept their eyes and ears open for anything suspicious as they travelled. The road had been abandoned and desolate for months and seemed to extend into the forest. Destruction lay ahead with toppled trees and new growth. Stella looked to Ari for directions as they came to a split in the road. She had felt dazed and disoriented the last few days as her mind grew more tired than her body.

Ari began to pull out the map when he suddenly stopped, his head snapping upward. Stella watched him as he watched the trees. Adjusting her own gaze, she turned to see where he was looking to see the furere silently creep closer to them. The shoulders hunched and hind legs bent before springing into action. Locked in place, Stella watched it soar through the air.

"Stella!" he howled.

Ari's legs carried him quickly as the furere charged out of the woods toward Stella. Their black masses, slick and sharp, were cutting through trees and bramble easily as their speed increased.

Stella pulled down the rifle and fired. The shot echoed in the sky as the bullet lodged in one creature's body. It paused only momentarily as it ran into the rod of the gun and wrapped its claws around the barrel, biting into the metal furiously.

Stella dropped the gun as a massive wolf, the same as before, stepped between her and the furere. She watched the wolf's limbs stretch upward as its legs straightened, eyes on par with the tops of the trees.

Her mouth fell open at the sheer size of the wolf before her. She wondered, momentarily, if the canine had been that large when she first saw it. If so, had she been so far out of it that she hadn't noticed the animal's gargantuan frame? The earth shook, making Stella wobble, as the wolf moved.

The wolf knocked the creature back into the tree line with one swipe of its paw. The furere screeched furiously as the wolf snarled, nose tilting down toward it.

Stella covered her ears and stumbled backward. It was a different sound than before. Not so hollow and terrifying. But the snarl of the wolf overpowered the furere and shook her lungs.

The wolf lowered its shoulders, moving purposefully and readying itself. The wolf's teeth glinted in the sun, snatching the furere and clamping around its body as it plunged toward the wolf.

Stella watched in horror as the black monstrosity, smaller than the previous ones she'd come across, howled painfully. The face of an older man ran through her mind's eye. The wolf dropped the furere when the whimpering stopped.

The furere lay in the ditch, bleeding tar through the grass. Stella once again saw the older man lying there. She shook her head. When she looked again it was a furere.

Sniffing the air, the wolf relaxed. Stella's mouth fell open as the wolf shrunk from twenty feet tall to Ari dusting himself off.

"Excuse me?" She felt her lips move before she could think about what she said.

"Are you okay?" Ari approached her quickly.

"Me?" she crackled.

"I don't think he knows." Galen warned her. "I was wondering myself."

"Knows what?" Ari turned to him.

"Never mind." Stella reached into his pocket and pulled out the map. She looked at it briefly, though her mind wasn't quite sure she was reading it correctly. "I guess we go right."

"Yeah," he said hesitantly as he looked at the corpse before them.

"You need to learn to protect yourself, Stella. Hiding isn't working anymore and you're too distracted now," Charon said.

"I agree," Galen said.

"It would be handy. But that wolf was pretty cool, eh? I think he's my guardian angel. I didn't even know what I was going to do once I got to you… then poof!"

Stella didn't think as she folded the map. "You're the wolf."

Ari choked. "It was a good ten feet ahead of me."

"No," she said. "It was you."

He shook his head defensively before saying, "impossible."

"Is it?"

"Yes."

Offering him the map back, Stella's arm was extended shakily. He snapped his hand out and whipped it from her grasp. Bursting, although for no logical reason she could discern, her voice and words were out of control as she yelled. "Think about it! Why does the wolf only come near you? Why didn't we hear about this wolf on the news when things were just starting? Georgian Bay? Amazon?"

"Okay, it's definitely a little weird. Hence, guardian angel."

"Just a little weird?"

"There's no point in arguing this at the moment," Charon said. "There are more furere headed this direction. We've attracted their attention with your shouting. I, for one, have no pleasure in killing them. They've gone through enough."

"We will be discussing this." Stella snapped angrily toward Charon. "Why didn't you just tell me?"

"You're not yourself," Charon said. "Ari has done nothing deserving your wrath, nor have I. Calm your mind and we'll proceed on our travels."

Pausing, Stella realized she had taken her anger out on both Ari and Charon. Truthfully, she was angry and frustrated with herself. Though, him keeping the knowledge from her was cruel.

"You knew who I was when we crossed paths on the street," Stella said. "I know… what we—"

"We can discuss that later," Charon said.

Swallowing hard, she took a step forward along the road and past them to hide her face. The memories of the fourth queen, her fourth rebirth, were bubbling to the surface. Able to recall the electric emotions swiveling between the two of them during that time had brought her further from despair. Though she now wondered if the emotions were truth or fantasy. However, she had driven their worlds to disaster all on her own.

"You can hate me," she said.

"They are nearly here." Charon ignored the comment. "They can hear us."

"Of course, they can." Stella stomped down the road. "They used to be fae!"

"Wait… what?" Ari looked at her, his jaw dropped as his feet crossed each other. He tumbled and stared at the three of them when he stopped walking.

"Let's talk about this later." Galen drew his sword.

"Right now, you're the only one that can't protect themself," Charon said to Stella. "Time to run. That I'm sure you can do."

Indignation rose like bile before a screech of the furere hit her ears and a different kind of emotion pulsated in her veins. Knowing Charon was right she took off without a word.

"Go on," Charon said to Ari. "You'll be useful if they catch up to her."

Ari chased after Stella without a word. She heard his footsteps behind her and she was guilty for snapping at him but remained silent.

***

Charon stood next to Galen, who looked down at him quizzically. "You don't want her to learn how to fight?"

"Keeping her with us at this moment will only distract us." He admitted frustratedly. "Aurella is far more suited to return her magic than either of us."

"Sword doesn't require magic," Galen said.

"To take down a furere, she would need some," Charon said.

"Some, but not much," Galen said. "I assume you'd rather Aurella take the lead because she worked in the mansion?"

Galen stretched his shoulder as he watched ten furere darting through and between trees. Removing his swords from their scabbards his arms swung readily as if stretching the muscle.

"I am leaving it to Aurella because she was entrusted with the task centuries ago."

"Will you call Stella queen?" Galen was curious as he watched the furere swing from branch to branch and scramble through the dirt toward the two of them.

"I do not yet know." Charon removed his bracelets as they formed long, clear blades. "The magic seal will determine the right to sovereignty from here on out."

The furere closed the gap rapidly. Both sides were prepared to clash though the furere moved closely, threading through each other like thread being woven. Galen's eyes watched them move seamlessly together as though one unit.

"They've become smarter," Galen said.

"Everything evolves." Charon noted with a glance over at the caelum.

"Not like it will help them survive right now."

"Perhaps not," Charon snorted. "Yet they adapt."

The furere swarmed out of the woods, their lanky, black forms slinking toward the two men. Jaws opened wide to reveal long tongues and serrated teeth. Their throats expanded and released shockwaves of shrill cries.

***

Stella looked back as her feet carried her as fast as they could. The image she saw took her aback. She imagined two ancient warriors prepared to battle. She almost laughed as she remembered they really were ancient and about to battle.

Fear seeped into her veins as she watched the furere circle them. Charon was already in the air, slicing the beasts open. It was almost as though he were dancing with the blades he held. Galen was far less graceful, simply tearing them apart after snagging them with his sword if it weren't a fatal attack.

"Keep going!" Ari yelled at her.

He grabbed her and yanked forward. She stumbled and looked at the road ahead. Ari was forcing himself forward, but she wanted to go back. She could smell them now that they were close. Stella gagged at the wretched scent as she pressed onward. The howling from her left took her by surprise and her head whipped to look.

A long, jagged mouth came toward her and she pushed Ari forward while flinging herself backward. She rolled away and came back up as fast as she could.

Another furere crawled out from the car down the road. She tried to breathe, but the smell kept lurching her stomach until she finally vomited across the road. These ones were more wretched than any others she'd encountered.

Ari was on his feet trying to distract the furere from Stella as she watched the one from the vehicle creeping ever closer.

"Behind you!"

Ari spun toward the furere as it drew its talons and unhinged its jaws. Stella watched Ari's body morph into the ginormous black wolf and clamp down on the furere as it tried its assault.

She wondered if she could get into the other's mind and control it. Resisting the urge to vomit, she looked it in the eyes.

Its base emotions were catastrophic and unruly. They bounced from rage to fear, then sadness.

"Stop." Stella mouthed the words. The command was hardly audible, but she knew it was just loud enough for the furere to hear.

The blank confusion and hate, fear and malice, its spitefulness was written over its face. She read it, felt it, and pushed further, suppressing vomit as the smell began distracting her from her goal. Telling herself to focus, its jaws inched closer, taunting her.

She went as far as she could, but nothing stopped the furere from desiring her flesh. Disappointed, she wrapped her hand around her small knife. Stella swung it upward into its throat and kicked as hard as she could.

It howled desperately and leapt forward, only to be crushed by a massive paw. The black wolf snarled and clamped down on the head, tearing it from the neck.

Stella could smell the blood more strongly and gagged again, bile rising from her stomach to the back of her mouth. The wretched scent of decaying flesh and rotted intestines was overwhelming.

Watching Ari return to his natural state sent shivers down her body as she sat on the pavement. Slowly moving her gaze to the dead furere her body felt new shudders. The corpse was broken as much as she was.

"Have we reversed roles? Why are you on the ground?" Ari asked.

Slowly, Stella rolled to her feet as he gawked at her. She was tired though her desire to reach out and touch him, hear his thoughts, grew in her chest despite knowing better than to try. His aura was sparking with frustration.

"She made them," Stella said as though it explained everything.

Stella was frightened to look him in the eye but did anyway. He was waiting, his shoulders back confidently, hands on his hips, for her to continue. His expression told her she was nuts but resisting all the urges in his body to bicker with her.

"The fourth queen," Stella progressed reluctantly, "I'm… reincarnated, or part of her, or something. I'm not entirely sure how it works. But she tortured her own people. She enjoyed it. The woman was amused by cutting open flesh and peeling it off to pull out bone and snap it. She was pleasured by their suffering. She forced them to consume their own flesh. Galen was right when he said psychopath and sociopath… she was horrible."

Stella could feel herself breaking down as she recalled the memories. She would have heaved the contents of her stomach had she not already done so.

Her disgust with herself, her past self, rose higher with each new memory. She feared becoming that person in her current body. She knew her actions then had consequences now. She was coming to realize this was her responsibility yet remained unable to do anything.

"You two don't know the meaning of the word run, do you?" Galen asked on their approach.

"Are you alright?" Charon stood next to Stella and touched her shoulder gently.

Shaken, she turned from him. Her body felt sick as she walked away. Once, his touched would have been a comfort. Now it felt shameful.

"I don't know anymore," she muttered as she passed the bodies of the furere. She watched their corpses, their forms shifting from furere to people, as she eyed them.

Chapter Twenty-Four

The spring air was cooling as night fell, surrounding the group in darkness as they huddled in an abandoned garage.

Charon kept himself a distance from the others as his mind ached for peace. The world had lost its harmony as it became overrun with humans. Even the fae world had lost some of its charm as the population grew, not just in numbers but with malcontent. His reprieve was always in meditation though lately he found himself ruminating on memories.

He listened to his heart pump blood through his veins as his magic pulsated in rhythm. Slowly, his mind turned from the thrumming of his body to memories as he brought them to life as if they were the present moment.

His eyes were on the mansion; it was bright and alive. The building shone and glimmered in the sunlight as vines wound its way up the columns. The entire place emanated with life, pulsing out of the very woodwork that it was founded upon.

Stella was bringing a dead rose bush back to life as he moved about the garden idly. He had never seen her use magic in such a way. She pulled it from the earth and put it together with a simple wave of her hands. Nature conformed to her will as easily as people breathed the fresh air.

"She is quite beautiful." Aurella admired from afar. "What kind of magic does she possess?"

"All magic," he said.

"All?" Aurella was incredulous, eyes widening.

"She isn't limited to elements or spells; using them makes the magic far more potent."

"Kind of like you?"

He looked down at Aurella. Her face, as always, was smiling and bright. She contained a warmth to her that many fae never possessed. He always wondered if it was a facade to trick people into liking her, but he had never seen a future where she was malicious.

"Similar," he said, absently nodding.

"Except you're still more powerful." Aurella bit her lip nervously as she imagined what the pair of them could do if they combined magic.

"And yet there are things out of my control."

"What does that mean?"

"It means, I cannot change what has happened nor can I change what will happen." His eyes grew dark. "I love her despite it."

Aurella watched him carefully, feeling her burning gaze, he in turn looked down to her. He looked at her closely as she squirmed under his watchful eye.

"You know what's going to happen," she said.

"It's already begun, she made this."

He opened his palm and showed Aurella the gold symbol. It glinted in the sunlight, the etches of life and death engrained in the magic. The force radiating from it both entranced and horrified her. It held pieces of someone's soul and she could see the etches of them bound for one-hundred-year increments, designed to be released one after the other.

"What did she do?"

"She believed she was prolonging her life."

"But restarting from infancy each time? I, for one, would never want to do that."

"It would not have been my first choice either," Charon said.

"So, did she prolong her life?" Aurella looked back at the young woman.

"No." Charon's body stiffened. "She viewed her timeline and saw a painful, gruesome scene in her mind's eye. Though she never completed the vision. Instead, she ran through ways to escape it and each one inevitably became worse than the last."

"How reckless," Aurella said.

"It was the first time she had been able to connect to life threads," Charon said, the words heavy in his mouth. "She reacted without speaking to me."

"I idolized her as a child. There have always been legends of her beauty and abilities. She is one of the eldest fae in our history, next to you and a few others. Yet even she was consumed by fear?" Aurella watched the woman from afar with curiosity and fear. Her admiration was dwindling with this information. "What will you do with the charm?"

"It needs to be guarded." He offered it to her and she stared down at it before gawking up at Charon. "Made to believe it is no more than a family heirloom, a trinket, but important for familial reasons. It cannot be lost."

"What do you suggest?" She wrapped her fingers around it hesitantly.

"Fae-el."

"Fae-el," she gasped. "Can they be trusted?"

"Create a line," he said.

"What?"

Aurella's steps faltered as her face snapped toward him. His expression was a blank canvas, though she shrunk in the depth of his power.

"If you create a line of fae-el and bestow the offspring with that symbol, they will cherish it. Eventually it will return to her."

"Are you mad?" Aurella's eyes grew large. "Fae-el are a bad idea. Why create more?"

"Perhaps they are," he said as he walked away from her. "But unless you can think of something better, this is what we have."

"I will not procreate with a human," Aurella said. "This spell is lethal on its own. She has already doomed us. How can you ask me to create fae-el?"

"Because this symbol is important," Charon said. "It must be kept out of her hands and my own, lest we attempt to change the course of time further."

He watched Aurella storm away from the mansion. He pitied her, sorrow filling his heart, but his eyes turned away and to Stella once more.

She was happy in this state, but he couldn't help wondering just how long that happiness would last.

Charon's eyes opened and he saw the glint in the moonlight. Ari wore the symbol on his jacket as he knew the line would. He hadn't thought such a young person would be the one carrying it, though.

Chapter Twenty-Five

Stella was silent as they passed through a small town. It was strange to see the deserted houses and businesses. Remnants of society echoed against the walls, cars and through the broken windows and open doors.

Few people remained, but those who did stowed away in basements and cellars. Stella could feel their eyes leering at them as whispers threaded the air.

"Should we stay here tonight?" Ari piped up as he looked at the more stable buildings.

"There are people here," Charon said. "It may not be the best idea."

"How many do you think?" Galen asked.

"Maybe a dozen. They're spread out across the block."

"A few on the roof," Galen said.

"Think they'll shoot?" Ari cut in nervously.

"Possibly. But they seem to be more scared than violent."

Ari moved around the group toward the abandoned bakery. Stella's eyes were cautiously watching as he walked toward it and glanced at her. The glass under his feet crinkled as he moved inside slowly, his eyes wandering.

She watched him brush cobwebs away from the corners as she too moved forward. She watched him leap over the bar and through the serving area. He looked sad as he ran his hand across the counter, pushing dust as he moved.

Stella stood at the entrance and waited. His eyes turned to her and she smiled softly, patiently.

"My parents owned a café," he said. "I miss them."

"I know you do," Stella said.

"I still don't know what happened to them."

Stella chewed her lips and checked in with him visually, his face was scrunched as he grew lost in his mind. "You might never know," she said.

"I'm aware of that."

A hushed sneeze turned their heads. Someone was in the back room. Stella and Ari looked at Galen, who shrugged, then at Charon, who was fixated on something above them. Stella sighed and entered the shop, flinging herself over the counter and preparing for a fight.

Ari smiled. That was the woman he had envisioned when he first saw her: tough and unafraid.

He moved to the other side of the door and pushed it open quickly. He jumped into the doorway; Stella close behind.

"Ack!" He cried out as he grabbed the handle of the axe before it could swing down.

The man stumbled forward and reached out to Stella; his hand balled into a fist. She swiped it away and pivoted around him quickly. She grabbed his wrist and continued to pull him as she put pressure on his elbow. He went directly to the floor and she knelt on his back as Ari tossed the axe aside.

"I guess that's your police training."

"More or less," she said.

"Get off!" The man wriggled as he shouted.

"Are you going to attack us again?"

"Get off," he said.

"Well, that's not an answer." Stella put a little more weight on him. She could feel his muscles tighten beneath her weight and grip, a small smirk curling her lips.

He wheezed as he tried to escape. "You're on my property!"

"There isn't exactly a sign saying people live here," she snapped. "Are you going to be still?"

The man growled before relaxing under the pressure. Once he was calm for a time, Stella looked at Ari and nodded. He shrugged his agreement and stepped back.

She eased the weight and released the man. He massaged his arm as he sat up, suspiciously watching the pair. He must have seen a deteriorating girl, maybe with some sickness, and a boy that was the exact opposite, virtually untouched by the world.

"How have you survived? They raided all the cities and populated areas."

"Turns out they don't like thyme," he said, rolling to his feet.

"As in the spice?" Ari tried not to laugh; it was unbelievable.

"Yeah, the spice. We've been growing it in planters and gardens. Anywhere there's soil. The garden center had bags of seeds."

"I don't see any." Stella moved past him, back to the main area.

"That's because we've been moving," he said. He continued to massage his arm, glowering their direction.

"Think he's going to try killing us?" Galen called from outside.

"No," Ari hollered back.

Stella was already making her way to the main area of the bakery as Ari shook hands with the man. They emerged from the back room, but the man leapt backward into the wall as he saw Galen by the doorway. His eyes bulged out of their sockets and his mouth hung widely. His chest bounced as his breathing increased.

"Wha-what is it?"

"I'm not an it," Galen said.

Ari patted the man's arm before proceeding. "That's Galen. He's cool."

"He's… massive."

"Yes. He is at that."

"Well, can we agree to be civil?" Stella began following after Galen as he strode down the street and away from the bakery.

“You don’t plan on staying?”

“No,” Stella said. “We’re travelling.”

“Is it safer that way?”

“Not really,” Ari said. “But we keep our cardio up.”

Stella kept her eyes from rolling as she turned to look at him. He was smirking at her and she couldn’t help but grin. Apparently, he hadn’t forgotten her comment.

The man walked into the street with them. “Where are you headed? What’s the connection here?”

“Between the four of us? Let’s just say it was unexpected, to be honest,” Ari said.

The man was trudging along the broken road. His hands were shoved deep into his pockets and his shoulders were hunched but not fully. There was still some pride left in his bones. “Are you taking more?”

“No,” Charon spoke firmly.

“Right. Closed house. Got it.”

“I don’t think you’d enjoy it anyway.” Ari comforted him, glaring in Charon’s direction.

“I wasn’t thinking of me. There are a couple of convicts living in our community and, to be honest, I’m not totally comfortable with them.”

“Have they done anything… untoward?” Charon said.

“Surprisingly, no. But I feel like I’m waiting for the pin to drop.”

“They’ve been useful?” Galen turned his head.

“Somewhat.”

“Then you might as well keep them around,” Charon said.

Stella didn’t look back. She was focused on finding a quiet place to rest for the evening. There were a number of places to pick from, but only a few that would be close in proximity to the people while still far enough away from them.

"Dad?" A boy in his mid-teens jumped out of the back of a truck. "Who're they?"

"Travelers. This is Charles and I'm Travis."

"Hello." Ari waved.

"Yo," Charles said. "Are they staying with us tonight?"

"We'll find space away from your people," Charon said, cutting in quickly before Travis could respond.

"There's a gym and a rec center," Travis said. "Turn right at the next street and take the last left at the end of that one."

"Thank you," Charon said.

"I should tell you though, the monsters put up a warning. You'll see it along the road."

"A warning, eh?" Galen said, sounding intrigued as well as concerned.

Stella's eyes turned to him. She knew, as he did, the furere were far more intelligent than humans assumed. She felt the weight of responsibility as their actions were the result of hers. Her heart hammered with anxiety as they steadily made their way to the warning. Taking a deep breath, she turned down the first street without faltering. She needed to see.

With some parting words, the others slowly made their way down the broken road. Judging by the dust, it was not frequently travelled. However, there was a trace of fresher prints, smaller than most — curious youth, no doubt.

Their footsteps echoed in the vast space. The eyes of the locals remained on their backs. Their dread and fear pulsated toward Stella and she felt it wrack her body. She began to understand why she travelled north. It wasn't just a calling or an urge anymore; it was the desperation the world was feeling. Every single living entity was begging for an end to the madness.

Her feet kicked up dirt as they made it to the end of the street. She looked left and swallowed hard. Mutilated human and animal corpses hung from posts, wires and bone crosses. They littered the road. Her mouth went dry and tongue like sandpaper. She suppressed gagging as she slowly scanned the rows. There had to be hundreds, if not thousands, of mutilated corpses before them.

"My God," Ari murmured in disbelief.

"How many other places are there like this, do you think?" Galen turned to Charon, who was also dumbstruck by the sight.

Charon's hands shook. His mouth hung open as his body tightened by the shock. "Where there is one there is bound to be more."

"This is across the globe, you mean," Ari asked, breathless.

"I reckon," Charon worked to retain his composure.

"Why haven't we seen this sooner?" Galen asked.

"Likely because we were avoiding cities," Charon said.

"Well, at least we know what they've been doing with the bodies," Ari said.

"Some at least." Stella exchanged glances with Charon. The look in his eyes told her that he was abhorred by the sight but not entirely surprised… like her.

"You don't seem too astonished," Charon said.

Opting not to continue the discussion, Stella walked away. Memories of the college cafeteria surfaced, and she stared at the rows of mutilated corpses. Her eyes studied the bodies weaved together by bones and wire. The tethering protruded from the rotted flesh and skeletons though pieces were beginning to fall off. It was as vicious as the food court. Definitely a warning to the living people.

"Why would those people stay so close to this?" Ari's gaze shifted behind them.

"Nowhere else to go," Galen said.

"Or this isn't the first they've seen," Charon said.

Stella forced her feet to move. Not only were they sore and begging for rest, but she was scared to see more. She knew her mind was failing her. The sheer lack of concern in the bakery combined with her lack of sleep was becoming dangerous as more memories entered her consciousness.

She needed to bring herself back to who she was—who she always aspired to be. This broken girl was not that. Nor was the woman who created this disaster. Neither were meant to be the final piece of a puzzle.

She drew the deepest of breaths and allowed the ragged, wretched stench of decomposing corpses and dried blood to invade her senses. It nearly awoke a rage in her as exhaled. But that fervor gave her strength to tread the gauntlet.

She passed by the rotted corpses, eyes directly forward, and attempted to give them no more acknowledgement than need be. They could be buried peacefully once there were no more furere to desecrate the dead.

Flies and scavengers could be heard getting their fill. It led her to imagine the sounds of their flesh deteriorating as their lifeless souls howled in protest. They wanted to live yet spared themselves the agony of such cruelty by accepting death.

***

Charon had not seen these in his visions and was disgusted by his inability. Had he not done enough to guard the gates of the tortured? Could he have prevented this before the spell was designed and the symbol cast? Seeing the future was one thing… stopping it was another.

His eyes turned to Stella. The woman he had loved was whole and complete on her own—even if she had been unable to see it. The pieces of her throughout the centuries, her mere rebirths, were far more dangerous on their own. One needed compassion to withhold rage; wisdom to control childishness and recklessness; courage to dissuade cowardice. To separate each was deadly in its own right. The shattered, hollow personifications created a world that mimicked these states. Though the fae fought to save both the magical and human sides, there was nothing they could do to stop the timeline.

Charon's gaze shifted to Ari. He too was unwittingly headed north. His family had held the symbol safe for hundreds of years, but he knew nothing of it. That would need to change before it was too late.

The recreation center was growing closer. The roof was collapsed, but they would be able to manage a small place for rest on the edge of an exit.

They paused at the parking lot and examined the building. None wanted to face the road, so they began to walk the around the structure toward the tree line.

Stella didn't feel safe. She imagined the souls of the corpses watching and waiting from their perverse gravesites. They too desired retribution.

Galen pressed his weight into a door and it slowly creaked open. He walked through and pushed fallen material to the edges.

He nodded. "This will do."

Chapter Twenty-Six

Stella found herself wandering the perimeter of the recreation center and forest. She was chewing her lip incessantly, debating what she should do. The closer she moved to Georgian Bay, the more urgent the feeling in her chest became. It was weighing her breath more heavily than ever.

The trees slung shade from the lowering sun, but their leaves hung silently. There was still no wind to be felt or heard. The only movement was a small creature amidst the woods. Stella turned her gaze toward it.

A squirrel with a large, bushy tail and big, dark eyes came into view before pausing. He was smelling the air for danger before moving again. It could sense her.

"I'm sorry." It looked in her direction before scurrying away.

She lowered her eyes and went back to walking the perimeter. Stella moved between roots and moss slowly as her mind percolated. Her feet remained steadfast as she walked quietly among the trees. She was slowly weaving outward, moving further from the light and safety of the fire pit outside the doorway. She could hear the voices of her companions murmuring softly to one another.

They were worried about her. She wasn't herself.

Understandably, she felt her sanity slipping away. Like the previous adaptations of herself, she didn't feel whole. She had seen most of her predecessors' memories. Except in this life, her final life, there were no mental asylums or castles—only chaos and destruction.

She stopped at the brink of a small cliff and peered down… only about two stories. Not enough to kill her but definitely enough to do some damage. To hurt.

She wanted to reverse the knowledge she had obtained at the mansion. Her instinct was to know, but she regretted that decision. Knowing who she was, what she had done, hadn't helped her. It had merely made her troubles more persistent and brought her failings forward.

Sitting, she watched the moon crawl across the sky. Stars began to emerge, their appearance calming and beautiful. Her mind stopped swimming, and she drew a breath. The sky, in this pure moment, brought her back to her first thought about Galen's eyes. They were the night sky without clouds that would otherwise hinder the heavens.

Her mind then travelled to Charon. His were the opposite. They glittered as well, but they were such a ferocious blue, like a clear summer day. More like diamonds hidden in the ocean waves if she pictured them in her mind's eye.

She shook her head to clear her thoughts.

In the distance an owl called, and Stella listened to it echo over the sky. She knew it was hungry but there were so few critters left that it might starve to death… if the furere didn't catch it first.

Sighing internally, she couldn't rationalize the actions of her past selves. She empathized with Charon. She would feel just as guilty for not stopping it when there was a chance to. But worse, to be unable to hold things together.

"You really shouldn't think about me." Charon sat next to her slowly, his feet hanging over the edge. "I can feel it."

"What?" Stella turned to him, surprised she hadn't heard him as goosebumps climbed her arm.

"You feel compelled to go north," he said. "I am compelled to you."

"Are you telling me someone is continuously thinking of me?" She would have laughed had it not been so absurd.

"No."

There was a long pause between the two of them. He was more solid in this world than the other, but there was still something otherworldly about his form that she couldn't quite grasp. He was smiling to himself before sighing.

"I was trying to protect you," he said. "I apologize."

"It's impossible to protect someone who doesn't want to be." Stella leaned up against a tree.

Charon licked his lips and stared down to the bottom of the cliff. His hands were relaxed but she felt the nervous energy stemming from him.

"Do you understand my fears?"

"I'm not going insane. As much as I may feel like it…"

He chuckled. "That's not quite what I meant."

"What did you mean?"

"I meant… knowledge can be useful or a hindrance," he said, resignation in his words. "It is a heavy burden to walk with."

"Ignorance is bliss," Stella said.

Charon looked at her gently. "Knowledge is power and it can weigh equal to guilt."

"Do you feel guilty?"

"I do."

Stella took as deep a breath as her lungs and stomach would allow. His body was inching closer.

"This was not your fault."

"Perhaps…"

"You are not responsible. You weren't the one who tortured people, fae, until they were unrecognizable in both physical and mental form. You weren't the one who used magic to turn them into creatures. You weren't—"

"But I was the closest person to stop it."

"Maybe," Stella said. "But why did you need to carry that responsibility?"

He looked her way, and she met his gaze. Even in the darkness of night his eyes shone. She could feel his fear and warmth swimming together.

"Surely you understand," he spoke quietly before rising to his feet.

She watched him leave, her heart aching for their losses. He carried himself well but was beginning to show signs of exhaustion. She wished she could return his former life to him as she began to understand not only his fear but his quiet, resilient love.

Stella turned and rested against the tree. All her memories of him were vague, as though they were not hers, but she could tell well enough what they had once been to one another. She still longed for his smile and, more so, his touch. She missed the gentle caress of his hands across her back and the sound of his heart beating against her ear.

Her hand reached across the roots and her fingers grasped a small flower distractedly. It hadn't quite bloomed yet already appeared to be wilting. She frowned to herself. Even the plant life would soon die out. Her head turned upward to the treetop. What was becoming of the earth?

She let her fingertip run across the closed bud and wished it to bloom, her mouth uttering small words of encouragement. She watched, mouth agape, as the wilted plant grew tall. The flower's petals began to open wide, white sparks floating from it in the effort. She watched the sparks dance between the flower and her hands. The flower's stem grew nearly an inch, the sparks humming melodically.

The flower seemed to face her as she drew her hand back. She kept her eyes on her hand and watched the white sparks flitter between fingertips and palm. Her heart jumped excitedly. It had to be magic. Was it returning to her on its own?

Chapter Twenty-Seven

Stella found herself restless after returning from the forest. She awoke nearly every hour, eyes groggy and crossed, mind spinning in turmoil. When it felt like dawn was approaching, she uncurled herself and sat in the doorway with Galen.

He peered down at her. "Did you get any sleep?"

"Nothing rejuvenating," she groaned through a stretch.

"That's unfortunate."

She sighed heavily and wrapped her arms around her knees. "I feel off."

"The world is off."

Hiding her face, she muttered, "it's my fault."

"Well, partially," he said. "Fear is powerful. But you, right now, aren't totally responsible."

"Huh?" Her head sprung upward.

"The original version of you was complete," Galen said. "But something terrified her, and she used magic to live longer. That magic, however, absorbed the different facets of her being and split them between eras; shards to be birthed every one-hundred years with the passing of the previous one. Each one missing a piece of her."

"How do you know that?"

"I have many books. Some from Charon, some from pixies and many from wizards. I hold knowledge others don't or, in some cases, cannot. I knew the moment you faced me who you were."

"That explains the open nature you showed us on your property." She rubbed her face. "Though you were fairly hostile at first."

"I wanted to see your reactions," Galen said with a smirk. "Do you even understand Ari's motivation for going north?"

"I barely understand mine," Stella said.

"If you take the magical object from him then his desire to travel there will cease." Galen sighed. "But that is your decision. You'll bring him or stop him. Either way you need the symbol."

"I still don't understand why I need to go to Georgian Bay," she said, shaking her head. "What makes that place so special?"

"You will understand as the remaining memories return," he said. "When your magic is given to you. We're waiting for that to happen."

"Ugh, right… I should have done that first instead of taking the memories of the fourth queen, that lunatic."

She was distracted as a piercing scream erupted into the air. Her head swung toward the small town as she jumped to her feet. Ari and Charon sprung awake, feet moving toward the door, while Galen sniffed the air.

"We should help them." Stella shot into the building and began ruffling through her bag for weapons.

"What do you plan on doing? You can't even do much for yourself let alone them," Ari said.

"That's rude," Stella said.

"He's not wrong, though," Charon said. "You may have gotten into the mind of a furere but you weren't able to control it, let alone kill it."

"Are you really going to the furere?" Ari said.

"Yes, and you're coming," Galen said.

"Excuse me?"

"You're going to react, as predicted. Which makes you useful."

"I'm not sure I'm comfortable with that."

"It's up to you, but I agree with Galen," Charon said, already heading toward the town. "Stella, remain hidden for the time being."

Galen was close behind Charon and taking the shortcut across the field. Ari sighed, glanced at Stella, then headed off after the two men. He was racing to catch up.

She watched them head toward the danger. Her shoulders hung heavily as uselessness filled her gut, and she wondered what purpose she actually had.

Stella chewed her lips nervously as her feet took her into the forest, searching for a proper spot to cover herself, heartbeat and scent. She kicked a stone as she went, angry with herself, as she seemed to revert to her former self.

***

Ari caught up to the others swiftly, his feet moving easily across the grassy terrain. As always, it felt natural, but this time there was a dangerous adrenaline rush in his limbs. He could feel excitement as much as terror in his veins.

The smell of the furere filled the area. The rot gagged them momentarily as they watched the creatures tear through buildings in search of victims. A few had already been caught, limbs here and there, likely from whoever let out the scream.

The giant wolf appeared, and Ari didn't know what was happening. He didn't recognize it as himself. It felt apart from him. It was also bigger than before. Its head craned to look at him, its deep, brown eyes knowing, before lowering itself to him. He shakily hesitated but whispered the words his father had often said to him as his hand reached out and touched the fur.

"Trust your instincts…"

He gripped the fur tightly and jumped up onto the wolf's back. Hunching himself into the beast, he held with both hands, his eyes just above the fur to see from the wolf's perspective as it identified its target.

The wolf snarled and leapt through the air. Long, powerful legs carried it across the expanse of streetway and onto the building. Its mouth bit down on a furere, the crunching of bones snapped in his jaw, and it jumped back down to solid ground as the roof began caving under the weight.

The wolf shook its head violently, the furere unable to escape, until the monster was torn in two and dropped like a raggedy doll.

A surge of furere came into sight, and the wolf dropped its shoulders, crouching to lunge at them. They screamed and screeched at it, eyes of

~ 167 ~

rage, as they raced toward it. The wolf growled and its legs snapped into movement, pavement kicking up behind it, charging into the enemy teeth-first.

Its giant jaws grabbed hold of one as the others leapt above it. They used the buildings' landscapes to climb high and push off, landing on the wolf and digging their talons and spikes into the fur. Ari felt the stinging in his own skin.

The wolf howled as it bit down on the furere and threw itself onto its back, rolling over the creatures and crushing their bones. The crackling and snapping echoed.

Ari saw the creatures laying on the destroyed pavement as his heart hammered nervously. They were trying to move, but their broken bones and detached tendons prevented it. More furere stormed the town as the wolf turned to face them. The wolf swatted several through a building with its tail as they lunged.

The sun began to come up over the town as the wolf charged forward. The furere leapt through the air, converging into one massive creature, and clamped down on the wolf's shoulders.

Ari felt the teeth dig into the fur and begin descending into the skin. He winced as it burned but the wolf howled and craned its neck upward. The black mass pressed further, Ari's paws sinking into the earth, and forced the wolf's shoulders to shake against the pressure.

Opening its mouth, the wolf snipped at the neck of the giant furere. It drew back, but the snap of teeth was enough to draw a stream of thick, black blood. Stumbling backward, it released the wolf but just as quickly gripped its own throat.

Angrily thrashing, it whipped itself at the wolf, arms now flying recklessly. The wolf straightened his legs and bound high above the buildings. The furere launched after it. The wolf howled loudly as the furere grabbed hold of its leg, Ari felt the acute, sharp pang of the claws digging into his own leg as he became one with the wolf. Buildings and forest were shaking with the sound and tried climbing up the body. Ari screamed as well, and they looked down.

The jaws of the wolf opened, and it swung its leg toward its own mouth. The creature catapulted directly into the waiting teeth, and the wolf closed its mouth with a defining snap. The bones snapped and the monster's screeching echoed for miles as it scratched and clawed for escape. The jaw cracked through the skeleton easily and split the furere into three, the wolf spitting the middle piece disgustedly.

Landing in the field past the buildings, the wolf sat easily and licked its leg, the sun's warmth beginning to cover the fur and heal the wounds. Remaining splinters pushed out of the skin, and Ari looked around him. He still saw everything from an outside perspective as the wolf faded. He was sitting, sucking his knee, as Charon and Galen approached.

"You okay?" Galen was cleaning his sword of the black tar.

"Yeah," Ari said. "That wolf is incredible though."

"As long as you're able to move," Charon said.

"There are perhaps ten people left," Galen said.

"Better than all of them dead," Charon stated as his blades of wind dissipated.

"I've never seen so many gathered in one place," Ari said, breath heavy, returning to his feet shakily. He watched Galen return to the forest, feet striding fast.

"You're right. There were at least fifty of them. They don't usually work in groups as they don't get along. It was rare to even see ten or twelve together."

"Are they getting desperate then?" Ari asked.

"Likely," Galen said.

"But what are they trying to do?" Ari was confused.

"They want to live again," Charon said. "They want revenge."

Ari remained silent. He didn't know much of their magical world. They returned to the campsite. It hadn't been touched, thankfully. Collecting their items, they headed to the woods. The sun's glow was illuminating a pathway.

They followed a row of deep vegetation through the woods. Ari looked beyond the green to see the dank and dingy surroundings. There was a drastic difference between the two.

"Her magic is returning." Charon murmured, mostly to himself, as he followed the path she unwittingly left. "Without Aurella. How?"

"Not fast enough." Galen sniffed the air, his eyes turning north. "I can smell them from here… hundreds of them."

"More like thousands." Charon shook, eyes turning northward.

"Thousands?" Ari's voice cracked.

"Easily," Charon said.

"I thought north was safer," Ari said.

"Is that what you and Stella believed?" Galen asked.

"It is."

"Then I am sorry, but that is not the purpose for our travels," Charon said.

"What is the purpose?" Ari asked. Charon and Galen remained silent as they shared a glance. Ari scowled at their secrecy. "How do we kill thousands of them at once?"

"Stella needs all of her magic returned to her."

Ari watched the large man stare down Charon with dark, pointed eyes. His eyes spoke volumes without saying a word. Shivers rippled down Ari's body as he watched them stand off silently.

"I have called Aurella," Charon said after the stare down. "She's not come yet."

"Clearly." Galen faced forward again, following the track of vibrant plant life. "However, it appears Stella's magic is beginning to return all on her own."

Chapter Twenty-Eight

The group stood from the cluster of people, in the midst of the night, as strangers danced and cried around a large bonfire. The flames raged high above their stature, and orange sparks flew into the night sky. The smoke moved upward, curling and dancing to its own beat.

The people howled, drums beating as they pranced, with their feet stomping and digging into the earth. Mud oozed between their toes with each step. Their words, a long-forgotten language, fell into the air heavily.

"What do you think they're doing?" Ari asked, his eyes large.

"They're calling to their ancient gods," Galen said.

"Are there gods?" Stella inquired, surprised.

"In a way," Galen said. "Fae, pixies, wizards… whatever you want to call them. There are higher energies than that. Consider fate one of them."

"Really?" Ari glanced at him.

"There are many magical creatures," Charon said. "Ones that are extremely powerful. I would say that, since everything is composed of magic in one form or another, humans are able to call magic using their own, what they like to call, intuition. What people perceive as magic, the unknown and unexplainable, is true magic."

"What are they saying?" Ari inquired.

"They're asking for their protectors to return." Galen headed away from the fire. "People return to their origins when they can't solve their problems. We shouldn't bother them."

Stella continued to turn and gaze at the group of people as they carried on their way. She wondered how they justified such recklessness when the furere would easily come and find them. The noise, light and the scent of sweat would surely make them stand out.

Desperation. A voice told her like an echo in the wind.

Her eyes snapped upward, and she saw just a glimmer of Charon's eyes as he turned forward again. Her mind twisted as their eyes lost contact.

She watched him more closely as they trekked. His body was becoming more solid with each day, yet he still retained an ethereal presence about himself. It was almost like Ari's aura but more intense, more separate from the world.

A low growl caught her attention. Before her were a swarm of butterflies. She looked around for the owner of the growling, but it was quite well hidden. She kept going, hand wrapped around the hilt of her knife.

"You're not welcome here," A low, ratchet voice called.

Ari leapt into action, grasping a broken branch and preparing to swing at the voice.

"Why don't you come out, Aurella?" Galen called back.

"You recognize me?" A white cat jumped from the shrubbery.

"Your voice," Galen said. "You've always enjoyed twisting your vocal cords."

The cat transformed into a woman. Her hair flickered in the moonlight. Stella couldn't be sure, but the girl's hair looked white. Her breasts, cleavage pushing up out of her shirt, bounced with each jump she took toward them. She was grinning ear to ear, revealing enlarged incisors.

"Another caelum?" Stella asked.

"Me?" She sounded equal parts amused and annoyed.

"Yes, you," Stella said.

"Aren't you a treat." The girl waltzed up to Stella and began circling her, sniffing as she went.

"I didn't realize you were actually coming," Galen said to distract Aurella.

"Of course!" Aurella burst before jumping into his arms. She wrapped her limbs around him in a giant hug. He patted her back gently until she finally let go and dropped to the ground.

"But travelling at night?" She frowned at him. "That is not safe!"

"Nothing is safe."

"Even the caelum aren't safe now," she said. "There are only a few of you left. They've found a way to kill even your people."

"Oh perfect," Ari murmured as he stood next to Stella.

"It's interesting to meet you." She pointed her nose at Ari with a sweet, slick grin. "A shifter…"

"Is that uncommon?"

"Actually, yes," she said. "Normally those who are only fae-el don't have those kinds of gifts. As for this one… the queen has returned."

"I'm not a queen," Stella said.

"Of course not." Aurella nodded, then turned to Ari. "But you shouldn't even exist."

"What does that mean?" Ari interrupted.

"You haven't told him?" Aurella sounded genuinely surprised. "What else doesn't he know?"

"Well," Stella began walking, "he still doesn't think he turns into a giant wolf."

"Okay. I see the wolf like I see all of you: as an external entity. Though, I will admit it was different last time."

"Disassociation." Aurella winked. "Fun. Where are ya'll headed?"

"North," Galen said.

"So, she is being called." Aurella's face turned serious, the smile faded away. She crossed her arms and examined the group.

"Yes," Charon said.

"How can she be called without magic?"

She ran and caught up to Stella who drew back even as Aurella pushed her face closer and closer. She looked at Charon momentarily but then back to Aurella, locking eyes with her. There was awe and intrigue — curiosity and anger. She was fearful.

"She's the most like the original," Aurella said. "How is that possible?"

"Factory reset?" Stella sidestepped and kept on her way.

"Magic doesn't really work that way." Aurella shot back.

"Doesn't it?"

"I assume it is because she was not born with the knowledge the others possessed," Charon said. "She also was not raised in the fae world."

"Does it truly have that much affect? I suppose it doesn't matter now. I must say I'm surprised though." Aurella started walking with the group. "Galen and Charon: guiding queen of the fae."

"Except I'm not the queen," Stella said.

"You don't believe so?" Aurella asked.

"I have no interest," she said. "Nor do I have need of such a position."

"Very intriguing," Aurella said. "Well, I may as well join you all."

"Please don't," Stella said. She stopped walked and looked at Aurella.

"Furere are gathering north," Aurella said. "You'll need me. Besides, I can teach you a little something about protecting yourself with your fae magic."

"Can you teach her?" Ari was serious.

"I can, well, not exactly teach, per say," Aurella said. "Her magic is precarious. Which is why Charon and Galen haven't tried. She'd probably end up killing them by blowing up a crater the size of New York City if they did. Though I reckon she's mostly been hiding when the furere come near."

"I'm right here," Stella said, scowling.

"Even better." Aurella smiled at her. "So… do you want to know what it's really like to be fae?"

"I think I already do."

Stella recalled the memories and she paused momentarily to consider. If the furere really were gathering, what was their purpose? What would they do when she arrived? Was it safer for them all to discontinue their current path? She bit down on her lip as she considered turning back.

A stabbing scream in her chest thrust through her heart as though her veins were yanked out of her. Stella couldn't breathe, her sight blurred, and her head spun. Bending over; her hands pushed into her knees heavily as beads of sweat pooled on her temples before dripping to the ground.

Stella forced herself to take one single step forward and the pain subsided in her body. Eyes were darting her direction and then away quickly. She ignored the looks and stood straight.

"So, do you want to see what you can do?" Aurella nudged Stella's elbow hard.

Stella glared at the new arrival. She was far too upbeat for such a situation. Furthermore, Stella's fear of becoming her predecessor sent anxious waves from her stomach to her throat. She had no desire to cause further pain.

"You'll need it to survive," Aurella said. "Plus, it's kind of fun."

"I have no interest torturing people," Stella said with a quick, sharp tone.

"That isn't what I meant by fun," Aurella said. "Not all fae are evil. Just like humans. The last version of you was a little cuckoo, if you know what I mean. She ended up in a sanitarium. The fourth queen was… shall we say, spiteful and angry. You're a little more… put together, given the situation we find ourselves in. Let me give you the magic back and you'll understand."

"Why couldn't it have been zombies?" Stella asked rhetorically.

"You'd have preferred zombies?" Ari looked over at her.

"I think I would have."

"Look… as much as I appreciate Charon," Aurella was now shouting, "you're the one who caused all of this! It should never have happened in the first place. Now you're the one who has to undo this. You destroyed my home, the humans' home, fae, pixie, animals… everyone's homes are gone because of you!"

"You think I haven't realized that?" Stella shot back angrily. Her lips quivered in anger as her hands balled into stiff fists. "I saw the memories.

You don't think I've been agonizing over that? What do you think me knowing magic is going to accomplish at this point?"

"Hopefully a whole heck of a lot more than what you can do without it," Aurella said. "You can do nothing without your magic. You let the fae generals and army die in battles that should never have taken place. All because you were scared to die. Well guess what — you have killed trillions of people because of your stupid fear! Start taking responsibility."

Stella's eyes burned at Aurella. While she didn't know everything, the words cut into her deeply. She knew whatever she had done in the past was the cause of the present, but she couldn't change it. She wasn't even sure she could stop it.

"We would very much appreciate it if you accepted Aurella's offer," Charon said. "And I would very much appreciate it if you stopped yelling, Aurella."

"My apologies." She stepped back; head lowered.

"It's fine," Charon said. "Stella, we'll continue north. You stay with Aurella. She'll bring you to us when you're ready."

"Excuse me?"

"I'm asking you to trust her." Charon moved closer. His hands rested gently on her shoulders; his face close enough to feel his warmth. "I'm also begging you to trust yourself. You aren't the fourth. You aren't any of them. Experiences shape us and these ones have created someone entirely different from any of the previous women you saw in those portraits. You aren't them. You are you. When you are whole again you will know everything. You'll realize what I know now. You will see what I see when I look at you."

Stella turned away. She wanted badly to believe in his words, but he was just as mad as she were. The world was not designed for people with good intentions… it was why destruction was much easier. But she did not protest his request.

"Alright," Galen said. "We'll see you around. Try to keep up, Ari."

"Wait, what?" Ari looked at him.

Galen began marching through the dying forest. Charon was close behind as they moved away from Aurella and Stella.

"Bye, boy." Aurella waved at Ari with a giant smile.

He walked over and wrapped his arms around her tightly. Surprisingly, she fell into his embrace openly. She could feel their heartbeats erratically pumping, but it was calming.

"Bye," he said and ran.

She watched his lanky body swiftly move through the trees until he was out of sight. The darkness became overwhelming with the two women standing side by side.

"Alright." Aurella nodded, pleased with the situation. "Let's take a little nappy-poo and then start fresh in the sunlight."

Beyond the point of arguing, Stella plunked down on the spot. She was tired but watched Aurella curl up in the roots of a tree. Stella saw her shoulders rise and fall with her breaths. She seemed to have no worry of attack as she stretched and relaxed.

"I can feel you watching me." Aurella opened her eyes. Their piercing blue shone in the darkness as her white hair curled around her face, bright against the moonlight. "Is there something you want to say?"

"There are many things I'd like to say," Stella said.

"Such as?"

"Why aren't we heading north?"

"Your magic is being given back to you. Rest will be essential to this. It won't be more than a day. Besides, magic will take us where we need to go and bring you back to them. You understand none of them can fight your war."

"I wouldn't expect them to," Stella said.

The two exchanged curious expressions. Stella locked eyes to see what the girl was feeling. There was still intrigue, but there was also admiration, of sorts, mingled into the sea of emotions.

"I knew you," Aurella said. "I saw you shortly after you created the spell. The first version of you. She was stunning and wise. She was so self-assured in what she had done. I think she was the only one who contained the original memories of your whole self."

Stella kept quiet, unsure what to make of the statement. Her mind still wasn't wrapped around what had happened in the first place.

"Charon only ever wanted to protect you," she muttered. "That was not his purpose in life, but he made it so and then he lost everything. That was not your intention, I'm aware. Funny what fear does to people, even the magically imbued."

She closed her eyes again and rested her head. Stella watched for a moment before also closing her eyes into a restless, saddened sleep.

Chapter Twenty-Nine

Stella's eyes opened slowly with the rising sun. She hadn't slept much but had heard Aurella's snoring as though they were next to one another. Quietly, Stella crept a distance away and drew several deep breaths. If she were honest with herself, disliking Aurella was illogical because she could give her the ability to stop the furere. Despite being responsible, Stella was terrified of what it meant to have everything she once was returned to her.

"Magic is in everything, but true magic is whatever the designer wants it to be," Stella's voice carried as she murmured to herself.

"Halfway true." Aurella's voice popped into the air. "There are limits. For example, Ari can shift into a giant wolf that heals itself. That's his only magic—it's contained within his aura. He cannot shift to anything else."

"So, how do I take what I can do and make it a weapon?" Stella asked.

"Well, there's a trick with you, darling," Aurella said. "You get all of your predecessors' abilities as well."

"I don't want those."

"Well, you need them," Aurella said. "Besides, they're yours regardless of your feelings. If it helps, think of them as the little boys who had crushes on you that you didn't like but couldn't help admire a little bit for their determination and cute tactlessness."

Stella inhaled sharply and stared at Aurella curiously. What did that even mean? The two women waited for the other to make the next move. Their standoff lasted several minutes before Aurella moved closer and jutted her hand out sharply.

"I want you to take my hand."

"No," Stella said.

"Come on," Aurella urged. "You don't want to disappoint Charon."

"Why would you bring that up?" Stella scowled.

"Take a deep breath." Aurella grabbed Stella's hand. "You're about to relive a few moments."

"What ar —" Stella began, but her words sputtered away.

They stood at the edge of the mansion's garden. Stella noticed it was bright, clean and the grass tended to. There were no graves yet and she could see herself in the doorway waiting.

"I've waited awhile," she said.

"My apologies, queen." Aurella curtsied sharply.

"You're… which one?" the woman asked.

Stella stood still; mouth unmoving. She couldn't decide if this was happening or if she was dreaming. Aurella nudged her.

"I'm Stella Martin," she said.

Smiling, the woman shook her head and wrapped her hands together. "Allow me to rephrase my question. Are you cowardice or courageous?"

"What does that mean?" Stella asked.

"Have you not seen your portraits yet?"

Stella vaguely recalled the inscriptions in the gold frames. Her tongue ran across her teeth as she attempted to remember them all.

"The last one was cowardice," Stella said.

"Then you must be courageous. When were you born?" the woman asked.

"I was born May twenty-third, two-thousand-three."

"Well, to make this easier you can call me Martin, not Stella. Since we are one and the same."

"Let's go." Aurella headed toward the house.

"This place is different," Stella said.

The mansion was alive with music and fresh air. In the distance, Stella could hear the birds singing to one another. It was pleasant, unlike the last time she was on the property.

"Yes." Martin welcomed them in and they proceeded to cross the garden. "I am the first, wisdom. I'm not the original, though."

"Who is the original?"

"She is the one who spoke the incantation," Martin said. "The original designed the spell; she weaved the symbol and she broke every rule the fae held sacred."

Stella considered the words as they stepped inside. The three women stood in the large foyer and Stella could see all the details she had missed previously. The remnants she had seen before were now shimmering and alive. It was all magic as the colours moved like water.

"There are three basic rules to magic," Martin said. "One: there are limits, both personal and natural. Two: you cannot change the timeline. Three: magic is nature."

Crossing her arms, Stella chewed on the rules. They seemed logical but she thought of those who thought rules were meant to be broken. Had the first of them been such a person?

"The first rule applies to each individual and the outside world," Martin said. "There is always a point where you've gone as far as you can. So, let's say the scale goes from zero to ten; the most powerful being the highest number and least powerful the zero. Humans are a zero to one scale, generally speaking. Fae-el are one to two. Pixie and caelum are three to five. Wizards, fae, sylph and furere are anywhere from five to ten."

"It's like depleting a battery?" Stella asked. "When a car battery dies you get jumper cables and give it a boost from an outside source."

"Exactly," Martin said.

"Why are wizards so high, they're human?"

"Humans, like any of us, can use magical artifacts to obtain magical skills," Martin said. "They learn, develop and enhance them. They can become quite powerful."

"Like this incantation you say our original used?"

"The symbol she imbued with magic, certainly," Martin said.

"What about fae-el?"

"Fae-el are usually psychopaths or sociopaths within humanity. The traits of the fae don't often bind with the human genome. Which is why there are such chemical imbalances. Humans haven't figured out how to handle them…"

"Then why procreate with humans?"

"Fae are bored easily," Aurella said. "It's particularly amusing for them."

"Not all fae are bad, Stella. Just like humans."

"I've heard that before now."

"My personal limit is a seven." Martin held out her hand and let flames lick the tips before flinging them up into the ceiling. "But I can use outside magic to increase that."

The fire didn't just move in swirls amidst the chandeliers. It turned to a bird. A phoenix swooped down to sit in the center of the room, watching the three of them. Its wings and tails burned away but never dissipated.

"That can bring me to about an eight." Martin smiled as the phoenix fanned away.

"I hit an easy five," Aurella said with a bright smile. "But I can get it up to a very close seven."

"You can go outside your body because everything is magic, your third rule," Stella said.

"Correct. There is a price though. The garden outside wilted when I went outside of myself. It will take some time to heal but, with proper care, it will return to normal."

"Can I choose what's affected then?"

"In some cases, you might. But often it comes from the easiest source for you to take from."

"Rule two then?" Stella shifted uneasily.

"The timeline. You cannot change it, no matter what you try. Everything that has happened was supposed to happen. Magic knew it from the beginning. It knows how it will end, even if we don't. So, if we see a future we don't want and attempt to change it, that decision was already recorded in the timeline."

"Our choices are predetermined then."

"Not in the least," Martin said. "We're presented with options. Depending on which choices we make, the timeline changes. It is never the same destination one second from the next."

"Then how can magic know the end?"

"Because… magic sees everything at once. It doesn't happen as we see it, progressing forward in a straight line."

"Is magic… God?"

"Magic is energy. It's our collective consciousness."

"Magic is nature," Stella said.

"Yes. Energy is magic. Therefore, everything is magic. Humans just haven't quite solved that mystery. With this setback, it will probably be another several thousand years before people make the connection."

"You assume there's humanity left," Stella said.

"Isn't there?" Martin smiled softly.

"Perhaps a few," she said.

"Then they can rebuild."

"So, I'm the sixth… in whatever spell was created."

"More or less," Aurella said.

"Is Charon correct in assuming that I'm different because I had no memories of my past live?" Stella asked.

"Because you were born as a human. Which didn't happen to the others." Martin chuckled. "They were also raised in the fae world, you were not. Aurella brought you here to open your magic. Properly."

"Why am I the only one born human?"

"Have you been told of the battles that occurred in the fae world?" Aurella asked.

"Somewhat."

"The symbol was meant to release each portion of your soul every one-hundred years," Aurella said. "But the war that raged in our land used copious amounts of magic. The delay between the previous one's death and your birth is likely because the symbol couldn't obtain the necessary energy to release your fragment. The energy it did find was probably only in the human world since we were preoccupied with battle after battle."

"Those battles were because of me," Stella said.

"The furere escaped," Aurella said. "Their prison couldn't contain them any longer. Charon's power was waning and he couldn't stop them."

"Charon lost his powers because of me." Silence filled the room as Stella watched Aurella shuffle anxiously. Stella looked between the two sadly as she asked, "what was the fae world like?"

"It was beautiful," Martin said. "What you saw in the human world was only half as stunning. The fall leaves glowed bright red and orange shades. Watching them fall to the ground was like watching stars fall over the sky. Stones and crystals were used for lighting homes and trails because they shimmered so brightly with magic."

"So, everything we dream of in the human world," Stella said.

"You'll remember it for yourself," Martin said. "Let's continue. Please stand on the center of the infinity symbol."

"Ari's jacket," Stella burst as she stepped to the designated spot. "It has a gold infinity symbol on it. What does it mean? Is that what Galen meant?"

"You'll find out."

Stella was prepared to retort snappily when a sharp, electric pain crawled up her body. She attempted to jump from it but couldn't move. Unable to blink, she watched Aurella and Martin circle her. They were doing something with their hands, but she couldn't quite make it out as tears blurred her vision.

Shockwaves coursed up and down her limbs and extremities. It shot into the back of her head. She tried to scream but couldn't breathe or move her tongue. Her vocal cords tightened so much she thought they would snap.

Then fire erupted. The flames licked her skin and permeated her flesh. She felt the current ride up her skin and into her hair and scalp. She could smell the burning of her skin but still couldn't twitch or howl.

At last blackness, seemingly night, surrounded her. She was enclosed in the sky and hung limply in the void.

"I give you everything you lost," her own voice echoed.

"I don't want it," she said.

"Be greater than you've imagined yourself." Stella could hear a smile in the words. "But feel free to be just as stupid as always."

Chapter Thirty

A canopy of leaves surrounded Stella as her eyes fluttered open. Her body was resting gently against blades of grass — the water rippled by her feet as the willow branches dipped below the surface. Wind billowed gently against her cheeks as she sat upright.

"Queen?" A voice chimed from beyond the branches.

"In here," Stella said.

The sound of rustling caught her ears, and her body spun toward it. Richard Antelucio. She watched him walk through the willow leaves and joined her next to the water. His eyes were still as Stella's searched the area.

"What can I do for you, Richard?"

"I simply came to see how you were feeling."

"You hated me in my original life, but now you care?" Stella laughed.

"I didn't hate you," Richard said.

"Could have fooled me."

"It is a heavy burden to carry every minute detail of a person's future without speaking of it," he said. His eyes were still, calm, as he stood by the edge of the grass.

Stella chewed on the words slowly. Her heart was tired despite being in the most peaceful place she could imagine. Resting under the branches of the eldest tree in the fae world, her life was rejuvenated. Physical energy restored her body, but her mind was restless.

"I'm sorry."

"I can't say I'm surprised by your actions," Richard said.

"Here, I thought I was unpredictable," Stella laughed sadly.

"You cannot hide from my gaze."

"If you saw what I would be then, why didn't you stop me?"

"The timeline cannot be changed," Richard said. "You should know that by now."

Stella began playing with the branches of the tree as he spoke. The leaves were dancing about her hands and coiling through her fingers and around her arms. The veins in the tree glowed with her energy as they moved.

"Yet fate is not predetermined," she said. "A concept that eludes me."

"We are presented with choices," Richard said. "They change from one second to the next based on decisions everyone else makes."

"So, I hear," Stella said. "Yet, magic knows which path we will take. This leads us to an ultimate end. Or will the planet never die?"

"The planet has been reverted and restored several times," Richard said. "The ice age is one of such means that the timeline ran through."

"So, the planet doesn't stop but we do."

"That may be accurate."

"How old are you, Richard?"

"I've been here since the formation of earth," he said.

"Yet you do not rule?" Stella was curious as she turned to face him. He was grinning and she couldn't help but return the smile. "Do you not wish to take the responsibility."

"I am not one to seek power," Richard said.

"I suppose you're not," she said. Her hand continued weaving through branches as they came to life around her fingertips. "I never knew I could do this."

"You knew," he said. "You merely forgot."

"How did I even come to this place? The last thing I remember is being in that darn mansion."

"You truly don't know?"

Stella walked around the trunk of the tree. Sun was peeking through the openings in the branches, and the warmth was welcoming. Though, it felt as though she were living a dream.

"You came here often during your first reign as queen," Richard said.

"I recall this place. But I'm not the first queen now... am I?"

"No."

"What is happening?"

Turning to face him, their eyes connected. His cat-irises were watching her clearly while she sought emotion. Though, instead of seeing his feelings, it was only her reflection that stared back.

"You cannot read me," Richard smirked.

"Clearly."

"Tell me the truth."

"About what?" Stella asked.

"What did you see when you accessed your life threads?"

"What did I see?"

Stella thought about his question. She didn't know what the vision entailed, and the harder she pushed for the answer, the more it seemed to vanish. It sat on the tip of her tongue as she kneeled before Richard silently.

"You're safe here," Richard said.

"What do you mean?"

"You're still scared," he said. "Fear blocks your mind."

She sat down and shut her eyes. The black screen before her was an unpainted canvas. No matter how much she tried to see something more, nothing appeared.

"Focus," Richard said.

Her breaths shallowed as a flicker of red bands formed. They danced like a string in the wind against the black background. Then she began to see it.

She was staring up at the sky, screaming in agony. Her stomach was rippling in pain as blood poured out of her lower extremities. She could feel her hips move unwillingly as more pain surged through her groin and up her spine.

The agony in her loins increased as another jolt of movement tore her flesh open. Sweat dripped off her face and into the dirt, her teeth clenching together to hush the shouts emerging from her throat.

Rolling to her side eased the heavyweight off her spine, allowing her lungs to breathe more easily. Her spine rolled up and down as shivers pushed down her legs. Another jab of pain to the groin sent Stella toppling flat against the earth.

Are my bones breaking? What's happening to me?

Stella pushed herself from the vision and gasped as her body fell forward into Richard. Chest heaving, she tried catching her breath.

"What was that?" Stella asked.

"You didn't finish the vision… again," Richard said.

"I can still feel it."

She shuddered, her blood running cold. Her body's flesh was still writhing in torment despite being free of the threads she viewed. Fear crippled Stella's body as pain pulsed like a heartbeat.

"What did I see?" Stella asked.

"Childbirth."

Stella froze. *That was it? That's all it was?*

Tears streamed readily, her face pressing into his chest as his hands pat her back gently. He shushed her in the overwhelming madness.

Stella's hands planted in the ground as Richard's body disappeared. Her eyes finally opened, and she realized she was no longer under the canopy of branches. She had returned to the dark, void space.

Chapter Thirty-One

Ari was slowly losing strength as Charon and Galen pressed him to run further. He finally stooped down and dropped his nose into a glittering river. Galen sheathed his sword as Ari reverted to his natural state. Heaving dryly, Ari could finally understand what they had meant. The wolf was still external but tiring nonetheless.

"Ugh." Ari let himself flop onto the ground.

He could feel the sweat sticking his clothes to his skin. He was an athlete, not a soldier—a social worker, not a battle strategist. Every time he pictured turning around, travelling south, his heart felt a knife prick. Sighing, he closed his eyes.

He thought then of his parents. They had always encouraged him and were proud of his accomplishments, even the smallest. They assured him failure was only failure if he quit or didn't learn from the experience. His body shook as he held back tears: they had to be dead.

His body was weighted to the ground as he heaved air through his lungs. Planting his hands firmly in the earth, he pushed up. His eyes met Charon's.

"Let's do this. If I'm really the wolf, I need to learn more."

"As you wish." Charon disappeared.

A strong hand grabbed Ari's shoulder and tossed him over the trees. Screaming and flailing, Ari suddenly wished for a sword. As he reached the peak, he opened his eyes and floated for minutes as he grasped the expanse of the province. The beauty mingled with the destruction; he could see a giant, black mass gathering some distance away. His eyes turned downward with his descent. More screaming and panic grabbed at his heart.

They wouldn't let me die... would they?

Shaking the thought from his mind as the tree tips came closer, Ari began howling.

"Shift! Shift!" he screamed over and over. He urged himself to change. He imagined becoming a wolf.

Slowly, his body began to meld and form. Tendons and muscles stretched and changed. His breaths become deeper. His eyesight shifted so he could see further and more clearly. He felt his legs and arms turn beneath him and he looked: paws.

Ari hit the trees with a loud thud, his legs bending with the landing, protecting the joints. Shaking off the broken branches and leaves, he sat down. His head sat over the treetops easily, allowing him to look every direction. There were birds gawking at him from afar.

"Interesting tactic," Galen said.

"It worked on the last one," Charon said. "Inadvertently."

Galen chuckled, "you'll have to tell me about that sometime."

"Hmm." Ari nodded and stretched himself out, trees bending against their will as his body moved. "This is weird."

"You're welcome," Charon said.

"So, what did you do to the last one?" Galen asked.

"Oh. The poor fellow went off a mountainside, to be honest. I was about to swoop in when suddenly he was an eagle soaring through the air."

"So, heights are the trick," Galen said.

"I think fear of inevitably dying, on a painful impact, is more like it," Charon said.

"Hey, you two." Ari began prancing about, shaking the earth with each step. "How tall do you think I am?"

"I keep forgetting he's still young." Galen's legs wobbled with the shuddering.

Charon swept himself up and floated in front of Ari, who stopped and looked at him.

"You're going to cause an earthquake if you're not careful," Charon said. "Not to mention attract many furere. Practice walking quietly if you're going to explore."

"Okay…" Ari said with slight nod as he began tiptoeing around the trees, careful not to step on any remaining animals. The creak of broken branches still caught animals off-guard, causing them to flee. Smaller vibrations shook as he managed to tread the area. Despite his massive size he felt light as he moved.

***

"I hadn't expected him to be the one carrying the symbol," Charon said. "I thought it would be someone older."

"How will you get the symbol back?" Galen asked softly as Ari moved a distance away.

"I'll remove it from the jacket," Charon said.

"He'll be upset."

"He can be upset all he wants." Charon said. "It'll protect his life."

"Once Stella's magic is whole, she'll be on her own then."

"That is the plan," Charon said. "It needs to happen that way."

"Then you will send her off and we'll return south," Galen sighed, exhausted by it all.

"Correct. We merely needed to get her as far as we could. We're very close."

"Ari won't be happy about that either."

"Once the symbol is gone, his purpose is complete." Charon looked over at the wolf. "His need will dissipate, and he can return to a more normal life. As normal as can be in this state."

"You're sure?"

"I am." Charon rested his eyes.

Ari was not his direct responsibility, but he was a descendant of Aurella. Which meant she had done as asked. Charon hadn't realized her magic would remain strong down the line and thankfully ignored typical psychopathic traits.

Charon's heart ached for Stella. It was the life in her eyes that drew him to her. Her soul was the only one that captivated him and could part him from his duty to their people. Despite the turmoil she'd caused, he couldn't bring himself to detest or loathe her. Fear was a natural reaction to death.

He imagined her wading through the River Tiber in the Empire of Rome. She would often tease the human men, having them call her "mermaid."

The memory brought a small smile to his lips. He had watched her often during that period. He imagined the humans, dangerous in their curiosity. Rather, she'd perpetuated their legends and myths about creatures that were unknown to their world.

He had approached her once, in the middle of the river, when no mortals were nearby to see them together. She was, per usual, quite bare skinned, and her lashes clung together with the water. Her golden eyes were glowing as though they were flames when she spotted him.

"Do you care for a gander?" she teased.

"You do not hide." Charon sat above the surface of the water. "I wouldn't need to request such a thing."

"Yet you have hardly approached." Her lips were turned upward, eyes glinting.

"Would you prefer I greet you more often?"

"I would indeed. You intrigue me."

"Do I?" Charon smirked. "I intrigue a number of people."

"I can imagine." She dipped under the surface and popped back up behind him. "Are you of the Antelucio family line, by chance?"

"Myself? I am not."

"Hmm," she circled him, "yet you seem to possess extraordinary power."

"Perhaps I do." He reached out to her mid-stroke; his hand combed through her hair.

“Do you like my hair?”

“I do. It reminds me of the golden fountains.”

She paused briefly before clamping her hands over his knees and pulling herself up to level her face to his. She squinted as their eyes made contact, her chest teasing his garments, as she locked herself in place before him.

“You speak of the fae capital’s royal garden,” she said.

“I do.”

“Very intriguing entity indeed,” Stella murmured, more to herself than him.

His hand coiled around her shoulders and pulled her in, his lips grazing hers teasingly. Their eyes, locked to each other, waited anxiously and searched for answers. Charon inhaled sharply and allowed their lips to press together.

He felt her heartbeat jump before falling into a steady, but quick, pace. He could feel every emotion she had ever felt and would feel. Charon pulled back slowly, knowing already what her future would bring and yet… he had oddly welcomed it.

His eyes opened when a thunderous rumble shot overhead. The clouds were darkened, and the men were surrounded by a thick smog. He stood quickly and looked for Galen and Ari before his eyes turned skyward. Stella’s limp body was hanging above them, held to the sky by lightning and magic. It was gathering around her dangerously.

Ari and Galen approached and stared as they stood in the eye of the encroaching storm. Galen was already preparing to move away, but Ari was frozen still in his shock. Another crackle in the sky shook the earth beneath their feet and several trees uprooted in the wake.

“Ari!” Charon’s voice burst in an equally thundering boom. “Run! Get out of here!”

Ari’s eyes turned to him before acknowledging what to do. He turned on his heels and fled into the smog as lightning struck below Stella.

“Aurella…” Charon muttered to himself as he sped away. *This is not what I would call careful.*

He watched Galen moving rapidly through the trees as more shockwaves shot through the forest. Charon slipped and caught himself on a branch. He turned downward to see water dredging from far below the dirt to the surface.

A howl sent his eyes toward Ari. Fire was blocking his path and he was trying to find a different escape. The wolf's fur was straight back along his spine as the he sought a way around the flames.

"Above!" Galen hollered. "Go over it!"

Charon saw Galen watching the scene and, while he didn't entirely agree, it was perhaps the best solution at the present. Ari's hind legs bent heavily before pushing off the ground and launching him high into the storm clouds. The smog was beginning to close in, and Charon knew he would quickly lose sight of the pair as he ran into the darkness.

"Charon! Don't inhale," Galen yelled over the noise around them.

Charon stumbled in his tracks. *What was the smog made of?*

He wrapped his shirt over his face and ran blindly through the forest. His heart was beating rapidly as his eyes teared up from the intense haze he was trapped in. Having had enough, he shot himself into the air above the trees and took a wild gasp for air before turning back, just for a moment.

Stella's body was surrounded by golden light, but every single element flickered with magic outside of that glow. He inhaled abruptly as every reborn version of her appeared. The original faded into view and looked at him. Her eyes were miserable and apologetic.

"Stella," Charon whispered. The wind carried it to her as the embodiments merged together in a twisting, scorching fury.

He could hear screams as her body was torn and then mended. The glorious golden light sputtered and cracked, raging outward in a spiraling explosion. Even he was no match for such power and was thrust further as the waves struck him.

His body hit the ground and he tumbled into something large. His back landed squarely, pushing the air from his lungs. Looking up, he realized it was Ari. Galen was already sheltered behind the giant legs and was reaching for him.

Charon quickly took the offered hand and the three hunched over as new blast headed their direction. Ari's paws dug deep into the earth to stay in place, but he was dragged across the earth, his exposed back taking the brunt of the explosion.

Charon leapt over Ari and pulled as much magic as possible from the earth to form a shield. It eased the percussion some, but they were still being pushed back. Charon wondered if this is what she had been truly capable of all along.

Thirty-Two

Ari reached out to touch Stella but was shocked by an electric charge when his hand moved within an arm's distance. With his hair on end, he backed away and crossed his arms with a scowl. His back was stiff from the rapid succession of explosions Stella's abrupt return caused. Regardless, he twisted to see Charon and Galen. They were standing nearby though neither seemed particularly concerned.

"She looks dead," Ari said.

"If she were dead, there would be no barrier between the two of you," Galen said with assurance as he sat. "This could be a while."

"Where's the woman we left Stella with?" Ari said.

"She'll probably be along shortly," Charon said.

Ari watched the man lay across the grass casually. Charon's arms were stretched overhead, and his hands pillowing his head.

Ari was exasperated and snapped, "Don't you care?"

"She's fine," Galen said. "It's when she wakes up that we'll need to be on guard."

"What does that mean?"

"It means we don't know if she'll panic or if she'll have her head attached correctly."

"Either she'll be herself, or she'll be a little cuckoo," Ari said.

"Essentially," Charon said. "There is nothing to do but wait."

Ari plunked down and crossed his legs with a heavy sigh. He could feel the tightness in his muscles. His body had healed relatively quickly after the flames, but he still felt the pulsating, throbbing ache of the beating he'd taken.

"It only took you a couple days to figure out, but at least you can choose when you shift into a wolf now," Galen said.

"Right," Ari said. "I'm constantly hungry now."

"Well, it does require energy," Charon said.

"You could forage?" Galen offered.

Ari couldn't argue with about that. They had forced the wolf out of him, although the methods were questionable, and now he didn't just see the wolf as an external force, but he was the wolf. They had covered a vast amount of terrain in such a small timeframe as well. It had been astounding how quickly he moved. Though, he wondered why they still travelled by foot if they had magical powers.

"If we can travel faster, then why don't we?"

"What good would that do if we're not skilled enough before arriving?" Charon countered the question with a slight grin.

"You mean me?" Ari asked.

"Naturally," Charon said.

Ari looked back to Stella's body and decided to ask a burning question, "why haven't the furere come?"

"She probably killed any that were nearby," Galen said, chuckling. "My assumption is the rest couldn't get through that smog. Of if they tried, they killed each other thinking it was something else."

"Could they be scared of her power?" Ari asked.

"I'm not sure they have that much mental capacity left," Charon said. "But we should be prepared for their emergence regardless."

He accepted the answer and began pacing the woods though his eyes continued drifting to the new landmark created in the wake of the explosions. It had been quite the sight. Not only did the forest burn, but the water pulled up from the ground in massive waves. The force of the liquid yanked the roots from their webs in the ground. The fire and water had spiralled together, though never touching, until the trees burned to a cinder and washed away.

Ari drew a heavy breath and reluctantly fell to a seated position on the ground as he waited impatiently for Stella to awaken.

***

Charon and Galen exchanged knowing glances. They understood their journey was at an end. If Stella failed, they would need all the skills they had to survive in the new, harsher world. They, however, had not told Ari they would begin south after Stella awoke.

Charon was waiting for a moment to remove the symbol from Ari's jacket. He wore it constantly, and there couldn't be too much time between the removal and Stella's departure. He needed to be sure Ari wouldn't notice either. The young man would strike up a fight with him and likely chase after Stella if she were still close enough.

Theoretically, Ari could go to the rune with her, keeping the symbol in tow. But he knew Stella wouldn't want him to take such a risk. She had performed the spell to save herself and what she believed would also save others particularly those she loved.

But the spell backfired in ways she couldn't have predicted. Instead of living longer, she merely caused the magic to rupture and had millions of life threads cut short. Her decisions in each rebirth assured that as she became increasingly less herself.

He shook his head. The heaviness on his shoulders had weighed him like an anchor for five hundred years, a burden that grew heavier every century she was reborn.

Except, he could not find the sixth. There had been no time for him when the gates were preparing to unseal. Rupturing magic itself had never been done, and she caused it twice over. Once, when she cast the spell and created the symbol, and again when the damned fae she'd created emerged from their hidden fortress.

Small ruptures in magical gates happened regularly; earthquakes, volcanic explosions, tornados, tsunamis… magic too strong or too weak could cause any number of disasters. Especially when those seeking to change the timeline or their own fate decided to experiment. It could not be undone. If one was meant to die, they would die one way or another.

His eyes moved back to Stella's limp body. From the corner of his vision, he could see Ari also watching her. They felt an eerie lifelessness to her that was stifling. Who would she be when she awoke?

Chapter Thirty-Three

Inside Stella's mind, thoughts were not her own. She struggled for power as the darkness carried her to places far from the ordinary mind's reach. Memories that were not hers sprung forward. Emotions she didn't recognize overwhelmed her. It was a thought that she had felt nothing until this point.

She saw five of herself surrounding her as her feet touched something solid. Wind echoed across her bare skin as she reminisced of Vasilis. His skin was the sweet touch of a cool breeze. He was the gentlest of souls, though sharp-tongued when required. His power need not be boasted, it was apparent.

Water dripped and ran across her curves. It seeped into her bones and weighed her down. It chilled her, making goosebumps run over her skin, hair stand on ends. She shivered in the cold as the liquid ran up and down, crossways, ignoring gravity.

Fire licked and singed the edges of her body. She curled her toes and winced away from the flames. They teased her before rising over her, surrounding her. She could smell the burnt hair, and her lips snarled. Flames licked her back, and she tried to move forward, but they closed in on her.

Roots covered in dirt ran their way up her legs and around her body. Her muscles tightened and weakened as they drained her of fight. The roots were living through and because of her. They kept her body trapped.

Metal sweat from her pores. It etched her body and hardened in a heated shield. Her body began cooking inside it. The more her body heated up, the more she sweat the metal that layered heavily upon her. She would have dropped to her knees were she able.

"Hello, Stella," a voice said.

Stella's eyes opened, and the elements slithered to their owners. There was no light. No darkness. It was a simple, vast, empty space: clear. The area came to life as a waterfall sprang before her and trees after that. Her eyes turned upward as a bird flew across the blue sky. Feet turning slightly, she scanned the space curiously.

"All this… for that one?" she heard an angry mumble.

"Half a millennia," a third uttered.

"We should kill her." One stepped forward.

"You cannot kill her," the fifth said.

"Enough!" Stella shrieked.

She thought her heart would leap from her mouth, tearing through flesh and taking her voice from her in its wake. Her legs could not hold her, and she dropped to her knees breathlessly.

The one who had stepped forward smirked and muttered, "I kind of like her… in a weird way."

Stella looked at her, lip curled in a snarl. "Well, apparently, we're all the same person. Except you are the ones I would tear from my flesh and destroy."

"Well," she took yet another step forward, laughing, "if we're all the same person, we all have a part to play in who we are."

"Let's just get this over with." The first one reached her hand out and touched Stella's shoulder though Stella tried to shrug it off.

"Get what over with?"

The others placed their hands on her skin and began to chant. Stella couldn't make out the words. It was a language she did not recognize except for the final word.

Moirai.

Stella's eyes opened, and she gasped for air. The cold seeped into her body as life came back to her. She blinked multiple times until her sight cleared and she could make out the blue sky above her. The pain was pulsating up and down her body, an electric river through her veins.

With no control, she screamed in agony and bent in on herself as her muscles tightened involuntarily. She felt like her body was strangling her from the inside out. It took all her energy just to let out a howl of pain before she felt the release.

She could hear yelling, crackling as the pain escaped her body in a surge of energy. It was as though lightning cracked its whip to strike her. She could feel the heat and smelled the smoke of burning wood and flesh. But soon, the scent of the ocean filled her nostrils before she sank into a pool of water.

Still unable to move, she felt herself drowning. She couldn't make it to the surface but couldn't find the bottom either. Spasming, her body shuddered from the chill. It felt as though hands were tightening around her heart and lungs.

Mind racing with images, past conversations, as their magical powers began to release. Stella's mind raced with images and conversations, thoughts turned to her first meeting with Ari, she had noticed the gold embroidery on his jacket.

She thought of Charon. His bright, blue eyes stunned her. The first time she had seen them, her heart skipped a beat. Tears stung her eyes as pieces of their history came back to her consciousness.

Her eyes opened as strong hands reached around her shoulders. She knew exactly who it was as the sunlight came ever closer. They flew from the water and above the trees. She gasped for air, arms hanging limply at her sides, chest convulsing as she dispelled water.

"Breathe," Charon said.

She sputtered as the last of the water withdrew, and she leaned her head back into his chest, catching her breath. His arms, and heart, were steady while he pressed her close to him. The wind seemed to catch and hold them in the sky, balancing between the heavens above and the earth below.

"How are you here?" Stella asked, turning to try and see his face.

"You came to us," he said.

His eyes, ahead and undiscerning, finally looked at her delicately. He barely smiled, but she could almost see the curl in his lips. Her ear touched his collar lightly, and she locked eyes with him. She felt his turbulent emotions rush him.

Relief and sadness overwhelmed Charon. But when he looked at her, she could still feel his affection and devotion to her. Not to what she was or what she represented, but to her as a person. Her heart warmed as she paused at the moment to take those particular emotions in.

"Aurella transported you to us with the infinity symbol since Ari is still carrying it with him," he said, pulling her from the emotions. "It gave you back your powers… it returned you to who you once were."

"The gold symbol on the floor," Stella choked.

Her head rolled downward. She could see a giant crater and lake below them. The surrounding area was scorched, smoke rising from miles away. Clearly, it had been her unintentional creation. She lifted her eyes back to him, momentarily ignoring the disaster.

"I recall everything," she crackled.

"You should," he said.

Their feet were planted on the ground next to the new lake formation. Ari was gawking at her from the other side while Galen was laughing.

Stella looked into the water and to the burned landscape. "I did that."

"You did."

"I'm sorry for everything." Stella turned her whole body to face him. "I was unfair."

He looked away, sighing heavily. He glanced at Stella and shrugged before turning to walk away. He finally spoke up, "I'm not holding a grudge."

"You sure about that?" she asked.

He looked at her, his bright blue eyes shining. "Yes. There is no reason to put the blame on you. This was predetermined; past decisions lead to those present decisions leading to future decisions. I knew this was coming long before it happened."

"They told me the future can't be changed," Stella said. "But that the future is always changing depending on decisions. Surely mine… were wrong."

"You did what you thought was best. Without knowing the future wholly, you didn't know this would occur."

"But…"

"I do not resent you."

"But you don't quite forgive me either."

She couldn't blame him. She would probably be resentful and unforgiving if their roles were reversed. However, fixing what had gone wrong was the next step. Stella turned on her heels and headed through the thicket. Stella paused; she couldn't disappear just yet.

"Okay, what the hell was that?" Ari ran up to them.

"Those were her abilities returning to her," Charon said.

"Is she okay?" Ari asked as he stepped ahead.

"She'll be alright," Charon said. "Everything has returned to her."

"You mean their memories." Ari bit his lip nervously, then turned to Stella. "You okay?"

"Yes," she whispered.

She could smell Ari now. His scent was similar to Aurella's. She glanced at Charon and saw his grim expression. She nodded and concluded that was why he carried the magic she created. He was unwittingly its protector.

"You can become the wolf now," she said.

"Yeah. How did—"

"I can smell it." She explained and gave him a solid pat on the shoulder before she moved to the lake formation.

"How do you feel, highness?" Galen asked quietly.

Stella stared up at him wondering if he knew the truth behind the title, he called her by. Galen was intelligent, and given his expansive library at his disposal, she surmised he must be aware.

Though, looking at his black eyes, she only turned her mind inward as she met him for the first time after her first rebirth.

It was days before her coronation, when a sceptre would be placed in her hand and a crown atop her head that she saw a handsome man with blue eyes wandering the capital city idly.

"Va-Va..." She tried to speak his name, but her throat was caught in silence. His eyes turned to her, shimmering and blue, as a smile spread over his lips. She stared up at him, still speechless, as he approached.

"You do remember who I was," he said. "But you don't know who I am."

"I remember much," Stella said. "It feels like a lifetime since we've met."

"You needed to grow up apart from me," Charon said.

"I understand. Would you walk with me?"

"Of course."

Stella enjoyed the warm breeze as they walked along the waterfront. The magic scales left by the mermaids glinted in the sun. Trees were dancing in the wind as animals leapt from branch to branch. The fae world was peaceful now despite the terror it had faced during the Crusades.

"Was there something you wanted to discuss?" Charon asked.

"Why can't I say your name anymore?" Stella blurted.

"I gave up my name when I surrendered my sovereignty."

"So, magic prevents me from saying it aloud."

"Precisely."

Stella nodded slowly as she wrung her hands tightly. The wind was gentle on her skin as it brushed past her, Charon's hands reaching up slowly to brush her hair from her hair. She locked eyes with him and smiled sadly.

"Why make me queen? Surely you don't believe it's a wise decision."

"When I placed my birthright outside myself it was left to the threads of life to determine where it belongs," Charon said. "Not myself."

"Are you saying magic chose me?"

"Indeed. Have you begun to consider the consequences of your actions?"

She froze and shifted her eyes toward him. He was looking straight ahead calmly, no expression written on his face.

"It appears I may have blundered when I created the spell," Stella said.

"May have," he said, teasingly but tender.

"I'm still scared to die," Stella said.

"Most living creatures fear death," Charon said. "We carry the innate drive to survive."

Stella snapped from the memory to see Galen still watching her. Sighing, she cleared her throat and looked away.

"The only reason I was considered queen was because he surrendered his sovereignty to me," Stella sighed. "Do not call me that again."

Chapter Thirty-Four

The forest was coming alive around Stella, though she tried to keep her body from expelling too much magic. She could smell it in the wind and knew the furere would as well. While she was confident in her abilities, she didn't need further attention.

Her hands shook as she opened and closed them tightly. Her fingers were stiff and numb from lying unconscious for an extended period. They hadn't told her how long she had been out, but it was obviously longer than she realized.

She sat by the lake and ran her finger across the surface. Stella guessed she had pulled the water from the ground and plant life around her. The energy created a massive hole in the earth and then filled it up with underground water.

Charon approached her. "How do you feel?"

"Brimming with energy but exhausted. I forgot what magic was like."

"Have all your memories returned?"

"I have been alive nearly three thousand years," she scoffed. "Yet I have not lived…"

Charon sat and stretched his legs into the water with Stella. "You once did."

"Barely," Stella responded dryly.

"I recall the first time I laid eyes on you," Charon said, smiling from ear to ear.

"Oh goodness." Stella touched his face. "I'd almost forgotten the sweetness in your smile."

Her hand hung in the air momentarily as she withdrew and laid it to rest atop her lap. Her eyes turned down to see the bottom of the lake. It was far too deep to see properly, but there were already living creatures making their way there.

"I had missed the days before civilization," Charon's voice was far away.

Stella reclined so her back softly touched the earth. She could hear its vibrations in her ears and feel the hum through her bones. It wasn't as it used to be. She could recall the times before vehicles and trains were common before leaving their mark in the soil despite no longer running across the earth. The sound of chariots or footsteps was more familiar to her, but even that was not the reverberation now.

The earth was shaken in its core. How much longer would it continue to burn and sustain life, she wondered.

"You changed your name," she said.

"I became the legend of the Romans and the Greeks."

"Mm," she smiled. "The ferryman of the dearly departed souls."

"Indeed," he said. "I've been that for many centuries."

"How is the gate?"

"There is nothing more of it… not even rubble."

"Evaporated?"

"More or less. There was tremendous power that burst through the gate. The power was too great for there to be anything left."

"So, we have no prison whatsoever."

"Not that a prison would do us much use at this stage."

Charon began caressing her arm. She allowed the warmth to run across her skin. She could feel his calm, tender emotions enter her mind. His skin against hers felt like home.

"I know what you saw," he said.

His hand crawled up her arm until he wrapped his fingers around hers and held her tightly. His touch was different than it had been in the last few centuries. It felt warm. She had nearly forgotten the hum of his energy. The way his magic whisked around him was like wind in the sky. Memories she had treasured, though forgotten, were returning. She could feel his energy humming the same tune as hers despite knowing she hurt him.

"It had not been death," he whispered tearfully.

"I know."

She caught his eye and held on, brows creasing as they exchanged glances. Her heart broke as they exchanged the knowledge.

"And now, death is unavoidable."

"So, it seems." Stella would have laughed had it not been so painfully true. It still didn't feel as though it were her who created the spell. She was so young and now she would die with barely having lived in any lifetime. "I should have spoken to you."

"Too late."

"It is," she said, tears welling.

"What are you two doing?" Ari stepped through the bushes.

Charon released her hand immediately and tilted his head. Ari had deep circles under his eyes, and his shoulders were drooped.

Stella smiled sadly. She needed to get the symbol back and get him as far from Georgian Bay as possible. Her heart tightened at the thought of him dying because of her. There had been too much death and suffering already.

"Just resting," Charon said.

"Well, there's food."

Stella bit her lip when he disappeared into the leaves. Charon sat up and pulled his feet from the water. He began standing when Stella touched his shoulder. Pausing, he turned his eyes to her.

"I was cruel," she whispered. "How could I do such things?"

Charon rested his hand on the crown of her head and gently kissed her forehead. She felt pitied and detested the emotion.

"When we lack compassion, we become our most cruel self."

He moved away while she looked again to the lake formation. She felt small despite the power now flowing through her veins. Frustrated, she skipped a few rocks before forcing herself up to her feet and moving to the campsite.

Ari was half asleep by the time she walked into the circle. She fell into a spot and watched the flames crackle. Galen stuck a hot potato in her face causing her to flinch, eyes moving to him.

"That's mighty close." She plucked it from his blade and bounced it between her hands as the heat overwhelmed her senses.

"Wanted to make sure you eat something. How do you feel?"

"I'll be ready shortly." Stella bit into the steaming food wishing there were salt.

"Good," Galen said. "I can smell them moving in."

She looked at him, bright orange eyes glinting in the flamelight. Galen's head was tilted upward as he scanned the stars. Stella couldn't help but smile though she reached down and touched the earth's surface. "The earth's begun a different vibration. They are gathering at the rune, aren't they?"

"Yes," Charon said. "The rune you used remains where you stood… where it became the throne."

"The throne? Vas — Charon… what exactly happened? You did more than—"

"You do not need to worry."

Stella eyed him quietly as she finished the potato and leaned into a tree. If she were able to travel through time, she would change everything.

Decisions had to be made and could not be unmade. Stella's eyes closed, the humming of the world filling her. There was still no wind in the air… Charon still kept that piece of nature to himself, she thought.

Slowly though, she fell into a deep and needed rest. She dreamt of him.

He was sitting in his own private library when she approached. He placed the scroll on the table before him and looked at her before she had even uttered a word. His eyes were studying her curiously while hers eyed him mischievously.

"You're… clothed," he said.

"Do you dislike that?" She sat at the table.

"No," he said, shaking his head. "Rather, I find it particularly alluring."

"I do enjoy the silk. It's rather soft and sensual."

Her body sprawled over the hard-oak surface, the fabric spilling over the sides and swaying in the wind. Vasilis smiled at her and removed the scroll from the silk's touch. He put it back on its shelf and turned around to watch Stella with a smile.

"You are a strange woman."

She laughed, "but I am delightful."

Vasilis walked to the table and allowed his fingers to skim across the silk on her leg. She sat up and ran her fingers over his hips. She pulled them closer so he could gently kiss the side of her head, his hands along her back and shoulders now.

"What were you reading?" Stella asked.

"Just the ferryman."

"Oh?" Stella withdrew slightly. "The Roman?"

"Human mythology is fascinating," he sighed lightly. "If ever I were to change my name, I would take on his."

"Why? He carried the souls of the dead…"

"Precisely the reason," He whispered to her before he wrapped his lip gently around her earlobe.

"Ahh!" She giggled. "You—"

"Sir." A guard interjected as he entered the room.

They parted and turned to the soldier, his garbs folding and flowing together as he moved toward them swiftly. He was a general, one of the Antelucio, and he was particularly displeased.

"Richard." Stella smiled. "Always a pleasure."

"Woman," he grunted.

"You'll warm up to me eventually. I'm quite likeable."

"You are a troublemaker," he said. "I need to speak with you, Sire."

"Of course."

"I'll depart then." Stella pushed herself from the table. "Until next time… Charon."

"I do indeed like the name." He smirked before moving on to his desk.

Stella's eyes opened wide as she awoke. The night was silent and the air bone-chilling. She looked at Charon and smiled. It had been a good memory. She, however, preferred his true name. It suited him better.

She huffed a large breath and thought about Richard. Did he recognize her at the gym? She clearly didn't know him before her memories came to her, but she certainly recalled him now.

He was quite different from who she knew originally. The man had disliked her and had no regard for her feelings or thoughts. The Richard she knew at the gym was opposite. He adored her and often spoke of her as being like a daughter to him. She much preferred the latter.

She tried to push her magic out and sense him, but there was hardly any life to detect anymore. Instead, she found the furere. Shuddering, she recoiled and tried to press herself into sleep once more.

Chapter Thirty-Five

Stella aimlessly wandered the beach. She knew she needed to do more than pace but couldn't bring herself to do anything else. Her eyes were watching the bay as storm clouds rolled in. They seemed to echo hatred toward her as they covered the sky, taking away the bright blue.

Finally snapping, Stella's hand shook, and she drew a deep breath. It filled her lungs and belly until she couldn't expand any further.

"What am I supposed to do?" she screamed as loud as her voice would allow.

Her voice carried into the sky toward the dark clouds. She watched them roll toward her, along with a hoard of furere. Shaking her head, she tried to escape her reality. They wanted to take from her what she stole from them, and she knew it was justified.

Her body shook as the storm clustered and merged into giant beings. Furere were barreling toward her, screeches and howls filling the air. They were livid, shattered souls.

"I won't apologize," the fourth queen said. She walked by, her black crown dripping with their blood. It rained down her face and bodice, magic swiveling around her and creating a thorned and sticky dress. "They tortured me first."

"You did this to yourself. You chose cruelty."

"They impaled us with a burning blade. They marked our skin with knives and nails, writing spells and taunts. They refused to acknowledge our voice as a queen." Her voice scratched and hissed loudly. "The second and third queens included. I gave them less than they deserved."

Stella observed the pain in her body. It sat over her heart and down to her hips. Her flesh hot in the flames and stinging. The fourth queen's eyes were filled with fear and malice. Her cruelty sprang from her in a sharp, raging desire for revenge. She could feel the same pain now. Stella could now understand.

"They took the only thing you ever desired," Stella said. "They made you barren and they made it purposefully painful when they stole it. The fae are tricky, and you ensured they would know your pain… but you destroyed another world doing that."

The fourth shook with rage, hands clenched into fists. Her eyes darted to Stella as she howled, "I did nothing to them until they provoked me!"

The air filled with stillness between the two queens. The furere echoed what the fourth screamed, manifesting as red, bloody rain falling down in giant globs.

"It was only fair." Stella kept her face passive, but her heart cried for the woman before her.

This broken, angry woman had told herself repeatedly that what she was doing was fair and just. They took away her only desire in that lifetime, so she needed justice. There was a price to pay for their actions. She had burned for revenge, but her mind was clouded by rage as she sought justice. There was no compassion in this fragment. That had already been born and lost.

Wars raged for centuries but what came of them?

Stella had seen millions of deaths firsthand, all for the sake of power, God and gods, greed, entitlement, legends, justice. She bit her lip as images flashed in her mind's eye of knights and soldiers storming into battle, swords drawn and bows flexed. She could see the ocean of red that their feet and legs sunk into. The earth was ravaged by wars and murder all for the sake of an imaginary power that people would attain. This was all to maintain their vanity.

Her body had once shaken with both admiration at their willingness to die for their cause and grief at the pain they caused due to it. The war she created was incidental of her fear to die and it had spun too far out of her control.

The previous five incarnations of her soul had all played a part in the attempt to live longer. This version wouldn't see twenty years and would never know of love beyond the physical.

She remembered the fear that filled the college as the media began showing furere swarming the streets. She felt the panic that students and teachers alike tried to hide as they locked themselves away. Sometimes teachers were protecting students, but other times were self-serving. Over thousands of years, nothing had changed in the ways people justified self-preservation.

Stella knew her own fear. She could feel her body recoiling at the memories as the red rain splattered on her. She was covered in blood while the furere steadily moved closer to her. But to finish this was a different fate than she wanted. She nearly wanted to die at their hands now.

"Stella?" Charon's voice was steady in the downpour of bloody rain.

She looked back to see he was untouched by the red. He walked toward her, and she looked up at him, eyes lost and seeking answers, pleading for compassion and understanding.

"Wake up," he said. He lifted his hand to her face and poked her forehead.

Stella sat bolt upright; breath panicked. Her heart battered her chest and she looked around. Ari and Galen were still asleep. Charon was standing over her, his frame casting deep shadows from the blazing fire.

"Why don't we walk?" He offered his hand.

She took it and he pulled her up. He was stronger than she recalled. She wondered if the memories had faded or if this world changed him more physically than it appeared? She tried not to think of it yet she felt her cheeks heat up.

They headed away from the campsite and into the trees. Charon stopped when they came to a clearing, still within eyesight of their sleeping companions.

"I never blamed you," Charon said.

"Maybe." She took an extra step away. "But I can't help wondering what this will fix."

"You don't think anything will change? Are you thinking there's a different way out of this?

"I don't know if there is," she said. "Why don't you find out?"

"I don't want to see the threads," Charon said.

"I don't know if this will do anything. The world is broken."

Stella leaned up against a tree, hands behind her back. Nearly three thousand years old and rebirthed six times… each time growing up and relearning. Her memories were clouding before her eyes. Her actions had consequences that were difficult to live with.

Charon stood calmly, patiently as she struggled internally.

"I don't regret my love for you," he said. "But I do wish you had come to me."

"I was rash," she said.

"Why didn't you feel you could approach me?"

"I was scared and I panicked," Stella said. "I feel like we're running in circles. You should never have needed to seal the gates or stand vigil."

Charon shrugged; his shoulders weighed with a burden that neither of them could change. "I would say my moirai had a different idea."

"My destiny, my moirai, was cruel," Stella said, her voice cracking.

"You are allowed to forgive yourself," he said. "But you will not… I know you far too well. You would feel you have further betrayed yourself, betrayed me."

He lifted his hand and ran his fingers through her hair soothingly. Charon stepped in and gently pressed his lips to her forehead.

Stella kept her eyes on him. There was some stubble growing in, but the muscles in his neck and jaw were as she remembered: strong and defined. She blinked as her face flushed, expression giving her away as he inched closer, bringing their hips together gingerly, his hand resting on the small of her back.

She tried to steady her trembling body against the tree. They had never touched like this in past five hundred years. Stella slowly reached up to touch his face and trace his outline.

"You'll take care of Ari when this is all said and done?" she nearly begged.

"Ari will be fine," Charon said, fingers tangled in her hair.

"You won't come after me." She realized it sounded more like a command than a request, so she reached up and touched his face delicately.

His angelic features were softened. He had been difficult to read when they first met, but she had grown accustomed to his small shifts. A muscle rising or falling on the left of his lips; an ear perking up; a shift in his stance... though most would never see them. But it wasn't just his eyes that gave him away now.

She felt his skin against her fingers as they ran from his ears to his collarbone. She wanted to recall his warmth as she passed on. The palm of her hand searched over his shoulder to the back of his head, fingers bristling against his hair.

She heard his mind as she traced her hand over his skin.

You won't be gone forever.

She wrapped her other arm around his side and up his shoulder blade. She could feel the definition of muscle built perfectly around his structure. His skin and flesh wrapped around the scapula perfectly and she gently followed the outline.

Charon's arm slunk around her body, embracing her tightly but sensitively. Their bodies pressed into each other and she buried her face in his shoulder. She felt comforted hearing his heartbeat. It thrummed musically in his chest. At least some things had not changed.

Magic is forever.

"I truly missed you," she whispered.

A small sob croaked through her mouth despite her vain attempt at controlling her breath. Stella felt Charon hold tighter as though he could put all her broken pieces back together. She could feel his emotions rising and falling like the ocean tide hitting the sand as he bounced between her feelings as well as his own.

Stella allowed her hands to run across his warm skin, allowing her to feel his thoughts as though they were her own. Rather than specific words, she felt that he didn't fear death but would embrace it wholeheartedly. Though, she sensed, he lacked faith in her ability to do the same.

"I am defeated," he said.

"You stand as you always have," Stella said.

"No, my moirai is to stand alone. I spent lifetimes without you and then centuries after your spell. Is it selfish of me to wish you would stay?"

"I've never heard you speak that way," Stella said. "Is your love for me so strong you would abandon your senses and leave the world as it is?"

"Perhaps it should be left this way."

"You don't believe your own words," Stella laughed, though there was a pang of sadness hidden beneath the sound.

"No, I don't. Though I wish I did."

"Will we ever meet again?" Stella asked.

"Magic is forever," he repeated.

"If I don't die, this cycle repeats… again."

"You have lived as a mortal," he sought to understand. "What have you felt as a human?"

"I felt buried in a society that forgot people. I felt love and joy and pain all the same, though. At least, what I imagined were those things."

"Humans forgot magic long before this began."

"Magic has destroyed us."

"Magic has saved us in the past and will save the future as well," Charon said.

Stella shook her head with a small smile. She was supposed to be the optimistic one. Who was this new man holding her? He felt the same, but his words were different.

She fell apart, voice melting into wails as she clamped down on Charon's chest. As her body shook violently from weeping, he remained a constant rock. He smiled sadly—*there is no need for tears*—as he allowed her body to react as it needed.

"I'm so sorry, Vasilis," she pleaded for forgiveness, finally able to speak his true name. "I should have let it be."

"If this is all left in the world's time, it is better to be here with you than to waste away alone, never feeling your love for me again."

Stella was scared to let go. She was afraid he would drift away like her dreams. That he would be gone, and she could scream and never be heard by him. That he would seek her and she would never hear him.

She felt torment seep from his body as everything he had held onto for a thousand years poured from his aura. The magic cycling around them was creating a small cyclone. But at the core of his grief was a glimmer of love. Stella wondered how he could still possess such depths of affection for a woman who put him and every other living being in such a cruel world.

She pushed away to look at him, her face was red and sticky from crying. He turned his head further down and locked eyes with her. She was indeed destructive with all her emotions and fears, yet her empathy and life had always shone the brightest.

He leaned down, pulling her head upward, and locked his lips onto hers. It was small but passionate. She smiled as they parted briefly. The salt from her tears teased her senses as she cried. It wet her lips as she kissed him again with the most tenderness and passion she could muster.

Charon pressed forward until her back leaned into the tree trunk. Breathlessly, her leg hooked around his thigh and he lifted her up. Stella wrapped her legs around him as he held her against the tree. His lips left traces of tingling magic as he etched his way down her neck to her collarbone. Pressing his lips into her chest, he felt her heart race as he etched magic into the skin.

She took a quick, raspy breath as the magic heated her body. Her blood pulsed electrically throughout her body. It wasn't just her heart beating anymore; his magic was surging inside her flesh, and she crumbled. Her teeth clipped down on his shoulder, and she cast a small spell, infusing their magic together.

It spun together like woven threads. As if a threat to tear them apart emerged in the darkness, they pressed their bodies together more fervently. Stella's back began chipping bark from the force of the pressure as the earth around them awoke. Life began growing as the dead flora rejuvenated and sprung up. Leafy green vines and flowers were sprouting rapidly around the pair. The tree, once burned, began to come back to life as its leaves grew back, and its roots dug into the earth in search of water.

She rested her arms on his shoulders, hands caressing his neck, as they paused. Slowly, she kissed him and allowed the magic to dance between them.

He let her down and rested against her as he caught his breath. The magic weighted them like a warm blanket as they held onto each other. Their magic entwined their bodies in the air and submerged them into their life threads. The magic danced in the night air as fireflies drew close; they desired the touch of magic they'd long been deprived of.

"It's been centuries." Stella could taste the sweet hint of strawberry. Her spirit was alive and moved swiftly as she pictured the future world. The centuries since they'd shared spiritual energy, magic seemed to fade like distance memories.

It was almost strange to feel that connection again. It was familiar enough to be comfortable at least. Stella had severed it when she cast the spell that tore her piece by piece into the symbol. Another punishment for her actions.

Stella pulled away from him. "Go back to those people. They asked for protection. You might not be a god but you have power. You three may be all they will ever have… regardless of the outcome."

He snorted.

"Even the humans didn't self-destruct as terribly as I have," she continued pathetically. "Of all the wars they've raged, this is the worst they've seen, and they don't even know why it happened. It should have stayed in our world."

"The two worlds are combined now," Charon said as he drew back.

"Even so," she frowned, "do you think moirai laughs?"

"Have you not yet realized it?"

"Realized what?"

"We are each our own moirai. We are our personification of fate."

"We are our fate." Stella nodded slowly, a half-smile cracking her lips at the irony. "By the choices we make."

The world grew quiet as they looked at one another. Stella knew it was time and he needed to release her… rather, she needed to release him.

"I should go." She could feel the sun beginning to rise. "Before this becomes more difficult."

"I agree."

"Thank you for coming so far." Stella was smiling now. "Tell Ari that as well. Will you tell him about the symbol?"

"I will." He smirked and handed her the golden infinity. "After all, he should know why there's a giant hole in his jacket."

She unwillingly pulled away, feet swaying beneath her unsteadily. It felt stark cold as she moved from Charon. She turned, kept her eyes forward and began walking away.

"Nothing for Galen?" Charon asked.

Stella looked at Charon one last time. "Tell him the book he wants is in the mansion."

Their eyes said volumes as they parted. She could not turn back around as her eyes filled with tears. She could feel them wet and overflowing. Her body was heavy as she moved. If she turned now then she would never move forward.

She knew his eyes were glued to her until she drifted from his sight. She could see him listening carefully to her steps as she completed the journey alone. What did her stance tell him? She wondered if it revealed all her secrets and desires.

Would he know she was still terrified to die but that fear was nothing in comparison to hurting him?

When the sound of footsteps behind her waned she knew he had returned to the campsite and she continued onward to her fate and justice.

Thirty-Six

The sun had been up for nearly an hour. Ari was awake and poking his hand through the leather jacket. Perplexed, he eyed Charon through the hole and scowled.

"I assume it was you who took the embroidery out…"

"Indeed."

"Why?"

"What do you know of the spell that Stella cast?" Charon asked him.

"Nothing really, except that she was reborn five times over five centuries. What I know is what I saw in those pictures."

"Well, Stella is much older than that," Charon said. "Her soul is nearly three thousand years old. She was driven mad by an incomplete viewing of her future and she made that symbol in desperation. I gave it to Aurella to protect and ordered her to continue the line of protectors—half human and half fae."

Ari crossed his arms, eyes clouding over, in frustration. That meant more humans were used by fae. It seemed to be a natural action for them at this point. Their disregard for humans was irksome.

"The symbol on your jacket is the original item," Charon said. "It's why you felt drawn to the bay. There's a rune at the bottom of the water that the symbol used to complete itself. Stella has to break the symbol on it to break the spell — though curse would be more accurate — she created."

Ari's mouth hung open heavily as it dawned on him what Charon was saying. He was the fae-el lineage meant to protect the symbol. It wasn't a family heirloom. It was a trick.

"She split her soul and gave them to the symbol. Then she called out her final words at Georgian Bay, locking the power in the symbol and rune. She cannot have one or the other to break it; it must be both."

"Then my family has spent centuries safe-guarding that damn symbol," Ari said. "Then me, as myself, have been heading up here for no reason."

"No," Galen said. "You gave Stella time and you allowed yourself to grow."

Ari stomped on the remnants of the fire and then turned away from the pair. He chewed over his next words carefully. He found himself having a difficult time accepting that Stella needed to be alone. The girl he had watched over the past month had gone through massive transformations.

"She's going to die?"

"Yes. That is what's meant to happen. It's moirai."

"She used the term moirai once," Ari said, recalling the portraits. "What does it mean?"

"Moirai is the personification of someone's fate," Charon said. "Destiny is not within our control. But moirai is personified through our actions, desires, thoughts and words."

"Then mine was given to me without my knowledge."

"To an extent we all face that dilemma. You still made your own decisions though," Charon said. "However, your family was protected in many ways because you were given such a heavy burden to carry."

"How do you figure?"

"Your family has never been poor. They've never had a disease steal their life. Medical bills were paid for by anonymous donors and education has always been covered through scholarships."

"What about my family's mental condition?"

"What do you mean?"

"Galen told us that most fae-el are sociopaths and psychopaths."

"Yes, they tend to be," Charon said. "However, with Aurella's magic, the wiring and chemicals in the brain can be subdued to an extent. Not entirely eliminated but at least offer some sort of block. I assume she took efforts to achieve this."

His eyes turned opposite as he imagined Stella walking alone. He wondered how she must feel being lonesome on the road to death. Reluctantly, he began to follow Charon through the forest.

"She's accepted it," Charon said.

"Has she?" Ari faced forward once again.

"The world as we know it was gone a long time ago," Charon said. "This is how she can make amends for the destruction."

Ari watched the man stride away. His chest burned with anger at the thought of his family being manipulated and used for centuries. Now his own journey turned out to be futile in the long run.

***

Charon's feet touched the earth softly as they traveled away from the masses of furere. The stink of them had begun filling the air days ago. But they weren't interested in attacking their small group. Instead, they gathered together in their reckless anger.

His mind touched on memories as they walked. His lips turned upward into a tiny smile as he recalled his favourite of Stella.

She was first learning a new magic that she discovered in her veins. But she was far from adept at it. Controlling an element was difficult enough, but to wield them all and then learn about each was not for the faint of heart. She was easily the most powerful being he'd ever met.

Not even he possessed such extreme abilities and he too was born of magic. No parents or family... simply existence. Having lived a millennium longer, he had a good deal of time to discover himself and his abilities outside of human eyes.

She had seemed to him a child in many ways. She was born in a different world than he had appeared. There were human and magical eyes to behold and admire her.

In her growth, she often forgot humans were not the same and did not possess such skills. He smirked, remembering how they called her a goddess. A word that eluded her at the time, but he knew they thought her magic was that of a god.

He pulled himself into the memory and lived it again.

~ 223 ~

Stella was dragging herself out of the ocean, hair and clothing clinging to her skin, after a failed attempt at controlling the water. Her eyes were dark, lips curled into a frown.

Her feet touched the beach and she screamed, feet kicking up sand. "Curse clothing!"

She spun around and faced the water, plunking into a cross-legged sitting position. Her arms were crossed, and she was angrily huffing at the ocean. Muttering to herself, she began wringing out the fabric.

"Stupid ocean… mind of its own…"

"Don't be so tough on the ocean," Charon said, walking out of the trees.

She glanced but didn't turn. He strode up and sat down with her. He gave her a sidelong glance and smirked.

"It's like you haven't learned magic before now," he said.

"I have used substantial magic before now," she snapped. "Apparently water isn't that easy."

"Well, you are trying to tackle an entire ocean."

She finally turned to look at him. Her face softened and she half-smiled. His eyes, per usual, were calm and bright. She wanted to reach out and touch his skin but refrained.

"Are you suggesting I start smaller?"

"It wouldn't be the worst idea."

"I've gone from glasses of water, to streams, to ponds, to a small lake," Stella sighed and flopped into the sand. "To conquer this would be… unheard of. Even for those with a true affinity for water magic."

"Yes," Charon said. "Even those with such gifts rarely control the ocean water. They say it's imbued with its own magical properties and mind."

"If you're referring to Moses, I'd say the fae showed a great deal of mercy," Stella said. "It took nearly fifty of them to part the Red Sea."

"So, it did," he said. "Yet here you are… trying to conquer an ocean."

"Any suggestions?" She turned to him again, eyes locked on the curves of his back. "Or just more glib statements."

"I am not glib," he said. "I do, however, enjoy watching your attempts."

"Of course." She exhaled heavily. "Why must I wear clothing?"

"You should get used to it." He laid back as well. "People do not much like impropriety."

"That's why they have brothels and whorehouses." Stella snorted. "Such hypocrisy."

"Try it again."

"Ugh. Fine." She forced herself up.

"Go on." He gave her a gentle nudge on the hip.

"Should I go without… clothing?"

"Wear the clothing," he answered dryly. "You have plenty of dry dresses."

"Fine then." She walked back into the water.

Charon sat up and watched. She stood hip height in the ocean and began to relax. He watched her shoulders rise and fall with her breath.

Her hands ran across the surface as water began to rise in pillars at her command, slowly moving away from the surface. The rest of the ocean calmed as she bestowed the use of her magic.

He cautiously watched, ready to leap from any tsunami that may crash down on them once more. But her magic was steady thus far.

The pillars soon turned to shapes that moved with her hands. She brought them up and down, left and right. She moved them around her body.

Charon saw her chest rising and falling more quickly. She was using enormous energy to control mere litres of water. He turned to the forest and could see she was pulling outside energy into her. The leaves were withering and beginning to drop.

His eyes went back to her and she dropped her hands into the ocean, the shapes disappearing. The rest of her body soon followed her hands into the water.

"Stella!" He snapped to his feet and flew to her swiftly.

She was sleeping when he brought her above the surface. He shook his head, nearly chuckling at the sight. She had pushed herself into a hazy sleep from fighting the ocean.

"You are something different," he whispered to her unconscious body.

Chapter Thirty-Seven

Stella walked through the forest and listened to the world around her. The trek was silent as she moved through the trees. It was strange to hear only her feet crackling and lungs breathing.

Her eyes scanned for animals, but there didn't seem to be any remaining. There were no footprints or droppings as far as she could tell.

The heat from the sun was raising her own temperature. The days were growing hotter as summer weather began rolling in. Stella lamented, knowing she would miss the hot, golden days ahead.

Rolling her neck and shoulders, she paused and looked around. She could sense the furere more strongly, smell their decaying bodies, as she moved closer to Collingwood.

Sitting gingerly on a fallen tree, Stella let her palms run across the surface. She took in every curve and ripple in the bark. Her skin took in every single sensation with exhilaration.

"What am I doing?" She asked.

As if on cue, a deer walked by and paused. Its ear flicked as the eyes looked at her. Stella drew a careful inhale, her hand rising slowly, as she watched the doe. Blinking back tears, she waited to see what would happen next.

"Don't suppose you know?" Stella laughed.

The deer was cautious as it approached. A smile, albeit sad, crossed Stella's lips as she waited. Stella could feel tears brimming her eyes as her heart beat wildly.

"You are beautiful."

The doe's body grazed up against her legs, causing a sense of peace to glide up her legs and chest. The warmth was welcoming as cold tears touched her cheeks and dripped off her jaw. She sniffled and wiped her face as the elegant creature stood before her, its eyes steadily watching her.

The deer poked her snout toward Stella, and she rested her palm against the fur. It was soft and comforting.

"At least you're alive," Stella whispered. "I can still save you… right?"

As her hands ran through the fur, she felt her magic begin coursing up and down her arms. The air around them flickered, and she reached across to touch her back. Stella smiled as she realized the doe was pregnant.

"Look at you. There is a reason behind this mission."

The doe turned its face and began wandering once more. Stella watched it go, her body rejuvenated. Facing north, she tilted her head upward and took in the sun.

Her magic was returning in steady, even doses. The earth was humming vibrantly around her as Stella released her magic. She watched nature grow around her in rising, swirling plant life.

Beautiful.

Pushing off the tree, her feet planted firmly in the earth, and she dusted her clothes off. She turned around to see it completely alive. Branches were protruding from the base with bright green leaves glistening in the sun.

Stella began her journey once more, a slight pep in her step. Seeing another living creature, and bringing a dead tree back to life, provided her with hope.

Her mind turned to memories as she marched forward. It was strange to have thousands of years of memories in her mind. It was even more odd to not experience brain fog. Each one was as clear as the summer sky above her.

Thinking of Vasilis, his sky-blue eyes consistently sparkling, she nearly laughed at the name change. He really had chosen a mythical name. She hadn't expected it though she should have, as he was always full of surprises. Grinning, Stella's mind wandered in and out of memories until one particular stayed at the forefront.

"You're here," Vasilis called, jogging toward her.

"I am."

She watched him maneuver easily toward her. His arms stretched as he climbed down a sheer cliff. The waterfall was steadily streaming next to him, and droplets landed gently on his body. Stella stared, grinning, at the man descending the rock wall.

"Why didn't you just fly?" Stella asked.

"Where's the fun in that?"

Vasilis landed in the sand and rubbed his hands together under the water. The grime wiped away easily, and he looked at her, eyes glittering.

"Since when do you have fun?"

"You are the only person I will allow to see this part of me."

"Am I?" Stella asked.

Her heart fluttered as he waltzed toward her, shoulders swaying gently. The ease in his step was such a vast difference from how he presented himself to others.

"I feel honoured," she said.

"You should."

His arms surrounded her tightly, pulling her into an embrace. Stella took in his scent with a deep breath. Arms wrapping around him, she squeezed him tightly. The feel of his body pressing into hers sent a tizzy down her flesh.

Vasilis ran his fingers through her hair, untangling it as he went, as he gently pecked her cheek. Enjoying the warm, softness of his touch, Stella turned her face upward and gently kissed his neck. She slowly traced her way up to his lips and kissed him fervently.

Hands pushing into the small of her back, he lifted her up, and she locked her legs around his hips. Propping her elbows on his shoulders, there was a brief pause as the wind whistled through the cove. Stella's hair whipped with the wind, and she rested her forehead against his.

The running water echoed loudly as it wound its way downstream. The forest surrounding them was lively and full of magic. Pixie buzzed above them, loudly chattering, as they soared between the trees. Their wings left traces of magic that, in turn, helped the plant life glow vibrantly.

Vasilis gently placed her down and began walking; her hand settled gently inside his. The sway in their step was light as they passed by small, magical homes. Emerging from the woodwork and toward the stream was a wizard; Vasilis slowed his step to greet the man.

"Your majesty," the wizard said, nodding curtly.

"Sir." Vasilis smiled. "You know who I am… who might you be?"

"My name is Merlin."

"Truly?" Vasilis was surprised.

"Indeed, your majesty."

"You may call me by my name, Vasilis."

"As you wish," Merlin said.

"Wizards don't often frequent this area. May I ask what brings you here?" Vasilis asked.

"I hear the village has a sickness," Merlin said.

"I've heard nothing."

Stella felt his muscles tighten, so she looked up at Vasilis. His shoulders were drawn back and his jaw clenched.

"Would you care to join?" Merlin offered.

"A human village?" Stella asked.

"Do you dislike them?"

"No," Stella said. "I don't love them either."

"Would you say you're indifferent?"

"Indeed."

"I am not indifferent," Vasilis said. "I will join you. I would like to see the village regardless."

"Then, shall we proceed?"

The wizard moved along the water's edge beside the pair. The river flowed far as they traced it down to the human village. It was small, huts with smoke curling into the air and a few vendors sitting on the outskirts leading inward. Stella's eyes discerned perhaps eighty houses and one church.

"I suppose the house of the Lord is Catholic?"

"I have not been here before," Merlin said, eyes turning to Stella. "But it is possible."

"I would assume it's likely," Vasilis said.

"Why do the humans insist on religious?"

"Do you ask in jest or sincerity?" Merlin asked.

"Sincerity."

"It is my belief they need faith to survive," Merlin said. "Humans require answers, and gods, religions, provide that. Can you name a culture that doesn't have a deity in their history?"

"No, I suppose I can't."

"Is it your belief there is no God?" Merlin asked.

"I don't know what I believe," Stella said. "Civilizations rise and fall like waves, regardless of prayer to gods."

"The timeline does carry forward," Vasilis said. "Regardless of faith."

"If there are gods," Stella began, "then do you suppose they ignore prayers because what's meant to happen is predestined?"

"If that were the case, then how could they be gods?" Merlin asked.

"Because gods are all-powerful."

"Precisely."

Stella looked to Vasilis, who was smiling, as they neared the village. Though, the scent of illness hovered over the landscape like fog. She scrunched her nose as she looked at the small town. Even the fields, their crops, seemed to be infected by the plague roving through the people.

"Could it be in the water?" Stella asked.

"You can sense it as well," Merlin said.

"I can smell it," she said.

"As can I," Vasilis said, his eyes scouring the terrain. "But it's not coming from the water."

"I agree," Merlin said. "It is a curse."

"Curse?" Stella said.

Her eyes shifted uneasily to the houses. If there were a curse, then a witch also resided nearby. Stella considered the fae, but her people were more pranksters than murderers.

"Who would curse a village?" Stella asked.

"Anyone with a grudge," Merlin said.

"You there!"

All eyes turned to a burly man approaching them, moving swiftly down the road. His grey hair was bouncing behind him as he walked fast.

"Do not enter!" he commanded.

"What troubles you?" Merlin said, still moving closer.

"There is disease here."

He stopped and planted his feet in the ground. His hands were crossed over his chest like a barrier. Stella observed him quietly, from afar, and looked into his eyes. He was protective, frightened and melancholy.

"What are the symptoms?" Merlin spoke up, his face and body relaxed.

The man's face creased suspiciously before answering. "Fever, chills, nausea."

"Death toll?"

"Nearly a quarter of the village," the man said.

"Are they contained?" Vasilis asked.

"They are."

"In the church?"

"Yes."

"Then we have no problem," Merlin said. "Your name, sir?"

"Tybalt," he said.

Merlin walked over and rested his palm on Tybalt's shoulder heavily. Stella watched the brief exchange in silent curiosity. Vasilis pressed forward, Stella in tow, as they crossed into the town. Terrified and wary eyes watched them from a distance.

"Do they know what we are?" Stella said in a hushed voice.

"I don't believe so."

"I can feel their anxiety."

"Shh!" Merlin turned and shot a glance toward Stella.

"Apparently, you're not quiet," Vasilis whispered, a chuckle rising from his throat.

Stella kept her mouth shut as they passed the houses. As they approached the church, she looked up the steps and noticed the door was barred shut from the outside by a giant log. She squinted at it thoughtfully as her feet faltered.

Their thoughts, screaming silently, were surging toward her like a hurricane. The people locked in the church were begging to live, crying for freedom. They pleaded for the doors to open, even just a little.

Stella kept her eyes on the ground as Merlin walked the steps. She felt her breaths change to rapid, scared gasps. Her hand fell over her chest as their emotions overwhelmed her body, soul and mind.

She could feel Vasilis looking down at her curiously. Tilting her head upward, she gave him a half-smile to ease her own pain.

"I can feel it," Stella said.

"I see." Vasilis gripped her hand tighter. "Can you proceed?"

"Yes."

Vasilis took the steps with a small grunt and assisted Merlin and Tybalt lift the log from the bars holding it steady. After placing the log upright against the wall, Merlin opened the church door, and a steady flow of deathly energy wafted out.

Stella clasped her hand over her mouth and nose but couldn't overcome the stench. Her eyes looked inside as rows upon rows of people lay sprawled across the floor. Blankets were mouldy, rouged with blood, and appeared to have forgone cleaning for weeks.

"Who is taking care of these people?" Stella asked.

"The priest has been trying," Tybalt said.

"Have they received fresh water, clothing?"

The priest emerged. "We do what we can."

"Are there… corpses inside?" Stella thought she smelled the rotting flesh.

"Yes. I have been praying over the remaining, but there has been no respite."

Stella's hand clenched into tight fists before turning on the ball of her feet and walking around the building furiously. Did humans lack such intelligence that everyday necessities of life were forgotten for the sickly? Her lips turned up as she snarled.

"You are right to be angry," Tybalt said, rounding the corner of the building.

"They need fresh air, clean bedding, purified water," Stella said. "Locking them in a church without providing such fundamental items is preposterous."

"I suppose you worked with a doctor," Tybalt said. "Or was it a witch?"

Her eyes shot up as she realized her magic was tingling in her hands. He was watching her like a hawk, hatred filling his eyes.

"Even if I were a witch," Stella began, enunciating each syllable, "would it be so terrible?"

"It is against God!" Tybalt said.

With that statement, he spun and left Stella alone. She leaned up against the wall and sighed, humans were fickle and judgmental, but she couldn't help but desire helping them.

She swished her hand gently in the air and uttered a small healing spell, "vivifica."

The air shifted inside the church, and she could hear rustling as they began breathing clearer. She smiled to herself and began trekking toward the forest. Rustling in the grass turned her head. Vasilis was gaping at her in confusion. He moved closer and tucked her arm in his.

"How could you be so reckless?" Vasilis hissed.

"They were dying."

"He already believed you were a witch."

"Any woman considered beautiful is thought a witch, regardless of her actions," Stella snipped.

"You play recklessly in the human world. You may have cured them temporarily, but the curse still remains."

"Yes," Stella said. "Once that decrepit odour has dissipated, you should be able to locate it easily."

"It?" Vasilis asked, his eyes shifting to their surroundings.

"You can sense it, can't you? It's an object."

"I concur."

"I'll be going," Stella said. "I don't believe I'm welcome."

"I will see you when I return."

"Yes, you will."

Stella continued on her march into the forest. She could feel multiple eyes on her as she left, but she refused to turn and look. The judgment was apparent in their auras spanning beyond their gazes. Once inside the forest, a pixie hoard came to Stella and floated alongside her.

"You have interfered once more," the pixies said.

"You have also meddled in human affairs," Stella said.

"But that is expected of us."

Stella glanced sidelong at the gathering. She was always impressed by their ability to collect themselves into a human figure and work as one.

"Why would you heal them?"

"Because it was the right thing to do," Stella said.

"Your magic is great," the pixies said. "But you should tame yourself. If not for your sake, then for Vasilis. He is the king—he cannot afford scrutiny because of his affiliation with you."

Stella looked at the sky, pulling herself back to the present time and out of her memories. She had been warned more than once to control herself, and she hadn't listened. Now, she walked alone toward her own doom.

Chapter Thirty-Eight

Stella was more herself than she ever had ever felt, though the memories flooded back to her had been exhausting both mentally and physically.

She kept her shoulders square as nature answered her body without instruction. She could feel everything. The earth pulsated its magic in bounds as it fought to live against the furere destruction.

Knowing she was destined to die… she shook her head. How could she use magic to try and change earth's timeline? Such stupidity. And now millions had perished as a result of her actions to save herself.

Rule two: you cannot change the timeline.

As a foolish young fae in love, she thought she could break all the rules and stay with Vasilis forever. She almost smiled at the stupidity.

She became absorbed in the memory that created the symbol. She took a gold necklace, a vine from the forest and plucked flowers with long stems and braided them together to create the infinity. A small spell of fire to bind them together and water to harden it. She carried it with her, placing her utmost wishes into half of the infinity.

In the other half she left pieces of herself one by one as moments happened. Wisdom to give her a solution when the time came. Childishness to ensure she would always be lighthearted. Compassion to soothe the souls of those she cared for. Rage to obtain justice for the people. Cowardice to protect herself from harm. Courage to always do the right thing.

She looked to the sky, freeing herself from the memory, and imagined Vasilis looking at her. For the first time in half a millennium he would be proud… not shattered.

As she exited the forest, she saw the new world. Crumbled buildings and desolate gardens. Stella trot down the abandoned streets. Unmaintained, they were cracked and falling apart. Some buildings and trees floated in the air. Scorch marks teased the walls, roads, cars and decimated plants. The fae and human worlds combined. Had it not been for the furere, it may have been beautiful.

She could hear the furere now, gathered nearby. She drew a deep, calming breath as she moved toward the scent of the beasts and water.

"Death is only part of the story," she said to herself.

The strength of their smell took her aback, making her gag as she rounded a corner. It was worse with thousands of them gathered in one place. It was overpowering. She lurched forward as vomit spewed onto the asphalt.

When her eyes turned upward, the cloud of them hung over the bay, hissing and howling. They screeched in unrelenting, eternal pain. The constant torment loomed in their bodies and minds. She knew precisely what they wanted. They sought revenge. They waited for her now.

As she got closer, she realized the bodies of those they murdered were not food. They were hung as warnings along the beach. Even more carcasses and skin were sewn onto their own flesh as they tried to take some of their semblance of life back. Except now, the flesh was deteriorating and rotting with no life to hold it together.

They had made puppets of animals and humans with their skin and flesh sewn onto their own oily hides. The spikes ripping through the rotting flesh kept them hanging at all angles.

Tears rolled down Stella's cheeks as she saw her madness in the flesh. The destruction and hate that she had in her life stemmed from the fear to die. From trying to change the timeline.

"There is nothing you can do about it now," she heard someone say.

She turned and looked at the collection of butterflies. She smiled at them wistfully. The pixies were best at hiding themselves as insects. With their small stature they could get away with it.

"You're here to fix it," the voice spoke.

"I am," she said. "How long have you watched?"

"We were there when you made that symbol. We have seen everything. That is what we do."

"I suppose it is. Tricksters and storytellers."

"Time to release that symbol, Queen Starlight," Aurella said. Her voice echoed as she appeared over a mound of rubble.

Stella looked over; the girl was smiling at her crookedly. She was just as joyous looking as ever, her eyes watching everything around them unfold.

"I was wondering when you would make an appearance."

"Here I am!" She started to walk closer.

"I was never meant to be a queen," Stella said.

"You were a queen, not because they chose you," Aurella said. "You were a queen because destiny chose you. You were born of magic but became a ruler by his sacrifice."

The pixie formed themselves into a person. "This was written before you knew it. Everything is predestined… we are given many choices, but each one is linked to a timeline out of our control. Only he knows them all."

Stella half-smiled at the words. Despite knowing what would happen in the future she was still created, born, and she was still very much loved.

"I'm relieved you truly love him, that your devotion remains," Aurella said, standing next to her.

"I have never stopped. I just wanted too much."

Aurella nodded, eyes glistening with tears. "No one has ever loved him the same way. Not even me. He is difficult to care for but he is the most valuable treasure of either world."

"He is… something else, alright," Stella chuckled.

The clouds darkened, sky thundering angrily, as the furere began to sew themselves together in a hopeless entanglement. They cried as they destroyed themselves. They howled in delight as they killed each other and stole the limbs for their own.

"I do not fear death."

"You fear not knowing what comes next," Aurella said in a hushed tone.

Stella looked at the mountain of furere. They were in more pain than she had ever been. Their magical presence was creating an abnormal fluctuation. It was distorting the earth at its core.

"Why did you choose to transform them?" The pixie asked.

"I was furious, jealous. I wanted to teach them a lesson. I was bored of mere torture so I took to magically attaching them to other creatures to see what would happen. It was horrendous."

"You never could control yourself," the pixie said.

"I have lacked discipline much of my life," Stella agreed.

"I wish you farewell and trust you to make amends," the pixie said.

"I will," Stella said.

The pixie floated apart and drifted into the sky like kicked up dust. Stella's eyes watched casually until they were out of reach.

"You know," said Aurella. "I once admired you."

"Did you?" Stella laughed. "I don't think I was much to admire."

"Perhaps that is what made you so admirable?"

Stella couldn't help but laugh again and it felt good to release a bright vibration into the otherwise dim world. She faced Aurella and smiled.

"Thank you," Stella said.

"For what?"

"You saved me."

"Hardly," Aurella snorted.

"Why did you create a line of fae-el?"

"Because Vasilis asked me to."

Stella thought for a moment, chewing her lip, before proceeding with a response. The symbol was heavy in her pocket and she couldn't wait to be rid of it.

"Then you returned my magic because —"

"Because you asked me to, or are you still incomplete?"

"It's been a week since you returned my powers to me," Stella said. "My memories are bitter and yet kind. They are all tiring though."

"You have survived many millennia," Aurella said. "There is a great deal for you to recall. Just how much do you love him?"

"Enough to have destroyed the world," Stella laughed bitterly.

"That was not brought about by love."

"No, it was not," Stella said. "But what I'm about to do is."

"Goodbye then," Aurella said.

"Goodbye."

Stella walked toward the bay and felt the echo of their magical home thrumming beneath her feet. It didn't like the evil looming over it. It didn't trust her. The source of magic was trying to hide but all things magic could feel it regardless. Stella began to tread the water of the bay. Her eyes filled with tears as she watched the furere.

"Moirai," she spoke to the furere as she swung her hand toward them.

Wind called up and took the water three stories high, surging toward the furere army. Their eyes, black and angry, turned to her.

"Remember your magic!" she called up the water. It suddenly turned it to flame.

The flames licked around the furere as they stormed in her direction. They continued to screech and howl as the flames overtook them.

She walked further out onto the water, turning it to ice beneath her feet. She called the earth to her, and roots grabbed, trapped and tore apart the furere as they ran, swam or flew swiftly.

The first of the swarm reached her and she surrounded herself in her old armour. She was cast in the elements, her pupils dilating until there were no more colour, as she leapt over them.

Running, she brought the wind with her, slicing as she went. She felt each and every slice as if it were her own body. She felt the mutilation in her bones as she sent fire up their limbs.

She could see every individual entity underneath the black, putrid skin they had become. She saw the cruelty and malice she forced them to endure. She saw pieces of flesh ripped away with teeth. She saw irises cut hollow. Stella saw the evil as if it were taunting her, telling her she was wicked even if she stopped them now.

A scream tore through the black menace as she stopped the flooding images. Everything turned to ash around her as she released her own magic and absorbed the earth's energy surrounding her.

A black stream went straight upward to the sky, covering the sun, hiding the earth. It was like night had descended on them. The darkness poured from her like water from a well.

The furere launched into her and scraped through the surface of the ice into the bay below. They sunk deep as her magic surged and screeched around her, disintegrating them whenever they neared her. In their madness they killed themselves against the black stream of magic flying into the heavens.

She smiled as an epiphany rose in her mind. Vasilis had always been nearby, a silent guardian. She couldn't fathom why he had not said anything to her as she pressed her armor away from her skin. There was no longer a need for it as her physical body fell apart.

As they began to peel apart, layer by layer, Stella's body ripped apart. Her skin stripped off like scabs until there was no skin to remove. The coolness of the water did not save her from the burning of the flesh that tore and scratched away from her limbs.

She convulsed as bones snapped. She nearly let go of the magic but could still feel them. The furere, their anger and resentment, were still battling themselves and her power. Unable to breathe, her chest convulsed and seized helplessly in the water.

She called the rune to her and the infinity symbol burned itself into what was left of her chest. Her breath let go as her howling into the water bubbled to the surface in magical waves. Her mind replayed the months since their release from the fae world. Every encounter she had with them had been a miracle to survive.

The furere finally flowed away, as though sand on the beach, from the magic she released until she could feel them no more. The source of magic in the rune called to her. It hummed musically through the water as it sat in the seabed. She was barely more than bones, tendons and ligaments.

Eyes open, she used what energy she had left to magically push her way deeper. When she saw the bottom, she tore her fingers into the symbol and pulled it from her chest. She watched the blood that had left her body ripple in the water like thread caught in the wind. It was like peeling her own heart from its place under her ribs. The pain swallowed her, and she began to lose vision.

She rested the symbol on the diamond rune outstretched to her. She held it in place as she found a small reserve of air in her lungs.

"Moirai," she spoke into the water as it exchanged places with the air.

The entire capacity of her magic flew at the gold infinity. The water stretched far at the outburst, letting her gasp for air at last as her body fell to the bottom of Georgian Bay. She sputtered out the water and rested a hand on either side of the symbol, the center sitting heavily on the rune. She opened her eyes and saw it was the throne from the capital city of the Fae. She almost laughed.

"Everything is magic," she sputtered while the symbol bubbled and sizzled. "Magic is everything. I undo you and all you represent."

She pulled downward as she fell to her knees. Her weight and the release of the spell cracked it in two against the diamond throne. The symbol melted and flowed down the seat until it dried and was scattered into nothing more than sand. The wind moved away, and the water crashed down to sweep everything away, cleaning what was left of the filth of black magic. The throne shattered in the water's crash.

Stella faded away, remnants of her body thrashing with the current. She gave up control, allowing the water to lead her where she belonged. No more than a terrible, yet beautiful, memory.

Chapter Thirty-Nine

Richard stood far from the magic but close enough to watch. His magic protected him from the shockwaves. He watched the last of the furere flutter away into the sand as Georgian Bay's water rose higher than any structure humankind had created. He watched it tease the atmosphere, breaking the black clouds away and revealing patches of sun.

The light glimmered through the bay and created the illusion of sparkling diamonds in the water and air. He heard the words Stella spoke and knew she had finally made a decision for herself, for her life. He had waited a thousand years to see her become everything he knew she could be.

The air shifted as the symbol broke. He shut his eyes and allowed the tension to ease in his own body. His emotions filled and emptied. The world was returning to how it should be. The fear, anger and hate were subsiding. It was allowing him to rest at last.

The earth's core, still shaken, began vibrating electrically. It was similar to how the world once hummed.

"Thank you," he said.

He watched Stella's soul shoot from the surface of the water and knew where it meant to go. Instead, he called to it.

Afterward

Charon looked at the portraits in the large office. She had always been beautiful, even in her worst state. Yet she had no control of her emotions. Her lack of discipline had always been alarming yet charming in its own way.

He left the room, the sixth and final captioning of her finally hung. Ari looked at him solemnly. He was still upset she hadn't said goodbye. The hole in his leather jacket was scarcely stitched up. Charon supposed he kept it as a reminder.

"It will become easier," Charon told him. "It has already been many years."

"I know." Ari closed the door, eyes on the portrait, before heading down the hallway and outside.

Charon went down the hallway to the new balcony. He watched the small gathering of humans and magical creatures in the garden. He could never recall a time when they cohabitated peacefully.

"What are you thinking, Vasilis?" Galen asked.

Charon looked at the caelum and gave a small shrug. He had kept his lineage quiet, yet Galen seemed to know everything.

"How long have you known?"

"Since we met," Galen answered. "Did Stella know?"

"She certainly knew what she wanted to and ignored the rest."

"She knew you are the king of all magic." Galen crossed his arms, neither angry nor pleased. "The wind. Father nature, as it were."

"If I am father nature then she would be mother nature." He sat on the banister.

"You could have prevented all this," Galen said.

"I cannot change the timeline." Charon spoke low. "This is how it was to be. I've seen every fate from every decision from every person that has lived. That is a curse like no other. To see her die a trillion ways and never one to save her. This was the only way in which she was restored to her brilliance and purity."

"Then you will be alone." Galen ducked under the doorway as he walked away. "But at least you're not entirely alone now."

"No. I'm not."

Charon could sense the magical creatures returning to him. They watched him from the forest, the garden and sky. They all looked to him. He was not a guardian. He was a king they had long forgotten.

Vasilis, of the wind, and the source of all magic before people recorded history. Before Stella had been born of magic and loved him. His decision to resign his sovereignty had been meant to save her. Instead, it made her a queen they did not want.

"Do try to love again," Galen said.

***

Galen walked through the mansion to his office. Aurella sat on his desk as he entered. He looked at her inquisitively. He had not been expecting her.

"I thought for sure you had died," he said as he sat in his chair.

She swiveled and crossed her legs, knocking items to the floor. She was grinning at him, her usual plucky self. She had a mischievous look in her eyes.

"It's been nearly twenty years. How have you hidden for so long?"

"Magic."

"We do like to hide behind that excuse, don't we?" He said and watched Aurella grin at him mischievously. "What?"

"I have a secret to share," Aurella whispered.

"What secret would that be?"

Aurella leaned forward and waggled her finger for him to get closer. He rolled his eyes and sat forward in his chair, waiting for her.

"It didn't kill her."

Galen looked at her curiously and then his jaw fell. He leapt to his feet, hands on Aurella's arms, and pulled her in. His nose jutted into hers as he said, "you'd best not be playing games, little fae."

"She is born of magic! Stella wasn't born the way we were. Which means… she can't die."

"Impossible." Galen shook his head and walked across the room.

"Not impossible."

"Then what had she seen that she wanted so deeply to avoid?" Galen spoke in a hissed whisper.

"She thought it was her death, but it was her life." Aurella insisted, becoming excited. "Childbirth. Blood, screaming, agony, pain, more blood… I too found it a particularly miserable affair."

"Then where is she?"

"Where do you think she is?" Aurella laughed. "She's in the bay."

"If this is true, why doesn't Va — Charon know?"

"I know who he is."

"How do you know Vasilis?"

"Because, he created me."

"You're his experimental magic." Galen nearly gasped at the idea. It had only been theoretical. Galen had no idea Vasilis had managed to create life from scratch with his own powers.

"Yes." Aurella smiled. "Magic is forever. He knows she's out there somewhere."

"Then why hasn't he sought her out?"

"Fear?"

Their eyes were locked as they considered possibilities. Galen realized he still had much to learn and Aurella knew far too much to hide herself again.

"I haven't sought her out because she is imprisoned."

Vasilis entered the study and Aurella and Galen turned to him. Galen's eyes were mistrusting, though he didn't sense any malice in Vasilis.

"It isn't time yet for her to be released. She is serving a sentence thanks to the Antelucio family."

Galen straightened and pushed his shoulders back. "The line of Antelucio has been long gone."

"Not precisely. Richard has been veiled. He made a decision and it provided Stella with a prison instead of death."

Galen's hands balled tightly. "If this is going to create another—"

"It will not." Vasilis cut him short. "The Antelucio are the timeline. More specifically, Richard is the timeline itself. He knows everything. He is magic."

The information hung in the air like fog. None wanted to free her from a prison yet all desired to see her returned. Though the knowledge that the Antelucio line was not fae, but rather, the magic entity that brought forth all life was astounding.

"Do we trust the Antelucio family?" Ari burst through a window and landed behind the group. "Can they be trusted?"

"They have only ever wanted the world to live peacefully. They understand far more than we do," Vasilis said.

"When will it be time?" Galen asked, arms crossed.

"I do not know," Vasilis said. "But Richard will see to it when she is meant to return."

Acknowledgements

Firstly, to all the readers, I sincerely thank you and hope you enjoyed the story. Hopefully you're excited for the next great tale.

I collectively thank all those in my life who have been supportive.

To my editors, Doug and Shanice, I thank you for perfecting my story and helping bring these words to life. Also, Harley, my wonderfully patient cover artist: thank you!

I must also provide a very special thank you to M, who pushed me to go after what I love rather than what was safe. Fear is inevitable. It is what we do when we face fear that creates or breaks us.

About the Author

Jennifer J. Lacelle has always been an avid reader and lover of fantasy, mythology and adventure. As a child, the genres she was permitted to read were generally limited to Christian topics. This did not, however, prevent her from coming to love the diverse range of stories available worldwide as she grew older.

She obtained a diploma in journalism from Cambrian College as well as a graduate certificate in communications from Georgian College. Furthermore, Jennifer has had nearly forty articles published to date — with more to come. She's also excited to share a wide range of stories with the world as she continues to develop her young adult novels.

Stay up to date and have fun with Jennifer on her social media.

Instagram: jenniferlacelle

TikTok: jenniferlacelle

Goodreads: Jennifer J. Lacelle

www.rambleandwrite.com

Cover Art by Harley Davidson

Instagram: adayics